"Tell me how you really feel," she asked.

It took a moment for Ally's words to compute. Bees were swarming through his thoughts. Slowly, Tag tuned out the buzzing and focused on her lazy-lidded eyes and swollen lips.

Ally. So, so beautiful.

Wayward strands of her silky black hair stirred in the breeze. She looked thoroughly...kissed. What had he done? A sick feeling rushed in, dousing the heat that had been muddling his brain only seconds before.

"Ally, we..." *We what? Not we, I.* What had he done here? What could he do? Apologize? She'd kissed him, yes, but he'd let her. He'd more than let her; he'd kissed her back without even an ounce of restraint and precious little self-control. And that wasn't like him. He'd never lost his mind quite like this before...

And she made him feel things he'd never felt before.

Dear Reader,

First of all, thank you for reading my books and reaching out in emails, on social media and through your reviews to let me know how much you enjoy them. I also love when you contact me asking if and when a certain character might be getting his or her own happy-ever-after.

I never imagined when I began this writing journey in Rankins, Alaska, that Tag James's story would become the most requested. But with each book, I fell a little more in love with him right along with so many of you. So I knew when it was time to tell Tag's story that he was going to have to fall for someone really special. I also knew that he was going to have to be knocked off his feet. Because he's awesome, of course. But also because he's a thirty-eight-year-old bachelor who's a bit set in his ways. Bachelorhood is beginning to feel like an affliction for him. I think Ally Mowak is the perfect remedy. I hope you do, too.

You can reach me by visiting my website, carolrossauthor.com. Or email me at carol@carolrossauthor.com. Or find me on Facebook, Facebook.com/carolrossauthor, Twitter, @carolross, and Instagram, carolross_.

Carol

HEARTWARMING

Bachelor Remedy

—

Carol Ross

HARLEQUIN® HEARTWARMING™

Recycling programs
for this product may
not exist in your area.

ISBN-13: 978-1-335-63358-3

Bachelor Remedy

Copyright © 2018 by Carol Ross

Printed in U.S.A.

Carol Ross lives in the Pacific Northwest with her husband and two dogs. She is a graduate of Washington State University. When not writing, or thinking about writing, she enjoys reading, running, hiking, skiing, traveling and making plans for the next adventure to subject her sometimes-reluctant but always fun-loving family to. Carol can be contacted at carolrossauthor.com.

For Janet.

Thank you. Without you, no one would even know it was me who'd written this book.

CHAPTER ONE

"How does it feel to be dirt free?"

"Honestly?" Tag James gave his cousin Bering a sober look and whooshed out a breath. "I totally lucked out. Can't believe that private investigator didn't find out about the insider trading or the body buried in my backyard. What an amateur."

Bering laughed. "I know. The background check seems a little over the top to me, too, but you know Jack."

"Jack" was United States Senator Marsh, longtime client and friend of Bering's, who was helping them prepare for Tag's future political run.

"Yes, I do. 'Find the dirt and clean it up before your opponent finds it first and smears it all over you.' I believe that's the quote?"

"That's it," Bering agreed. "Senator James…" the snap of the metal tape measure retracting in his hand was like a loud punctuation mark "…has such a nice ring to it." Wielding a pencil in his other hand, he drew a tiny line on the freshly painted lavender-colored wall in his daughter's bedroom.

"It certainly does," Tag agreed. Despite his outward nonchalance, the topic always caused a twinge of nerves. Plenty of time, he reminded himself, before he needed to start worrying about it. Lots of time to prepare.

Wordlessly, they each took an end of a bookcase and adjusted it to line up with the pencil marks and the units they'd already installed. Tag wound the screws through the brackets, securing the shelving against the wall. Neither earthquake nor climbing toddler would bring it down now. "Violet proofing," Bering's wife, Emily, called it, although with baby Brady walking now, Tag figured she would soon have to broaden the term.

He stepped back and eyed his cousin. "And you're sure you don't want that senator title for yourself?"

"Ha. Positive. We've had this conversation, my friend, and you and I both know I'd be no good as a politician."

Tag couldn't dispute that fact. His cousin and best friend wasn't exactly the most diplomatic person in the world. Besides, it was Tag's turn. Bering had saved the town of Rankins once from a proposed massive oil-development project. He'd formed and led the coalition against Cam-Field Oil & Mineral, and with the backing of Senator Marsh, they'd prevailed.

Bering had scored the bonus of a lifetime by meeting his now-wife Emily during the antidevelopment campaign. As relieved as they'd all been at the project's outcome, the experience had shown just how vulnerable Rankins was. Tag, Bering, their family and friends, virtually the entire area relied on the pristine natural beauty of the Opal River Valley in some respect for their livelihoods. His winning a seat in the state senate would provide long-term security for them all. And they'd agreed, Tag was more suited to political life.

"Anyway," Bering said, bracing his big hands on a shelf to test its sturdiness. "Jack says you're on the right track, doing everything you need to be doing. Just stay the course, keep your nose clean and we'll be ready."

"Got it. Stay out of the dirt."

"Although he did mention one small thing."

"What's that?"

Bering let out a chuckle and began stacking kids' books on the bottom shelf. "He said it could be helpful if Rankins's most eligible bachelor was to find a wife and maybe start a family."

Tag felt a familiar invisible hand reach inside his rib cage and give his heart a painful squeeze. This chest pinch had been happening more and more lately when the subject of parenthood came up, which was all too frequently now that Shay and Hannah, two of his four sisters, were married, as were his two closest cousins, Bering and his sister Janie. There were eight cousins in his generation on the James side of the family, and at thirty-eight, he was the oldest of them all.

The family bachelor. Everybody's cool and fun uncle, cousin, brother, friend. The childless bachelor. The one everyone could count on. And, somehow, somewhere along the way, he'd earned the moniker of the town's most eligible bachelor. Lately this unintentional status had begun to bother him. Tag loved kids. He'd always wanted a family, had just assumed it would happen one day. He'd meet someone and settle down and have kids. That's the way it was done.

He'd met plenty of someones, all right. Problem was, either they weren't quite right, or he wasn't, or logistics like work schedules and geography made a relationship too difficult. Or a combination of these resulted in the woman cheating on him. Okay, maybe that one was just Kendall, his last girlfriend.

"I'll get right on that," he replied drily.

Bering shot him a hopeful glance. "If you mean it, Jack has someone he'd like to fix you up with."

"No, thanks. No way."

"Why not?"

"Seriously? You have no recollection of life pre-Emily, do you? Dating is bad enough. Blind dating is...brutal. I try not to be offended by the matches you people think will work out for me. Being single should not be the only criterion involved. A couple of weeks ago, Shay set me up with this uptight mortgage broker from Glacier City who hates sports and is afraid to fly."

Bering grimaced. "I see your point. But until you start blind dating in the women's professional basketball league you aren't going to find a woman who can beat you at basketball. You do know that, right? You might need to cross that off your list."

Tag laughed. "Hey, I'll settle for a fan at this point. She doesn't even have to play."

"Tag!" Smashed, half-eaten sandwich in hand, Violet skipped into the room, her tousled blond curls and peanut butter–smeared cheeks the cutest thing he'd seen since his last visit three days ago.

"Violet, my flower, you woke up for me!" Tag picked her up and swooped her high into the air. Wild giggling ensued. Planting a kiss on her cheek, he asked, "You want to take a walk on the ceiling?"

She thrust the sandwich at her dad. "Daddy, can you hold this? Don't eat it!"

"I wouldn't dream of it." Bering grinned and took the sandwich.

Holding Violet securely at the waist, Tag flipped her upside down until her bootie-clad feet touched the ceiling. Still giggling, she carefully placed one foot in front of the other as Tag strode across the floor while she "walked" on the ceiling. When she'd crossed about half the room, he lowered her and turned her in his arms.

Wrapping her arms around his neck, eyes nearly the color of her name fixed firmly on him, she said, "I love walking on the ceiling. And I love you, too."

A chest pinch of mega proportions nearly made him wince. "I love you, too, flower." Tag wondered if men had biological clocks. A prick of sadness followed as he thought about his sister Shay and how desperately she wanted a child. She and her husband, Jonah, had recently suffered yet another adoption disappointment, and Tag was worried about the long-term repercussions on her. She seemed to be having a hard time recovering from this one emotionally.

"I think you're her favorite person, Tag." Emily stood in the doorway, eleven-month-old Brady on her hip. She followed that up with a quick "Don't tell your sisters I said that." Wearing black leggings and a long flannel shirt, her blond hair bunched into a cute, messy pile on top of her head, Emily didn't look anything like the corporate executive she used to be. Although by all accounts she was a wizard in her current job as head of the Rankins Tourism Bureau.

"Are you guys wrapping it up? Lunch is ready." Stepping inside, she surveyed the shelving they'd constructed and installed across one entire wall. "This looks incredible. It's even better than I imagined. Thank you so much for helping, Tag."

"Of course. Anytime. You know that."

A buzz in his pocket followed by a distinct-sounding chime indicated a text from his business, Copper Crossing Air Transport. This particular alert had his paramedic's pulse thumping because it told him that an emergency required medical evacuation.

"You need that sandwich to go?" Emily asked. His family members and most of his friends were familiar with the sound. And they all understood when plans were interrupted; there was no such thing as an inconvenience if it meant a life could be saved.

"That would be great, Em. Thanks." Tag frowned as he read the brief message. A tap on his phone sent a return text letting his crew know they needed to get the float plane ready.

"Bad?" Bering asked.

"Grizzly bear."

Bering winced and muttered under his breath.

"Oh, no!" Emily cried, one hand coming to rest possessively on Brady's back.

No further explanation was necessary. Everyone who lived in Rankins, or the rest of Alaska for that matter, knew what those two words meant.

So MUCH BLOOD. Too much to see exactly how much damage the bear had wrought. With nimble fingers, Ally Mowak probed her fifteen-year-old cousin Louis's wounds. The dressings in her first aid kit weren't going to go far, not with this amount of shredded skin. She slipped off her jacket as well as the thick fleece shirt beneath it. Using the knife she'd already wielded to cut away Louis's tattered clothing, she went to work on her own, arranging strips of cloth on the worst of his wounds.

"Quinn?" she barked at the other teenager crouched beside her. Zombielike, he stared down at Louis. "Quinn, look at me." Grabbing his shoulder, she gave it a shake. "See what I'm doing?"

Blinking slowly, Quinn managed to wrest his gaze from Louis.

Still cutting, she repeated, "See what I'm doing? How I'm making strips? I need you to do this with your sweatshirt, too. Do you understand?"

Blank eyes stared back at her. Ally feared he might pass out. Combat experience had taught her that the best way to handle a person on the verge of shock was to keep them moving— even better if you could give them a job to do.

"Quinn, I need your help here, kiddo."

Louis let out a moan, hoarse and full of anguish.

That seemed to spur something in Quinn, and he nodded. He removed his top and held out a hand. Handle first, she passed him the knife. "It's super sharp, okay?" she warned. "And hey." Gripping his shoulder tightly until dark-brown, terror-filled eyes met hers, she forced a confidence she didn't feel into her tone. "He looks worse than he is. We will save him. But this is important. We need these strips to stop the bleeding."

The sound of crunching leaves and snapping branches had her snatching up the bear spray at her side. Adrenaline flooded her bloodstream. Jessie and Ryder Shelton and their three monster-sized dogs, Colfax, Pia and Fife, emerged from the brush. Exhaling a relieved breath, she dropped the canister and focused her attention back on to her patient.

"That was fast," she said. "I expected you to come across the lake."

"The ATV was quicker." Jessie knelt on the opposite side of Louis, already tearing into the packs of dressings she'd brought along. "We have a stretcher."

Ally and her teenaged cousins Louis and Quinn had spent the morning fishing in Jessie's canoe on Jasper Lake. A road accessed the scattering of homes located on the south shore of the lake, while the wooded northwestern shore could be reached only by boat or trail.

As lunchtime approached, she and the boys had paddled to this remote portion to eat and enjoy the view. Quinn had suggested a hike up a scenic trail that followed a winding stream past Sullivan's Spring to Sullivan's Falls. Round trip was only a few miles, and because they'd made it almost back to the spring when the bear attacked, Ally estimated they were now half a mile from the lake.

Thank the stars, she had her cell phone. Double and triple thanks that she had service and Jessie was around to hear the call. Jessie and Ryder ran a dog rescue facility, where Jessie rehabilitated injured and abused dogs, and Ryder trained service dogs for the police and military.

Ryder silently went to work on Louis's neck and shoulder. After doing what they could on his front, they rolled him over so Ally could inspect his back. Relief surged through her. It didn't appear that the bear had punctured the chest or abdominal cavity.

"Tag James is picking him up in his float plane," Jessie said. "It's the fastest way. The Coast Guard could send a search and rescue team with a hoist, but it would take longer. I already called."

"Good." Ally was relieved. The less jostling around for Louis, the better. "Let's get him on the stretcher. I want to stop at the spring on the way to the lake."

TAG CLIMBED OUT of the plane onto the pontoon and stepped into the shallow water of the lake. A few splashing strides and the pebbles of the shoreline were crunching beneath his booted feet. He hurried to where his friend Ryder stood nearby.

"Ryder, man, I'm glad to see you and Jessie here."

Ryder was former military special forces and had medical training. Transport would go so much faster with his help since Tag didn't have to apply first aid and stabilize the patient. Already on a stretcher and covered with a wool blanket, the wounded teenager looked ready for transport. A girl was crouched beside him, holding his hand. Jessie stood several feet away, talking with another boy.

"Hey, Tag. Feeling's mutual," Ryder said, giving his hand a quick shake.

Taking positions on each end of the stretcher, they quickly loaded the patient inside the plane while Ryder filled him in on the details of the attack. Tag didn't notice the problem until they'd secured the stretcher inside. That's when the blanket shifted, and instead of fresh white dressing, he saw dingy gray-and-brown strips, almost like…

Peeling the blanket back farther, he found a mass of dirty, albeit neatly arranged, bandages. What in the world? Had they dropped him? If so, why hadn't they cleaned him up?

"Why is he so dirty? These bandages are filthy."

"Ally did that," Jessie explained. "Native healing thing. She says the clay in Sullivan's Spring contains antibiotic properties and helps stanch the bleeding."

Tag was familiar with the small mineral hot spring. Most people didn't even know it was there. It wasn't large enough to draw visitors. There were no deep or colorful pools to attract attention, but he'd heard about its purported healing properties for most of his life.

"Who is Ally?" he asked, although his keen powers of deduction were telling him she had to be the only other female who wasn't Jessie. Initially he'd assumed she was a teenager, maybe the injured kid's sister or girlfriend, as she'd been holding his hand and talking to him right up until they'd loaded him inside the plane.

Ryder's brows shot up. "Ally Mowak? You haven't met her yet?"

"No. Why would I have?"

"She's the new hospital liaison in Rankins. I guess, technically, she doesn't start until tomorrow."

Tag glanced over to where Ally was hurriedly stuffing gear into a backpack. Pretty, and like Jessie, she appeared to be of Native American descent, as did the two boys. She was petite and fit, her silky black hair tied back in a ponytail, and she wore no makeup. He supposed she might not be as young as he'd assumed.

"How old is she?"

"Young. Twenty…something. Early twenties. Old enough to have served in the Army, including a couple of combat tours. She was a medic and then came home to earn her paramedic certification."

"Huh." Because of his affiliation with the hospital, he knew a liaison had been hired. Flynn Ramsey, a doctor at the hospital, had told him because the position entailed overseeing medical transport, which meant Tag would occasionally be working with the new person. Up until now, the task had been tacked on to Flynn's already demanding schedule.

Tag watched as Ally slung the pack over her shoulder. The two women exchanged a brief hug, and then Ally turned and jogged toward the plane.

"Hey, pilot, let's go!" she called, a note of impatience infusing her tone, as if he was the one who'd been holding them up. Without waiting for a response, she waded into the water, climbed nimbly onto the pontoon and scrambled inside the plane.

Tag called out thanks to Ryder and Jessie and followed, even though he wasn't sure of their destination yet. Anchorage and Juneau both had excellent trauma units. Either way, he needed to call and inform them they were en route.

Turning around, he asked, "Alaska Regional or Bartlett?"

"Rankins," she answered without hesitation.

"Rankins?" Was she serious? The kid had been mauled by a bear. "Are you sure? It's a small hospital, and Juneau has—"

"I know how big the hospital is," she answered in a tone as crisp as an ice chip. "He's my patient. It's my call."

Giving his head a stupefied shake, he turned to focus on the plane's controls. The only thing that kept him from arguing was the fact that he didn't want to waste any time. The patient could be airlifted from Rankins if necessary. Although, at some point in the very near future, he and Ms. Mowak were going to have a conversation about patient transport protocol when he and his company were involved.

As Louis drifted in and out of consciousness, Ally held his hand, touched his cheek, told him stories, all the while closely monitoring his condition: listening to his breathing, checking his pulse, scanning every inch of him from head to toe and back again. There was some oozing through the dressings but no serious bleeding. She wished she could check the injuries on his back.

What she really wished was that she'd been there to protect them.

Ally had been lingering behind on the trail taking photos when she heard the boys' screams. She'd sprinted toward the commotion, but by the time she'd arrived at the scene the bear was gone and the damage done. Squeezing her eyes shut, she took a few seconds to appreciate how lucky Louis was to be alive. She still wasn't sure why his injuries weren't more severe. Ally was proud of him for keeping his head covered like he'd been taught, his scratched and raw forearms proof of the defensive move. A bear's powerful jaws could remove a person's entire face or crack the skull with a single bite, as easily as a nutcracker splitting an acorn.

Quinn said that in those few seconds of awareness before the attack he'd thought they were both dead. The boys had been standing maybe ten feet apart when they heard a noise in the brush behind them. They hadn't had time to do more than turn before three-hundred-plus pounds of muscle, claws and teeth were charging toward them.

For whatever reason, the bear had gone for

Louis first. As Quinn scrambled to retrieve his bear spray from the holster on his hip, the sow, seemingly distracted by something in the trees, had dropped Louis almost as quickly as she'd attacked and loped back into the brush. Probably her cubs, Ally theorized, as Quinn had seen two little ones scooting ahead of the bear's retreating form.

It seemed like only a few minutes before the plane was descending toward the waters of the bay adjacent to the town of Rankins. After a smooth-as-glass landing, they were ferrying toward the dock. Red and blue lights from the waiting ambulance were a balm to the gnawing worry in her gut. She'd thoroughly assessed Louis's injuries, but with the conditions and the limited resources in the field, she knew there was a chance she'd missed something.

With efficiency and care Ally approved of, the onshore team rushed Louis into the ambulance for the short ride to the hospital. She joined him inside and was soon handing her cousin off again, this time to a team of doctors and nurses.

Relief rushed through her when she saw Dr. Ramsey instead of Dr. Boyd. Like her, Flynn was new to Rankins Hospital but old to Alaska, meaning he'd grown up here, too. He was also sympathetic to traditional medical practices. He would understand the clay.

CHAPTER TWO

"IN THIS HOSPITAL, Ms. Mowak, we don't treat patients with dirt." Dr. Robert P. Boyd leveled his glacier-blue glare at Ally. He even looked like ice, she decided, with his white hair and snowy-smooth skin. The sharp edges of his shoulders and elbows jutted against his white jacket.

So much for her hope that Dr. Boyd wouldn't get wind of her use of clay on Louis's wounds. Poof went her plan to ease into a relationship with the chief physician at Rankins Hospital.

Ally already knew that an education, even one as extensive as a doctorate, didn't guarantee wisdom. Knowledge, sure. Wisdom, not so much.

Her grandfather, Abe Mowak, had been using medicinal clays on patients ever since Ally could remember. Clay from Sullivan's Spring was among his most valued. She'd collected some for him last time she'd visited Jessie, which was how she'd gotten the idea to use it on Louis.

"As an Army medic and a paramedic, I know you're aware of the proper treatment for lacerations and punctures of this severity."

"Yes, sir."

"Dr. Ramsey informed me of the fact that the patient is a relative of yours, but that makes no difference where medical procedures in this hospital are concerned. I acknowledge that Louis's mother, your aunt I understand, has no problem with it. But trust me when I tell you that family connections are no guarantee when it comes to lawsuits."

Dr. Boyd flipped through a sheaf of papers on the desk in front of him. Best guess, the file contained her résumé, Army record and reference letters. Then again, there could be anything in there—photos of his grandchildren, sudoku puzzles, his grocery list. The point was to intimidate her. Obviously Dr. Boyd didn't know her yet.

Flynn Ramsey, Ally's supervisor and friend, sat beside her. He tilted his head and mouthed a silent "Sorry."

"It's fine," Ally mouthed back and added a wink.

Dr. Boyd addressed her again. "In case you haven't had time to consult the hospital's policy, I've had my secretary highlight the portions..."

The reprimand continued, and after much

longer than necessary, he finally quieted and looked at Ally expectantly. Apparently it was time for her to respond.

She'd love to tell him exactly what she thought of his antiquated opinions, but she knew better. "Actions heal, words incite" was one of her grandfather's favorite sayings. But she couldn't resist trying to plant a seed, at least.

"Have you heard of the antibacterial properties of mineral clay, Dr. Boyd?"

"That's what antibiotics are for, Ms. Mowak. Perhaps *you've* heard of penicillin?"

Perhaps you've heard of MRSA, Dr. Boyd? The sarcastic retort tap-danced silently across her tongue. Ally knew that Rankins Hospital had battled a bout of the antibiotic-resistant staph bacteria a few months back. MRSA and other superbugs like it were a direct result of the overuse of antibiotics. But she didn't say that, either. She wouldn't want the inference to be that she thought Louis shouldn't receive antibiotics. Dr. Boyd seemed like the word-twisting type.

Then there was the fact that this was her first day on the job, a job she'd been training for and working toward her entire life. Her grandfather had sacrificed so much for her. No way would she let him down by getting fired before she even started. She knew that technically Dr. Boyd alone couldn't fire her. That decision would require a vote by the entire hospital board. But Dr. Boyd was the ultimate medical authority here at the hospital, and she knew that her job, as well as her overarching mission, would go so much smoother if she could establish a good relationship with him.

"Of course," she responded. "I'm a huge proponent of antibiotics when administered correctly. I'm grateful Dr. Ramsey prescribed them for Louis." Ally flipped an appreciative smile in Flynn's direction.

Dr. Boyd sat back and studied her. His long surgeon's fingers curled over the arms of his chair, where they twitched menacingly like two hungry albino spiders.

An awkward silence ensued. "Now, I realize this is your first day on the job as our new hospital liaison."

"Yes, it is, sir. And I appreciate your taking the time to go over these important rules with me. Working here at Rankins Hospital is a dream come true, and I assure you I'll do whatever is necessary to make a smooth transition, including rereading the handbook the hospital has provided and reviewing all of these highlighted notes."

Dr. Boyd sniffed and adjusted his glasses. "That sounds fine."

Ally thought he looked suitably defused, so she stood. "If there's nothing further then, I'm anxious to get to work."

APPROXIMATELY TWENTY MINUTES later Ally was still trying to calm down. Seated behind her new desk inside her new office, she read her new job description for about the millionth time. Certain sections seemed to glow from the pages, reminding her why she was here: *To facilitate patient care regarding medical treatment, procedures, hospital stays and preventative care... Appropriate consideration must be taken regarding the age, gender, ethnicity and religious beliefs of the patient...*

Simple words, yet so open to interpretation and incredibly challenging to implement. The knot already bunching in her stomach tightened. Did her grandfather know the monumental task she was facing here? Of course he did. She wouldn't be here if he didn't have faith in her.

From the depths of her soul, she believed there had to be a way for traditional and modern medicine to meet peacefully, to merge, even. Yet she knew, and both her grandfather's and her own experiences had taught her, how difficult the concept was for some people to accept. She hadn't intended to wave her opinions around her new workplace quite so blatantly, and wouldn't have, if Louis wasn't a relative.

A knock startled her out of her thoughts. Looking up, she saw a vaguely familiar male figure filling the open doorway. A tall figure, she couldn't help but notice—very tall and lean. The Mariners T-shirt he wore predisposed her to like him, and she couldn't help but appreciate the way it stretched nicely across his muscled chest. Longish dark brown hair curled over his forehead and at least a day's growth of stubble shaded his jaw.

Handsome face, she noted, but it didn't look like a happy one.

"Good morning, Ms. Mowak. Do you have a minute?"

"Sure. Come on in."

Long strides carried him into the room. "How's your cousin?"

Now she had the feeling she should definitely know him. "He's doing very well, thank you. He should be released in a day or two. Do you know Louis?"

One brow ticked up. "Just from yesterday."

"Oh, were you part of the medical team treating him?"

He gave his head a little shake. "Ms. Mowak, I *met* you yesterday. Pilot?"

"Your name is Pilot? I have a cousin named Jett."

One hand came up to scrub his chin. "No, I was the *pilot* who flew you and your cousin in from Jasper Lake."

That was it. "Oh, yes, of course. Mr....?" Had he ever said his name?

"Tag. Tag James. From Copper Crossing Air Transport."

"Sorry, I didn't...remember you."

"Yeah, I got that," he answered flatly.

Ugh. This was uncomfortable, although she wasn't sure why exactly. She recalled the brief interchange about which hospital to fly to and realized she might have been a tad short with him.

"Your landing was excellent, by the way. That, I remember."

"My landing?" He repeated the word like he hadn't quite heard her correctly.

"Yes. In the bay. You're obviously a competent pilot."

"Competent?" The word came out slowly while his brows dipped down along with the corners of his mouth. He looked baffled. He crossed his arms over his chest and kept them locked there.

Hmm. Was he offended that she hadn't recognized him? Or put out because she'd overridden his suggestion to go to a larger hospital? When she shifted into rescue mode, she tended to become hyperfocused on her patient and the circumstances surrounding the emergency at hand. And yesterday's patient had been Louis, a family member, which had heightened both her concentration and concern. She felt it unnecessary to explain this.

"I apologize that I didn't recognize you?" she said, and immediately realized that it came out sounding more like a question. Ally didn't believe in superfluous apologies, or conversations, for that matter. She found them both a waste of time, and hers was at a premium.

With more smirk than smile, he said, "I can assure you I am more than competent, Ms. Mowak."

Oh, brother. She should have seen that coming, pilots and their egos. Her second oversize ego of the day. At least this guy wasn't her boss.

"Mr. James, what can I help you with?"

"Please call me Tag. I'm here to discuss the flight yesterday. Do you remember anything besides my competent landing? Do you have problems with your short-term memory I should be aware of?"

Ally felt a stir of dismay. Carefully, she answered each question and then followed with one of her own. "Of course. No, I don't. And what about the flight?"

"Specifically, I'm here to talk about how your new position as hospital liaison affects me and the patients I transport, as per my business arrangement with the hospital."

"I see."

"Do you?"

"This is about the clay?"

"Partially. Not entirely. I have more than one issue."

Oh, good, she thought wryly. She was about to get grief from the pilot, too. Who was next? The charge nurse hadn't accosted her yet. But it was early, not even lunchtime. Patiently she waited for him to continue.

"If we're going to work together I think we need to establish some ground rules."

"I agree."

He got right to it. "I don't have issues with alternative medicine per se—herbal, Ayurvedic, naturopathic, homeopathic, acupuncture, Reiki or any other type of traditional remedy, for that matter, is fine with me. I don't care or interfere with what people believe or how they choose to treat their medical conditions. What I *do* have a problem with is when it directly affects my job, and more specifically, my ability to save a life."

"And you feel like my use of medicinal clay falls into the latter category?"

"I do."

"Please keep in mind that yesterday I was treating a family member in an emergency situation. I wasn't on the job."

"I understand that, which is why I'm here instead of in Dr. Boyd's office." He shrugged a shoulder. "Even though I do not understand why you would purposely put your cousin in danger."

"Obviously, I don't see it that way."

"Obviously. You can see it any way you choose. But for the duration of time that we'll be working together I need you to do it my way. My way is the right way."

"Noted," she replied calmly. "My turn."

"What?"

Ally almost laughed at his look of utter confusion. "You said we were establishing ground rules. You gave me yours. If this works the way I think it does, then it's my turn to outline my rules?"

Narrowing his gaze, he studied her like he was puzzling out this detail. His eyes burned into hers, and she couldn't tell if they were green or brown. Inexplicably, the back of her neck began to tingle.

"Do you want to have a seat?" she asked, partially to stop his perusal, partially to bring him closer to her eye level. If Dr. Boyd hadn't intimidated her, there was no reason this guy should. But it might be easier to manage if he wasn't hovering over her.

"Fine." Moving closer, he lowered his tall frame into the seat across from her.

Better, she thought, meeting his gaze head-on. Except now he seemed really...close.

Gathering her thoughts, she said, "When I'm out on a call and acting as the paramedic on behalf of Rankins Hospital my word is final. My way is the right way. I also have some ideas on how you can improve your efficiency. It took you too long to take off after you landed at the lake."

He scoffed. "Are you kidding me? The only thing holding up my takeoff was you chatting with Jessie while *I* waited for *you* by the plane."

Hands folded neatly on the desk in front of her, she went on. "I disagree. It took three minutes for you to get inside the plane and settled after I'd already boarded, and your dissension took at least another minute. Had you already been on board, we would have landed approximately five minutes sooner. I don't think I need to remind you how vital five minutes can be in an emergency medical situation."

Ally waited for him to respond, steeling herself for whatever came next. He didn't look angry or upset, though. In fact, he was completely still. Too still?

"Hmm. You know what? Coming here might not have been the best idea, after all. Because I don't need professional advice from someone who was still in grade school while I was getting my EMS certification."

TAG WISHED HE could take the words back before they were even out of his mouth. A flicker of something was there and gone from her face faster than the beat of a swallow's wing. Disgust maybe? Which he might deserve. Bering was right. Normally, Tag was the easygoing, slow to boil, diplomatic one.

Admittedly, he'd come here geared up for a possibly unpleasant conversation, but a professional one. Ally Mowak didn't seem to have any problem maintaining a professional tone, whereas he'd just blown it. Her expression remained as unreadable as a slab of granite, and he couldn't help but think he'd disappointed her in some profound way. Or maybe that was his own disappointment nibbling at him.

When she didn't speak, he let out a sigh and tried backtracking, "What I was trying to say is that I don't need anyone to advise me on how to do my job, Ms. Mowak. I've been at this a very long time."

"Ally," she said. "Please call me Ally. And the same goes for me." Shrugging a shoulder, she continued in that same serene, not-quite-condescending way that he was fast learning was how she spoke. "But isn't that what you're really doing here now? Telling me how to do my job?"

"Uh, no." He resisted the urge to scratch his itchy scalp because he sort of was, wasn't he? He hadn't meant to, not exactly. "That wasn't my intention, anyway."

"Did you or did you not see a woman who you interpreted as too young for this job and then decided that you'd teach her a thing or two? You, with your wisdom honed from years of experience, would come to the aid of an inexperienced, newbie female colleague?"

"No!" *That* he was not doing. "Nope. No way. Don't even try that on me."

"Don't try what on you?"

"There's no misogyny or ageism or sexism or racism or any other 'ism' going on here. I have four sisters and a boatload of female cousins, all of whom are younger than me.

Each one is equally as smart and capable as I am, more so in many, many ways. This isn't about any of that. This is about your workplace attitude, your approach and your lack of respect. After your behavior yesterday, I would have come in here today if you were an eighty-six-year-old man wearing a honey badger suit."

One side of her mouth twitched. Only slightly, and he probably would have missed the movement if he wasn't so intent on watching her, marveling at her composure.

"I don't see how my attitude plays into this. My approach was honed through four years of military service, a civilian EMS-P certification, and a decade and a half of studying and practicing under the tutelage of a renowned medical expert. And as far as respect goes, I subscribe to the 'respect is something you earn' school of thought. And you being here right now and complaining about nonissues isn't helping on that front."

"Your résumé already got you this job, Ms. Mowak. You don't need to recite it for me, and the fact that you are speaks to your insecurity, which I'm guessing has something to do with your attitude. Your approach is my concern because I have to work with you. And the respect I'm talking about is the respect you should innately have toward a fellow medical professional whose job and reputation you put on the line because you chose to smear mud all over a patient."

"It's clay." Her tone was flat, but her shapely black brows arched higher and Tag had no idea what that look was supposed to convey.

Waving a hand, he said, "Whatever. Since we're sharing our qualifications, I am going to give you a piece of advice based on my eighteen years of experience as an EMS-P, my fifteen years as a volunteer firefighter, and a lifetime as both a friend and a big brother. If you don't want people to notice your age, don't draw attention to it."

"You're the one who brought it up."

"That's true. But I—" Biting back the words he'd been about to say—*I'm not used to people questioning my skills*—he went with "I shouldn't have. For that, I apologize."

A head tip told him she acknowledged the mea culpa.

Exhaling, he checked the time on his watch. This meeting had been an epic fail, and he had no hope of turning it around at this point. He'd promised his sister Hannah he'd give her a hand with some repairs up at the ski resort this morning before his flight to Anchorage at noon. He needed to wrap this up.

"For now, I'm going to quit wasting both our time. Maybe we should meet with Dr. Ramsey and talk about our professional expectations?"

"That would be fine."

"Good. I'll set it up."

ALLY STARED AFTER HIM. At least he'd suggested the meeting with Flynn and not Dr. Boyd. She had no more time than that to dwell on it, though, because the phone on her desk let out a buzz. She answered it and proceeded to deal with the first call for the job she'd actually been hired to do. She tackled paperwork and fielded calls until lunchtime, when she placed one of her own to Louis's mom, her aunt Gina, who Ally knew was sitting vigil in his room.

Quinn was there, too, she learned, so she headed to the hospital's cafeteria and ordered cheeseburgers, fries and strawberry shakes for them all. In the room, she was heartened to see Louis already sitting up, laughing and chatting with Quinn. At least she'd made the right call regarding his injuries.

When her break was over, she said goodbye to her family and promised to stop by again when she could. The afternoon was spent visiting patients and their families, assessing their needs and making notes about any questions or concerns they had regarding hospital, hospice or at-home health care.

The interaction with patients revived her, reminding her why she wanted this job. Back at her office, she immediately began cataloging the patients' needs while they were fresh in her mind. One was ready for palliative care, so she called the hospice and set up a meeting for the patient and her family.

The remainder of her day consisted of more phone calls, emails, strategizing, and plotting out her to-do list and schedule for the next week. Just past six, a knock sounded on her door and relief flooded through her when she discovered this one had a much friendlier form attached to it than the morning's.

"Flynn, hi."

A dimpled grin transformed the young doctor's already handsome face into a combination of sweet and gorgeous. Too bad she thought of him like family. With no siblings of her own, he was as close to a big brother as she could imagine. Their grandfathers were friends, so Ally and Flynn had known each other since childhood.

Flynn's grandfather—"Doc," as he was more commonly known in Rankins—had always welcomed her grandfather's advice as a Native healer and doctor. Likewise, Abe had never had a problem calling on Doc when modern medicine was needed. A friendship had sprung up early in both of their respective careers, one based on mutual respect.

An image of Tag James flashed into her mind, embarrassment rushing through her because she realized in that moment that he'd been right about one thing: she'd been so concerned about his respecting her that she hadn't shown him the respect he deserved.

Lowering himself into the chair Tag James had occupied that morning, Flynn said, "Hey. Good job with Dr. Boyd."

"Thank you. I only wish all of my confrontations today could have gone as smoothly."

Eyebrows a shade darker than his seal-brown hair darted up on his forehead. "Uh-oh. What else?"

"Among other affronts, I was told I need to work on my attitude."

Scrunching his features into a grimace, he said, "Seriously?"

"Yes."

"Not by a patient, though?"

"Of course not! It was a colleague. Although, in thinking about it now, I may have deserved part of it."

"Well, honestly…" he drawled, pursing his lips as if thinking about the statement. "I'm not that surprised. You know you're not exactly warm and fuzzy, right? Outside of patient care, I mean."

"Yes, but I think basically this guy was telling me that he didn't like me. Right before he made a crack about my age."

"Ooh. How politically incorrect of him. I know how much you hate that."

"Right? He apologized, but for some reason I let it get to me. You'd think I'd be used to it by now." Working with her grandfather at his medical clinic, Ally had been given a lot of responsibility at a young age. She'd joined the Army at seventeen, but she'd looked even younger, so she'd grown accustomed to people asking about her age. At twenty-two, it was still a common occurrence. "I thought I was. But this guy…"

Why did she care what he thought? She didn't, she reminded herself. She didn't care what anyone thought about her. But she would apologize properly because they needed to work together.

"Never mind, I don't want to talk about it. I'm using my energy to focus on the future. And right now, I'm focused on that dinner you promised." Ally logged off her computer. "I believe fish and chips were mentioned?"

"Lucky you." He held his hands aloft as if

he were a prize she'd won. "That's what I'm here for."

She stood and stretched before stepping over to the corner behind her desk to fetch her bag.

"Speaking of the future— Do you want to go to a party with me this weekend?"

"What kind of party?"

"It's a welcome home, congratulations on getting your graduate degree party for my friend Iris. Casual, fun and there will be a ton of people."

A party was exactly what she needed to meet people, make some connections, become a part of the community. She wanted people to get to know *her* before hearing *about* her and reaching the wrong conclusions, although she knew the "mud story" had probably already raced through town faster than a staph infection in an untreated wound.

"That would be wonderful, Flynn. Thanks."

CHAPTER THREE

"WE'RE GOING TO the Cozy Caribou," Flynn said after they exited the hospital. By silent mutual consent, they paused to admire the water of the bay sparkling below them like freshly ground glass. Thick green forest fanned out from snow-capped mountains jutting upward in the distance.

"See that red roof over there?" He pointed toward the middle of town, and Ally couldn't help but notice the rectangular-shaped building situated roughly in the center. It seemed to be a pretty big place by small-town standards, certainly in relation to Saltdove, the remote village she'd grown up in, where there were exactly two "large" buildings, neither of which would ever be described as such.

"It would be difficult to miss. Let's walk?"

Flynn nodded and took off at an unhurried pace. "This kind of evening makes me remember why I love it here."

Ally agreed it was gorgeous. She'd only visited Rankins a few times before moving here, and she enjoyed the walk, seeing the tiny historic town through Flynn's enthusiastic eyes as he pointed out businesses and landmarks, adding fun facts and anecdotes.

And clearly, Flynn wasn't the only resident proud of their little town. Evidence of Rankins's heritage was everywhere. They passed old fishing boats and equipment, vintage logging and mining tools, all strategically displayed and interspersed with newer, attractive sculptures and wood carvings. Along with the eclectic mix of building styles, the layout provided a pleasing glimpse of the town's interesting and varied past.

Flynn said, "So, in case you don't already know, the Cozy Caribou is an institution here."

She gestured for him to go on.

"Half bar, half restaurant and all-around community gathering place, it can accommodate pretty much any event you can imagine— concerts, reunions, receptions, parties and meetings. They have karaoke nights and even an occasional poetry reading. Food is simple, home cooked and across-the-board fantastic, including the best fish and chips on the entire planet, and freshly brewed root beer that will make you forget your own name."

Ally grinned. "Sounds like my kind of place."

Flynn opened the door for her, and the second she stepped inside she knew it was true. The tension of the day began to recede as welcoming sounds bombarded them from all directions: laughter mixed with music while the slide-and-chime of dish on dish was accented by clinking silverware. Across the wide space and off to one side were a couple of pool tables. At the far end of the room a game of darts was in full swing. A group of women was seated at a large table nearby.

"Ah," he said, following her gaze. "Friends of mine. Come on—I'll introduce you to some of the nicest people. Most of them will be at the party Saturday, too."

They approached the group and Flynn turned on his grin, gesturing around helplessly. "Uh-oh, I think I'm walking into a girls' night thing here, aren't I?"

A pretty blonde answered. "Well, it is girls' night, but you can join us because you're not one of *our* men and only if you don't speak about any of them tonight. I happen to have argued with mine, and I don't want his name mentioned."

She reached out a hand toward Ally. "Hi, I'm Emily."

Ally shook it. "Hi, Emily. Ally."

Flynn draped an arm over Ally's shoulder. "So, everyone, like Ally just said, this is Ally

Mowak." He started with the opposite side of the table where two look-alike women sat side by side. "Ally, this is Hannah and Shay. Sisters, in case you couldn't tell."

To the women, he added, "Ally is coming to Iris's party with me this weekend." He turned back to Ally. "Hannah owns and manages Snowy Sky Resort and JB Heli-Ski. Shay is the owner of the Faraway Inn and Restaurant."

Anyone would guess the women were related; they both had long brown hair and nearly identical golden-brown eyes, over which the same sweeping brows arched gently. Matching smiles accented sculpted jawlines. Something seemed vaguely familiar about them, yet she was sure she'd never met the women.

Flynn was gesturing toward the other side of the table. "And this is Adele and Janie. Adele is Shay and Hannah's cousin and manages the Faraway Restaurant. Janie owns a knitting business and simultaneously wrangles five children, while Emily here—" he indicated the woman she'd already met "—is president of the Tourism Bureau." Next, he pointed to the woman seated beside Janie. "This is Laurel, owner and editor of the town's newspaper, the *Rankins Press*."

Ally felt like she'd walked into the middle

of a chamber of commerce meeting instead of a girls' night out.

"Nice to meet you, Ally," Hannah said with a warm smile. "Was Flynn saying somewhere in there that you know our sister Iris?"

"No, I just know Flynn. He knows your sister. Flynn and his grandfather are pretty much the only people I know in Rankins."

"How do you two know each other?" Laurel asked, glancing at Flynn's hand still draped over her shoulder. Ally was pretty sure she wasn't imagining the curiosity shining in more than one pair of eyes.

Flynn explained, "Ally is like a little sister to me. Our grandfathers go way back. Ally's grandpa Abe is friends with Doc."

A few more minutes of small talk went by before Flynn said, "We should go get a table. Ally started a new job at the hospital today, and we're both starving."

"Sit with us. Seriously," Emily said, "we'd love to have you. We're really not that strict on the girls-only rule."

The waitress appeared to deliver food. Flynn quickly placed their orders and rounded up two chairs while the women shifted and made room at the table.

Easy conversation ensued until a blond man with a bright smile and boyish good looks sauntered over to their table. "Hey, since Doc Junior here is horning in on your girls' thing, does that mean I can, too?" He twirled a finger around the table.

Adele scoffed. "Absolutely not."

"Women and *men*, Park. No boys allowed," Hannah said and bit off the end of a french fry.

"Ladies, come on…" he drawled. But his grin suggested that he loved the attention. "It's been days, hasn't it, since we've bonded like this? I know you've missed me." He seemed to be talking to Hannah and Adele, but they all laughed.

"So, Hannah, how about a game of pool?" he asked.

Adele laughed. Hannah's chin jerked up as if she was studying the ceiling, but she brought it back down quickly to peer at him. "Seriously, Park?"

"Yes! Please, Hannah. Come on! I've been practicing, watching videos on YouTube. Pretty sure I've got this."

"Fine. One game. No bets."

He huffed. "I know, I know. My betting days are over."

"Get me a root beer float, and I'll meet you at table two when those guys finish their game." She pointed at one of the tables currently in use.

"Awesome." Park hustled off, presumably to claim the table and fetch Hannah's drink.

Adele smiled at Ally and Flynn. "Park once lost $500 to Hannah on a pool bet. They were enemies for ages until Hannah saved him from a probable jail sentence and financial ruin. Now they're friends."

"I don't know that I'd go that far," Hannah said, but her voice held enough gentleness that Ally knew it was true. "He's on Snowy Sky's board of directors, but he's still a royal pain in the butt."

A shout rang out from the crowd playing darts, drawing the attention of most of the table.

Hannah turned in her chair and started to stand but immediately sat down again, wincing as she settled sideways on the seat. She busied herself riffling through her bag, but Ally wasn't fooled.

With the collective focus still on the dart game ruckus, Ally felt confident no one was paying attention, so she lowered her voice and asked, "Are you okay? Is it your knee?"

Hannah's eyes widened slightly before giving her leg an absent pat. "Oh…yes, it is, but I'm fine. Just an old injury."

"What type of injury?"

Her expression went blank in a way that

reminded Ally of herself when someone was prying into her business.

Ally bit back a smile. "Sorry, I'm not being nosy. Well, I am, but only because I'm a medical professional. Maybe I can…"

Before she could think of how to phrase the rest of her explanation, Hannah said, "Thank you for the offer, but I've seen so many doctors… It's a form of arthritis caused by having my leg crushed in a car accident and then pieced back together."

"What treatments have you tried?"

Hannah glanced toward the pool table where the guys were still playing before facing Ally again with a thoughtful expression on her face. "Do you… Are you like a naturopath or an osteopath or something?"

"No, nothing like that. I'm not a doctor. I'm a paramedic. Currently, I'm working as the hospital liaison and the emergency air medical coordinator. But I'm also… My grandfather, Abe Mowak, is a Native healer. He practices a form of holistic medicine, and one of his specialties is arthritis. I studied with him my entire life."

Ally knew she needed to tread carefully here. But she trusted her instincts and they rarely failed her. "This would just be a…discussion," she finally said. "Like I'd have with a friend."

Hannah seemed to ponder that before replying, "You know what? I'll think about it. Right now, I need to go humiliate Park."

TAG LIVED OUTSIDE Rankins on twenty-two tree-studded acres located approximately halfway between Bering and Emily's place, which was a few miles away, and the town of Rankins in the opposite direction. Two years ago, the property had become available, and Tag had snagged it. With a family in mind, he'd built the house mostly himself, a roomy two-story lodge-style home. There were four bedrooms, one of which he used as an office, two and a half bathrooms, a spacious living area and, according to his cousin Janie, a "kitchen that would make a foodie drool." He'd indulged in some extras like hardwood floors, exposed wood beams, copper sinks and a hot tub.

Upon finishing the house, he'd been surprised by two things: how much he looked forward to getting home each evening and how much he wished he had someone to share it with. Interesting double edge. Tonight, tired as he was, he was solely focused on the first, although it wouldn't happen for at least a couple more hours. He had a stop to make.

Mickey Patterson had been his high school basketball coach, and Mickey's wife, Sheila, his third-grade teacher. They owned the property next door, and even though Tag couldn't see their house from his, that still made them neighbors. Mickey's arthritis was gradually slowing him down, and Tag often lent him a hand with projects and tasks around his property.

As he approached the Pattersons' driveway, a brand-new for-sale sign on the opposite side of the road caught his eye, and he braked, slowing the pickup to a crawl. Why would Park Lowell be selling his property? A shareholder and member of Snowy Sky Resort's board of directors, Park had told anyone who'd listen that he planned to build his dream home out here.

He turned, traveling along the Pattersons' long gravel drive until he reached their home. Parking behind Mickey's rig, he then grabbed two hockey sticks from his back seat before scaling the steps of the porch.

Mickey opened the door before Tag could knock, stepped out and closed it behind him. Tone muted with anxiety, he said, "Thanks again for helping me out with this, Tag."

"You know I don't mind, Mick."

"She's real stubborn and uncooperative. I couldn't get her to so much as flinch."

"She's determined, I'll give her that. It might be time to move her out once and for all?"

"'Fraid so. I hate to saddle you with it."

"It's no problem." Tag handed Mickey one of the hockey sticks. "Let's go see if we can talk some sense into her."

They headed toward the small workshop a short walk from Mickey's house. Tag spotted the prickly female huddled calmly in the corner as soon as they entered the building. But, then again, a critter covered with quills didn't have much reason ever to get riled.

Twenty minutes later, without incident, they'd herded the wayward porcupine into a pet carrier.

Mickey seemed pleased. "Time for a beer?"

"Sure."

They settled at the dining room table. A Mariners game was on the TV in the living room beyond, and Tag noted happily that the team was up by two.

"Hey, I noticed a for-sale sign on Park Lowell's place. Know anything about that?"

"Yep. I guess he's selling. Goofy bird thinks he can get twice what he paid for it."

"Really?" It used to be that Park was always up to one money-making scheme or another, but after he'd tangled with Hannah over a ploy involving the ski resort, Tag had thought those days were past.

"Yeah, I ran into town to have coffee with Scooter Tomkins yesterday. It's listed with Nadine, and she told Scooter how much he wants for it." Nadine was Scooter's sister and the owner of Rankins Realty, the largest of the two real estate agencies in the valley.

"Huh."

"I know. I'm surprised, too. Supposed to start on his house right about now. Wasn't too happy about having him for a neighbor, but Scooter said some highfalutin couple already checked the property out. And I generally subscribe to the better-the-devil-you-know philosophy."

"Me, too, Mick," Tag agreed. "Me, too."

PORCUPINE RELOCATION COMPLETE, Tag finally pulled into his own driveway. He was looking forward to heating up the leftovers that Emily had given him, putting his feet up and watching the last couple of innings of the ball game. As soon as he saw his cousin Janie's SUV parked out front, though, he remembered he'd made another commitment.

Inside his house, he found Janie's son Gareth watching the game. A basketball, the teen's constant companion, sat on the sofa next to him like an important guest.

"Hey, sorry I'm late. I had to relocate that problem porcupine for Coach P."

Gareth laughed. "No problem. I just got here, like, five minutes ago. Where did you take it?"

"About ten miles up toward Glacier City. I'm hoping it won't be motivated enough to come back upstream no matter how tasty Mick's saplings are. You want some dinner before we shoot? Emily sent me home with enough lasagna for a week."

"Sure. Only a couple innings left in the game and it's tied."

A basketball scholarship was taking Gareth all the way to the University of Oregon. Tag liked to think he deserved a tiny piece of the credit for developing the kid's skills. He'd put a ball in Gareth's hands almost as soon as he could walk and then taken the brunt of Janie's ire when the toddler dropped it and face-planted right over it. Instead of crying, Gareth had immediately stood and patted the ball, giving credence to Tag's claim that Gareth was dribbling at nine months old.

Janie's first husband had died when Gareth and his younger brother, Reagan, were in middle school and she'd been pregnant with twins.

For two years, until she married her current husband, Aidan, she'd been a single mom. Tag and Bering had done their best to pick up the slack.

Basketball was Tag's sport, too, and he loved that it had become his and Gareth's thing. He wondered how much longer he could fool the kid into believing Tag was still the better player.

"Did you hear back about that camp?"

"Yep, I'm in."

"Awesome."

"Coach said the best thing I can do now is have a ball in my hand every day between now and next season."

"He's right about that."

"I need to work on my outside shooting. Which reminds me, did you hear we're having a basketball tournament on Saturday at Iris's party?"

Tag's three youngest siblings were triplets, of which Iris was one. Hazel and Seth were the other two. The party was at Bering and Emily's. Years ago, Tag and Bering had installed a regulation-sized basketball half-court. Games and tournaments were a regular and eagerly anticipated part of their lives.

Tag grinned. "That should be fun. Edible prize from the Donut Den?"

"Yeah, but Mom said we can't be on the same team anymore."

Tag scowled. "Who made her boss?"

"Emily. She put Mom in charge of the teams and the bracket."

"Well, in that case, we're screwed." As a former corporate executive for one of the largest oil and mineral extraction companies in the country, Emily's charm and organizational skills, combined with the sheer force of her will, left no room for argument.

Gareth chuckled his agreement. "Yeah, but the party will be epic."

CHAPTER FOUR

FRIDAY, THE LAST day of Ally's first week on the job, and she'd only been in her office a few minutes when Flynn popped his head in.

"Hey, you got a second?"

"For you? Always."

He came in and took a seat. "A couple of things. First—don't forget we have a party to go to tomorrow."

"I haven't. I'm looking forward to it. You said it's an outdoor thing, right?"

"Yes, and I'm glad you brought that up. Wear comfortable shoes."

"What, like hiking boots or flip-flops?"

"No, like sneakers. We'll be playing basketball. Bering and Emily have a half-court, and there's going to be a little tournament."

"Got it. That sounds fun."

"Next thing, we have a patient who is going to be transported to Anchorage this afternoon."

"Yesterday's rock-climbing accident?" Two

injured climbers had been brought in the day before after suffering a bad fall.

"Yes, a doctor in Anchorage is going to perform surgery on that shattered leg. I know you've had a long week and this will be your first transport. Do you want me to see if I can get one of the paramedics at the station to do it?"

"No, I got it."

"Okay, it's scheduled for two. When Tag arrives with the helicopter, I'll page you, and we'll go from there."

Ally's stomach did a flip. Tag James had been lingering in the back of her mind all week. She'd been waiting to hear about the meeting he'd requested with her and Flynn. She had polished her apology and wanted to get it off her chest.

Careful to keep her tone neutral, she asked, "He flies helicopters, too?"

"Yep. I don't think there's a flying machine out there that Tag doesn't know how to operate—small planes, float planes, big planes, gliders, helicopters. I don't know that he's licensed for commercial jets, but I'm sure he could fly one."

"Was he in the air force or something?"

"No, he's just really accomplished. In a family filled with overachievers, Tag is the standard-bearer. You remember him, right? He brought Louis in last weekend?"

She sighed and said flatly, "Oh, I remember him, all right."

"Uh-oh. Wait…was he the person who commented about your attitude?"

"And my age, yes. I have a feeling this is going to be a long day."

Flynn sat back in his chair and chuckled. "Huh."

"What?"

"Well, it's just that everyone loves Tag. Great guy. Pillar of the community type. He's also one of Dr. Boyd's favorite people."

"Figures," she muttered. "Pod mates, those two."

"Uh, not exactly. Tag is just easy to get along with. Usually."

"Hey, I'm… I can be easy to get along with, too."

"You can be, sure…"

Ally gave him her best menacing glare.

They shared a laugh, and then Flynn said, "Ally, seriously, it would behoove you to get along with him. Pull out the charm, which I know is difficult, but which I also know you're capable of."

"I'm going to try, Flynn. I promise." Wondering if Flynn had forgotten, she asked, "Did he contact you about setting up a meeting? We agreed to settle our professional, um, discrepancies under your guidance."

"Nope. Haven't heard from him, although…"

She waved him on impatiently. "What? Spit it out."

"It's a good idea, I think. He does have a lot of experience."

She scowled. "As do I."

"Hey, settle down there," Flynn teased, raising a conciliatory hand, fingers spread, palm out. "I know you do. All I'm saying is that medicine is collaborative, or it should be. You know that. You also know from working with Abe your entire life that not everyone thinks or believes the way you do. We talked about this before you took the job."

"I know. I do know that, Flynn. I just wish a different pilot was doing this transport today."

Slowly he tipped his head, like a thought was occurring to him. "This party tomorrow, it's for his sister Iris. Did you know that?"

"No." It figured. Just her luck. Small towns.

Flynn peered at her for a few seconds. "Is this computing? Those women you met the other night, at the Cozy Caribou? Most of them are related to Tag. He has relatives all over this town."

Ally's brain went into overdrive. This meant

Iris's sisters, Shay and Hannah, were also Tag's sisters? Meaning she'd initiated a discussion with his sister Hannah about her arthritis that, had the conversation taken place, would have included mention of alternative treatments.

Yikes. Based on their initial encounters, Tag would not approve. Ally was almost relieved that Hannah hadn't taken her up on her offer. Almost, because, she reminded herself, she didn't care what he thought of her. At least today's excursion would give her a chance to apologize before encountering him in a social setting.

A small smile played on Flynn's lips. "You know, most women in this town wouldn't consider it such a hardship to spend the afternoon with him."

"Oh, yeah?"

"Yeah, he's generally considered the one to catch around here."

"The one to catch?" She repeated the statement flatly.

"Rankins's most eligible bachelor."

What did that mean? That he was some kind of player or that he wasn't? "Huh. Well, I'm not most women, am I?"

Flynn barked out a laugh. "That you are not.

I gotta get going. Promise me you'll make nice with Tag James?"

"I promise I'll…try."

TAG WAS SURPRISED when he arrived at the hospital to find that the patient wasn't ready for transport. His inclination was to seek out Dr. Ramsey, although he knew the task now fell under Ally Mowak's job description.

With flashbacks of their last meeting flickering uncomfortably before him, he headed to Ally's office only to find that she wasn't in.

Tag gritted his teeth as he realized they'd never had that meeting with Dr. Ramsey. He'd headed back to the office that day and asked his assistant, Ivy, to schedule it. But that same evening Ivy had received word that her dad had died, and Tag had immediately given her as much time off as she needed to fly home to Nebraska to be with her mom, assuring her that all tasks would be taken care of in her absence.

Was it too much to hope for that someone other than Ally was assisting with the transport today? Dr. Ramsey or one of the other doctors sometimes accompanied patients, and he knew of at least two nurses who were trained to travel. He went to the nurses' station on the first floor—they always seemed to know everything—and asked about Flynn and Ally.

"They're both with patients," Marlena, one of the nurses, told him a moment later after making a call. "But Nicki wants to know if you're aware that you're more than an hour early for your transport?"

"I thought the pickup was scheduled for one."

"She was afraid of that. She says she called your office this morning to reschedule but got your machine."

"Ah." Tag nodded. That would explain it. He hadn't gone into the office this morning. And probably none of his crew had bothered to check the messages. He couldn't blame them; that wasn't their job and he hadn't asked them to. He made a mental note to give Ivy a raise immediately upon her return and headed to the cafeteria to grab a coffee.

On his way out, he ran into his friend Laurel Davidson, the owner of the town's newspaper, the *Rankins Press*.

"Laurel, hey, what are you doing here? Chasing a story?"

"Possibly. I have a line on a human-interest piece. What are you up to?"

"Killing time because of a scheduling snafu.

Ivy is gone, and my office is bordering on chaos."

"Speaking of chaos, I am looking for the new hospital liaison, Ally Mowak. You know her, right?"

Tag set his features to bland. "Met her. Briefly."

Laurel's brows jumped high onto her forehead. "And…?"

His answer was a little frown and a shrug to match.

Clearly not fooled, not that she ever was, she said, "You can cool the closemouthed, cagey act. I know you flew her cousin in from Jasper Lake after the grizzly bear attack. Tell me what you know, what you think."

"About what? I don't know anything. It was pretty intense, Laurel. The patient was her cousin, and we didn't spend much time chitchatting." Why did he sound defensive? Tag wasn't about to mention the controversy Ally had caused with the use of the clay, although he knew gossip had already flown around the hospital like a foot fungus in a dirty locker room. Heck, he'd heard it being discussed at the Cozy Caribou the day before.

Meaning Laurel already knew, which must have something to do with her being here. Her doubt-filled expression seemed to strengthen his deduction.

"Do you know her grandfather is Abraham Mowak?" Laurel asked.

"No…" Doctor Abe Mowak, the well-known, well-connected Native healer and advocate had a reputation for being…unconventional. How had he not made that connection?

"Yeah, we've got the granddaughter of one of Alaska's most renowned Native healers working right here in Rankins. I met her earlier this week before I realized who she was, and even then, I thought she was…intriguing. From what I've learned, she's been working by his side since she was a very young girl. And she's an Army veteran."

"Huh. Well, Laurel, it sounds like you already know more than I do."

"Big surprise," she teased. "I also stopped by to see Ginger."

"Ginger is here?" Ginger Weil was a mutual friend. In addition to being a professional photographer, shooting weddings, parties and portraits, she also took photos for the region's newspaper. She'd been diagnosed with ovarian cancer nearly a year ago, and it hadn't responded well to treatment.

"Yeah, they admitted her last night with an infection."

Tag felt his gut tighten with concern. "Is she staying?"

"I don't know." Laurel shook her head. "She doesn't want to. Poor thing. She wants to stop treatment and her family is not taking it well."

"Yeah, I talked to Jacob last week. He's not dealing with the whole thing in general. I think I'll head up there and say hi."

"She would love that. And so would Jacob. You should try talking to him. He likes you. Maybe he'll listen. I'll see you tomorrow at Iris's party, right?"

"Yep, her flight gets into Anchorage this afternoon. I'm picking her up after I drop off a patient."

ALLY HAD RETURNED from her lunch break to discover a request to visit a patient ASAP. She'd headed to the fourth floor to find a smiling nurse standing outside the patient's door, seemingly waiting for her arrival.

"Hi, I'm Nicki. You must be Ally. It's great to meet you finally." With a wave, Nicki moved to the end of the hall. Ally followed. "Ginger has ovarian cancer. She's done two rounds of chemo. They didn't work. Now she says she's through. Doesn't want to talk options anymore. Family is distraught. Dr. Ramsey thought a conversation with you might, um, encourage them to accept her decision. Ginger agreed." Nicki handed her a chart.

"Of course." Ally skimmed the details and headed into the room.

"Ah, Ally." Flynn smiled and waved her over. "Thanks for coming. I'd like you to meet Ginger Weil. Ginger, this is Ally Mowak, our hospital liaison. Ginger is a photographer, the most talented one I've ever met."

"Pfft." Ginger flapped a hand in his direction, but she was grinning. "Charmer. How many photographers have you met?"

Ally sent her a warm smile. "Hi, Ginger."

"Lovely to meet you, Ally. Welcome to our family meeting." Ally was surprised by both the twinkle in the woman's eye and the trace of sarcasm when she said, "Doc Junior here tells me it's your job to reassure my parents that I'm a grown woman capable of making my own decisions about my health. I'm looking forward to hearing someone with the proper authority do that."

Ally took in the two women huddled together off to one side. A beefy man with a gray buzz cut stood on the opposite side of the bed, not frowning, yet there was no trace of a smile, either. Massive arms folded over his muscled chest made his biceps bulge, and everything about him screamed military.

Flynn introduced the man and the older woman as Ginger's parents, Jacob and Kate. The other woman was their younger daughter, Cara, Ginger's sister.

Ally moved closer to Ginger. "I understand you've decided to forgo further treatment for your condition?"

"Correct." A confident nod accompanied her response.

"I'm sorry, but I need to ask if you understand what that means. Even though I know that your oncologist, and probably Dr. Ramsey, have already gone over this with you, I'd like to talk—"

"Yes, let's talk about it," Kate broke in. "That's all we're asking, honey."

"Any hope is still hope," Cara chimed in.

"Talking some sense into her is all we want," Jacob growled.

Oh, dear, this poor family.

"Platitudes are my favorite," Ginger whispered. Squeezing her eyes shut, she gave her head a shake before settling a determined gaze on Ally. "I'm totally fine talking about it. With treatment, my odds of beating this are less than two percent. Treatment would consist of more brutal chemo. The first rounds left me helpless and miserable and incapacitated and nearly killed me. But if I opt out of the treatment I could have three or four or as many as six or even eight months with relative quality of life. Way, way better than the chemo version of *quality* I've suffered through already.

"I could smoke weed—sorry." She gave her dad a pointed look before addressing Ally again. "I could legally partake of medical marijuana until I can no longer stand the pain. Then I'll hook up to a morphine drip and sleep peacefully until I die with as much dignity as dying allows."

"Stop talking about dying!" Cara barked, her tone bordering on a shout. "You have to fight, Ginger. Why won't you fight?"

Kate choked on a sob. "Ginger, honey, Cara's right. Please think about Ella. She needs her mother."

Jacob stood his ground, menacing and gruff, his blue eyes settled on the wall above Ginger's head. Ally's heart went out to him; she wasn't fooled by the man of steel routine. Why was it that the harder the shell, the more devastating the heartbreak seemed?

A passionate, circular conversation ensued, and Ally understood why Ginger had requested some help. She glanced at Flynn, whose only response was a gentle upward nudge of one brow.

Ally had experienced an uncommon amount

of death in her life. Palliative care was one of her grandfather's strong suits and Ally had shown a knack for assisting him at a very early age. She knew when a patient was making a decision for the wrong reason and when they were making it for the right one. As far as she knew, her intuition and experience had never steered her wrong.

Beside her, Ginger's eyes were shining and filled with anguish. The sight caused an ache deep in Ally's chest. She reached across and placed her hand over Ginger's, lightly squeezing her fingers.

Ignoring the others, Ally asked, "So, Ginger, now that you've decided, what are you planning to do with the rest of your life?"

The room grew silent while Ginger's eyes welled with tears. "You're the first person to ask me that…" Dipping her chin, she nodded for a few seconds before swiping at a tear on her cheek. "I've thought about this a lot."

"I'm sure you have. I know I would."

"It even has a title, this last chapter of my life. It's called Photographs and Memories, like the Jim Croce song. Do you know it? I'm plagiarizing, but I'll be dead by the time anyone figures it out so let 'em sue me."

Ally smiled. "Know it and love it. He's one of my grandfather's favorite singers."

"I want a few more months of taking photos and making memories. One last glorious Alaskan summer…" Ginger swallowed and nodded as if to blink back more tears. "I want to spend time with my daughter and take photos to leave for her. I want us to do things and make memories and document them together. Memories that don't include me sick and vomiting and so weak that I can't even hold her or read to her or sing Jim Croce songs…"

Ally squeezed her hand while she gathered her thoughts, awed by her strength and bravery and the beautiful poetry of her words.

"What I don't want…" She cleared her throat. "What I don't want is to lie in bed *wishing* out the window, you know what I mean? Lying there dying and thinking about all the things I *wish* I was doing? I want to do them, live while I can. So, Ally, that's what I'm going to do with the rest of my life."

"Ginger, that sounds just lovely." Ally lifted a shoulder. "I can't imagine anything better."

"Me, either."

"You realize that it will be painful? That, in the end, it could possibly be more painful than if you chose chemotherapy? Physically, I mean, because the cancer will be allowed to grow. Chemotherapy kills your good cells,

but it also kills the cancer cells and can pro-
long your life."

"I do. Dr. Fulton, my oncologist in Glacier
City, was brutally honest about that. I asked
him to be because I want to be prepared. But
I'll have quality time, that's the point."

"Okay, good. You get it. Your daughter is
lucky to have you. How old is she?"

"She's eight." Ginger reached toward the
bedside table, picked up a frame and handed
it to her. A photo collage, Ally realized, and
in each and every image there was a petite
girl with a heart-shaped face, wide smile and
lively eyes that were nearly identical to her
mother's, right down to the glowing inquisi-
tiveness in their startlingly blue depths. Some
images featured the little girl alone, others included her with a happy and healthy Ginger,
her grandparents, Aunt Cara and presumably
other loved ones. In some, there was a fluffy
gray cat.

"These photos are gorgeous. Dr. Ramsey
is right about your talent. And your daughter
is beautiful."

"She is! And smart and kind and artistic
and imaginative. All the things I dreamed my
child would be."

Ally stared into her eyes, pouring every bit
of support she could manage into the look and

the touch of her hand on Ginger's. "I dream of those things for my daughter, too, if I'm ever lucky enough to have one."

"Thank you for understanding," Ginger whispered.

"You bet. Have you applied for your medical marijuana card yet? I know some doctors who specialize in this area. They can work with you and suggest strains that are symptom specific. It's—"

"Wait! What? Aren't you going to try and talk her out of this? Jacob, do something," Kate demanded.

"Yeah!" Jacob erupted. "Hold on here for one minute! This is your solution? I thought doctors took an oath to save lives."

Cara was looking at Flynn. "Dr. Ramsey, is it possible she doesn't know what she's saying? I've read about how chemo can affect the decision-making process. It can make people confused and—"

"Cara!" Ginger cried.

Eyes bright with tears, Cara turned toward her sister. "I'm sorry, Ginger. I'm so sorry. I just… I love you so much. And Ella…" Her voice broke with a sob.

"It really wouldn't be like that, Jacob," Ally said calmly. "I know it's easy for me to say because Ginger isn't my daughter, or sister, but

I can tell you that I've seen hundreds of people die in my lifetime, both working for my grandfather's medical practice and from my time as a medic in the Army. The acceptance of an inevitability we all have to face at some point isn't necessarily giving up. It can be a way of taking control. And, without exception, it's one of the bravest acts I've ever witnessed."

The room went quiet. Jacob peered at her as if he'd only just seen her for the first time. Kate looked thoughtful. Cara's sobs quieted. Ginger was beginning to look tired, and Ally didn't blame her.

"How about if the four of us, you and Kate and Cara and me, talk about this down the hall? There's a private room right next to the lounge."

"Thank you," Ginger told her before fixing a pleading gaze on Cara.

Ally watched a light dawn in Cara's red-rimmed eyes and felt a rush of relief when the woman began nodding. "Mom and Dad, let's do that. Let's go and let Ginger rest. I think it might be a good idea to hear what Ally has to say." Tugging her bag up from the floor, she adjusted the strap over her shoulder and added, almost like an afterthought, "And we can say some things, too. Ask questions and…yeah. This will be good."

Nicki, the nurse who'd briefed Ally, seemed to appear out of nowhere. Tucking an arm through Kate's, she led her toward the exit. "Come with me. I'll show you guys where to go."

Ally's back had been to the door, so she realized someone else had joined them only when a man stepped forward, presumably to allow the family to pass. That's when she saw him clearly: Tag James—every handsome, frowning inch of him.

CHAPTER FIVE

TAG STOOD BESIDE the helicopter and watched Ally push through the doors onto the roof-top landing pad. Perfect timing—the patient was being loaded. She'd secured her silky black hair into a messy bun and tendrils were slipping loose in the force of the late spring breeze. A messenger-style bag hung diagonally across her body to rest against one hip, and she'd traded her hospital blazer for a sporty fleece jacket. She looked relaxed and happy.

And why wouldn't she be? She'd just worked a magical spell on Jacob Weil. Not that he could blame the guy. Tag had been rather spellbound himself. Emotion stirred in his chest as he thought about her compassion and empathy for Ginger.

Flynn followed a few seconds later, took Ally by the elbow and steered her off to one side where they conversed for a moment before Flynn patted Ally on the shoulder. She pivoted and headed in Tag's direction, and an almost panicky feeling assailed him as he reluctantly allowed himself to acknowledge just how pretty she was. He couldn't seem to take his eyes off her, and his lack of self-control left him vaguely appalled. It dawned on him that she was likely younger than his baby sisters.

"Ready, pilot?" She blew by him, throwing a tentative grin his way, and continued to the passenger side of the chopper.

He felt his jaw drop at the teasing remark. Flashes of her comments about his being too slow to take off spurred him into action. Once on board, he found her already checking on the patient. She slid Tag a glance and the playful half smile on her face made him go soft.

He couldn't resist a little teasing of his own. "You're not back there smearing mud all over him, are you? Cuz I think he's already set."

Her gaze snapped up to meet his, and the laugh that followed had Tag feeling like he'd won a little prize. She scurried forward to her seat.

"So, you take this strap—" He bit off the explanation of how to work the intricate seat belt when he realized that she already knew. He'd never seen anyone who could get buckled in faster than he. Until now.

Cocking her head, she gave him an inquisitive look. "You were saying?"

He couldn't help but grin. He buckled up

and after a thorough run-through of preflight checks they were ready for takeoff.

Adjusting his headset, he asked, "Hear me okay?"

"Roger that," she responded, and within minutes they were off the ground and on the way.

Seconds after he'd settled the helicopter at their altitude and cruising speed, Ally's voice came through his headset. "Before we start making awkward small talk I need to say something."

"Okay?"

"I want to apologize."

Sparing her a glance, he noticed how intently she was staring ahead, brow softly furrowed, and something warmed inside him because he knew she'd been rehearsing this.

"You were right the other day when you said I owed you respect as a medical professional. You were right, and I didn't give it to you and I'm sorry about that. I'm not usually so ruffled under pressure. I've heard—and I learned the hard way—that emergencies feel different when they're family. I don't like excuses for bad behavior, but that's mine for being short with you on the plane."

"That's understandable. There's a difference

between a reason and an excuse, though, and I understand—".

"Hold on, please," she interrupted gently. "I'm not finished. In addition to excuses, I'm not great at apologies, either. I don't have to be, because I don't make very many mistakes. But I've practiced this one so I'd like to get it out.

"I was going to wait for our meeting with Flynn, but you haven't scheduled it yet, and I don't want things to be uncomfortable between us today, not to mention that an emergency could happen at any time that would force us together again where on the spot decisions will have to be made."

"Ha. That must be nice, the not making mistakes part."

"Oh, I'm talking about my professional life, like where my job is concerned. In my personal life, I should probably just start every conversation with an apology."

He laughed.

"You laugh, but it's true. Interpersonal communication is not my strong suit. When you came to my office that morning, I'd just come from Dr. Boyd's office, where he gave me his opinion on the use of traditional medicine in *his* hospital."

"He's very old-school."

"And I'm new-school, which technically is

older school, but… Regardless, I'm more of a blend of the two, but I don't think he's interested in blending. Anyway, I am sorry for not speaking to you more professionally that day, as well. I promise it's not normally like me. If anything, I get accused of being too professional, too…stoic."

"Okay. Well, then, I'll return the favor and admit it wasn't my finest moment when I brought up your age, which inadvertently implied a lack of experience."

"Thank you. Apology accepted. That is a bit of a hot-button issue with me. It gets…old, for lack of a better word. I try to let my actions speak to my experience and usually it works. But I have my moments."

Tag resisted the inclination to point out that only experience would make things easier, but as he worked through her explanation he wasn't so sure. He tried to put himself in her position as a woman and a young, beautiful Native one at that. It was impossible to imagine what she went through, dealing with people's doubts and preconceived notions, and constantly having to prove herself. In truth, he'd probably be a whole lot more defensive than she was.

A million questions flashed through his mind about her age, her experiences and her life, which he suspected had already been an interesting one. But he wasn't about to ask any of them now. He didn't want her to think he had more doubts. He'd already messed that up once. Better to let his actions speak for him.

"I appreciate you laying all this out on the table. I tell you what, let's work it out later when we can talk more…face-to-face, so to speak."

A soft sigh sounded in his earphones, giving him the impression she liked the layer of distance the onboard communications provided. "Okay."

"So, I don't know if Flynn mentioned it to you, but we're bringing my sister Iris back with us from Anchorage."

"He did not mention it. How nice. Does she live there?"

"No, she's flying in from Washington, DC."

"She lives in DC?"

"She was living there and going to graduate school. Just finished and now she's looking for her dream job."

"Hmm. So, I've met two of your sisters, a couple of cousins and I think your cousin-in-law? How many of you are there, anyway?"

"Um, a lot." Tag hadn't known she'd met any of his family. He wondered what they'd thought of her. "Tons of cousins. Six kids in my immediate family. Me, Shay, Hannah and then the triplets, Hazel, Seth and Iris."

"Triplets?"

"Flynn didn't tell you Iris is a triplet?"

A glance at her told him she was pondering that. "No, he didn't. I don't think I've ever met a triplet. Where are the other two?"

"Seth lives in Rankins. But he's a professional fisherman, so he's gone a lot, out on the water. Works with my dad. Hazel is a travel writer and blogger. Very adventurous. She's currently in Mongolia."

"Mongolia? Wow. That is utterly cool."

He laughed. "I think so. Our dad? Not so much. He doesn't understand Hazel's desire to constantly put herself in harm's way."

"You probably get her, though, don't you? The adventure part, anyway?"

A bolt of surprise went through him and it must have shown, because she added, "Pilot is not exactly a low-risk occupation."

"But I'm a paramedic, too. Saving people cancels out the danger."

Her husky laughter filled his headphones and worked right into him, into places that had him thinking about her in a way he knew he shouldn't. *Too young for you, James*, he told himself. Too young and too…what? Different? Yes. Probably. At this point, he hoped so, because a reason beyond their age difference would help to put him off.

"Nope, doesn't work that way, cowboy. Floatplanes, dual props, gliders, helicopters all scream *risk taker. Paramedic* just says you also like taking charge and helping people."

Cowboy? Hmm. And how would she know he liked to fly gliders? Had she been asking about him? He found himself smiling; he'd never have guessed Ally Mowak had this fun, easygoing side. Despite his first impression and having questioned some of her beliefs, he liked her. She seemed like a good person with the intentions to match. That's why, when the time was right, he was going to give her some advice.

TAG JAMES LANDED a helicopter just as smoothly as he did a floatplane. Granted, a landing pad on top of a hospital probably wasn't as challenging as a lake. But what did she know about piloting? They both seemed difficult, and frankly, she was relieved the trip had gone so well.

They seemed to have put the clay incident behind them. And she'd learned from the Weils that Tag was a friend of Ginger's, so her unease over finding him in the hospital room was pretty much alleviated. For some reason, probably Flynn's comment about Tag's close relationship with Dr. Boyd, she'd assumed that he was checking up on her.

Hospital staff was waiting in Anchorage, and they handed off the patient to the medical team without incident before climbing back into the helicopter. Within minutes they'd taken off and then landed again.

"This is a private airfield," Tag told her when they disembarked. "Iris is taking a car from the airport and meeting us here. We probably have enough time to grab a sandwich if you're hungry? There's a…" He'd been checking his phone as he spoke and she watched his brow knit with concern. "Uh-oh. Well. Maybe dessert, too, it looks like. Her flight was canceled."

"Oh, no."

"Mechanical problems. They put her on a different plane, but she's going to be delayed a bit. I'm sorry."

"You should be more than sorry if you did something to that plane just to hang out with a girl for a few hours," she said drily.

She'd meant it as a joke, but for a half a second he looked alarmed by the thought. Then a slow smile spread across his face. Hazel eyes narrowed and swept slowly over her, leaving a trail of heat across her skin and a pleasant tightness in her midsection.

"That's funny," he said in a quiet voice, those eyes pinned on hers now.

Her throat went dry. "I just meant that you don't need to apologize for your sister's flight delay," she said, because she couldn't think of anything else. Why was the back of her neck tingling?

"But it's Friday, and you probably have plans. Now we're not going to get back until late."

"No plans. Unless you consider eating pizza and watching the Mariners game plans?"

Was it her imagination or did he look pleased by that answer? Considerate of him to be worried about ruining her Friday night. She had to concede that Flynn was right; Tag did seem like a nice guy.

"In fact, I *would* consider those plans. Very fine plans indeed. You wanna grab a bite and watch the game while we wait?"

She grinned. "Uh, yeah."

They walked to a nearby sports bar. Because it was early for dinner and late for lunchtime, the bar was quiet inside with only a few tables filled. Fellow Mariner fans were easy to spot in their blue-green and gray caps and shirts.

A sign indicated that they could seat themselves, so they grabbed a booth with a good view of one of the oversize television screens. A woman wearing a snug Mariners T-shirt and a tight denim miniskirt hustled over from the bar. She was attractive with thick, strategically applied makeup and blond hair up in a complicated twist. Her name tag said Rita.

"I'm sorry," she said, giving Tag an apologetic smile before pinning a gentle scowl on Ally. "But this side of the restaurant is for customers twenty-one and older only."

Tag blew out an exaggerated huff and reached for his wallet. "Will this madness never end? I'm getting so tired of it. I'm going to be twenty-three next month, or is it twenty-four? Hold on, let me check."

Ally laughed and dug her wallet out of her bag. She handed her driver's license over to the waitress. Rita was giggling and seemed far more interested in examining Tag than Ally's ID.

"Sure you are. Come on…" Cupping her fingers, she waggled them in a come-hither gesture. "Hand it over. I can spot a fake ID from a mile away. Sneaking into bars is going to get you into big, big trouble, Mister…?"

"James. Tag James," he supplied.

"Tag, huh?" Reaching out, she gave his shoulder a playful nudge. "You're it."

Wait… What? Was this woman hitting on him while Ally was sitting right here?

Rita thrust her ID in Ally's general direction with a flat "Thanks, hon." Eager blue eyes remained fastened on Tag. "Is this little cutie your daughter?"

Ally slid a hand across the table, threaded her fingers through Tag's and pitched her voice to sweet. "Wife, actually. Thank you, Rita, for your meticulous and painstaking commitment to the law. You're a credit to your profession."

"Oh…" Rita drawled, her pale cheeks turning nearly as pink as her lip gloss. "Um… you're welcome. Are you guys ready to order?"

They both asked for the special, the Mariner Plate, which consisted of deep-fried fish, clams, and shrimp with spicy slaw and french fries.

Ally turned her head and pretended to watch the game while Rita hurried off toward the kitchen. She hadn't thought this through, because now her skin was burning at every contact point where it touched his, but she didn't want to remove her hand in case Rita was watching. Tag's gaze was intent on her, no doubt wondering how many shades of psycho she was.

It took all of her willpower not to squirm. Was he upset? She should probably apologize for thwarting Rita's romantic ploy. But then the sound of his low, deep chuckle seeped into her, heating her from the inside out. She really liked his laugh.

He gave her hand a little squeeze. Her eyes felt heavy as she heaved them up to meet his. A rush of heat blasted through her at the intensity she saw there. She couldn't blame Rita. No doubt he had women hitting on him constantly. She already knew he did. As Rankins's most eligible bachelor, the title all but guaranteed it.

His brows shifted up along with the corners of his mouth. Eyes shining, green hues dominating, he repeated the word, "Wife?"

Subtly, she tried to extricate her fingers, but he held firm. "Stop that," he said, "I'm holding my wife's hand."

"You don't have to—"

"I do if you want to pull this off. Rita is over there telling her friends right now about the cradle robber she's serving at table seven."

Ally snickered and offered up a helpless shrug. "I'm sorry if I got in the way of something there. But the way she looked at me and then just dismissed me with the 'hon' and the 'cutie' and then hitting on you right in front of me? It was rude. Now you see what I was talking about earlier? I'll tell her the truth if you want. I'll even ask her out for you?"

"I'm not interested in her," he said in that warm gravelly tone that melted into her like honey on toast. She managed a weak smile and tried not to think about why that statement pleased her.

"And, I assure you, I can find my own dates. But you do realize that you are probably young enough to be my daughter?"

She knew he was teasing, but for some reason, she needed to make sure he understood. "Technically, I suppose, yes. But I'm also old enough to be a paramedic, an Army veteran and the hospital liaison—as well as your wife."

Like she'd hit a dimmer switch, his expression faded to serious. "Ah," he said, brushing his free hand across his jaw. "Are you sure this isn't still about our first encounter?"

Was it? She didn't know. The way his thumb was moving over her hand made it difficult to think. She did know that she wished she hadn't turned the look in his green-brown eyes from lazy fun to sharp and solemn. Although they probably should discuss the subject further, as they'd agreed. Face-to-face. She just wished his face, his hand, his voice and the rest of him wasn't so…unsettling.

"I don't know. You made that crack about the clay in the helicopter, but you never scheduled a meeting with Flynn. Are you going to give me grief going forward?"

He seemed to be thinking it over. "Oversight on my part about the meeting. My office assistant is on leave, and things have been a little scattered. Let's meet right now."

With a wink, he lifted her hand and brushed a soft kiss across her knuckles before letting it go. Ally's breath froze in her lungs because his lips seared her skin and her heart was beating this hard, rhythmic thud in her chest. Then he reached across the table to tuck a piece of hair behind her ear, and her pulse took off like a bottle rocket anxious for the Fourth of July. Husband-like gestures, she reminded herself; he was only playing a part. And for her sake, no less.

He took a sip of his water. When he spoke, his voice sounded low and a little husky, and she had to focus on the meaning of his words. "I do plan on requesting that you adhere to strictly modern medical practices in emergency cases where I'm involved. As we previously discussed, I understand that Louis is your cousin and that you hadn't technically started the job yet, so you've got a pass there. But in future cases, we need to be on the same page regarding treatment."

"You think because I used the clay on Louis

that I would discard modern medicine whenever I feel like it?"

"Well… I don't know. And it's not just Louis now, is it? You seemed pretty convinced in Ginger's situation, too."

Debates about medicine she was used to, so thankfully everything Abe had taught her kicked in. This topic she could discuss with complete confidence. She tried to decide how best to proceed.

He beat her to it. "Since you brought this up, I feel like I need to give you some advice. Despite our rough start, I have a good feeling about you, Ally. Aside from the mu…clay, Louis's evacuation went well. You made the right call regarding the hospital. And I admire the way you handled Jacob Weil. He can be pretty intense, if not outright intimidating. I know you had Ginger's best interests in mind. Anyone could see your compassion. Except…"

"Except what?"

"Except that I'm wondering if you're aware of Dr. Boyd's opinion on this subject."

"Which subject?"

"The subject of medical marijuana. He's very much against it."

"But it's legal now."

"Not at the federal level. And he lobbied hard against it here in Alaska."

"Ginger brought it up."

Tag exhaled. "I know, and like I said, I think you handled it very well. But you need to be careful."

A million invisible needles pricked at her skin. "Careful?" She repeated the word flatly. *Careful* was the opposite of what she needed to be in order to get her message out, especially when medical marijuana was a topic about which she should be able to speak freely.

"Yes, if you don't want people to think you're…"

She smiled and asked, "What? I don't care what a few people say, people who don't know the facts. All I want is to help people who want to be helped."

"You might not think you care right now, but even one person in a position of power can have a lot of pull. What if you lost your job? How would that help anyone?"

That part did bother her, the job-losing bit. She'd worked so hard to get here. Her grandfather had sacrificed so much. "Dr. Boyd can't fire me, not by himself. The board hired me."

"I know, but…he has a lot of influence in the hospital and on the board, and in the community, for that matter. At the very least, he can make your life miserable. Please don't think I'm being condescending here. I have no doubts about your skill and experience. But, on another level, I don't want to see you get yourself into a…situation. I'm afraid you might not understand how powerful bureaucracy and politics can be."

These words hit another nerve, reminding her of both her vulnerability and the importance of building a strong reputation. She might be young, but she wasn't stupid, not where her profession was concerned, anyway.

"Did you not hear the part where I spent four years in the Army?"

"That's one of the things I've been wondering about. How did you reconcile all of this? I can't imagine Uncle Sam being very tolerant of your alternative methods."

"My job in the Army was to follow orders. I was there to learn as much about modern emergency techniques as I could. The military is not exactly a flexible, open-to-change type of organization. Not when it comes to my cause, anyway."

He grinned. "But a small hospital in Rankins, Alaska, is?"

"It's a place to start." She shrugged, not willing to talk about her plans or her grandfather's. She just needed a little time to prove herself.

"A revolutionary." He winked. "What do

your parents think of your accomplishments and ambition?"

"Parent. One. My grandfather. And he is extremely proud. I am everything he hoped for. At least, that's what he tells me. So far, anyway." She couldn't help but smile when she thought of him.

"How…did your parents die?"

"No. My mom dropped me off with her parents when I was only a few weeks old. My grandmother died when I was three. It's been my grandpa and me ever since."

"Where is she now, your mom? And what about your dad?"

Ally fidgeted with her silverware. "Last we heard, which was a few years ago, she was alive. She was—is—totally messed up. Ran away when she was fifteen, had me at sixteen. I've never met my father." She grimaced. "I don't even like calling them my mom and dad because my grandfather is both of those things to me."

"Wow. I don't know what to say… I can't imagine what that would be like. I've been inundated with family my entire life. They kind of, uh, consume me. I'm so sorry."

Ally forced a smile. She was used to this reaction, and while she appreciated it, she didn't need it. She was fine. Mostly fine. Sure, a fe-

male opinion would have been, would be, helpful now and then. But her grandfather was
more than a lot of children had in two parents
and she was incredibly grateful for that.

"It's fine. Families come in all shapes and
sizes, right? So many kids out there have it
way, way worse than me. Honestly, I'm very
lucky."

Tag nodded, and the way his eyes were
searching hers made her feel…she wasn't even
sure beyond the fact that her skin was hot and
her throat felt tight. The pity in his gaze was
gone, replaced with what looked like admiration, maybe? She found herself hoping it was
that.

CHAPTER SIX

"How long is Iris staying?" Bering handed one end of a banner to Tag and backed away, unrolling it as he went.

"Not sure yet." Tag fingered the thick textured paper that said Welcome Home & Congratulations, Iris! He climbed the stepladder next to the gazebo in Bering's yard, pausing at the top while Bering scaled the ladder on the opposite side. He then tacked his end to the beam. "She's job hunting right now. Why does this paper feel weird?"

"It's some sort of super-biodegradable paper that Reagan made for a science project. The paint, too. He's going to put the whole works in Emily's compost pile after the party and then chart how long it takes to degrade and how it affects the surrounding…molecules or plant life or whatever. I don't know. Emily and Aidan are helping him."

Tag let out a chuckle. "Of course they are." Aidan was Janie's husband and Gareth and

Reagan's stepdad. He was also a scientist as well as Emily's brother.

"What kind of job is Iris looking for?"

Ally had asked Iris the same question the day before. Those two had hit it off like long-lost pals. Tag and Ally had walked back to the airfield after the game where they'd talked for hours before Iris arrived. She'd taken one look at them and asked if Ally was his girl-friend, which prompted them to share the story about Rita and their pretend marriage. Think-ing about yesterday's trip filled him with a disconcerting mix of exhilaration and anxiety, much the way he felt when he piloted a new aircraft for the first time.

He'd nearly jumped out of the booth when Ally reached across the table and took his hand. The feel of her skin on his had been in-tense, the force of his attraction catching him off guard. It had also kept him up way too late the night before, leaving him a little irri-table today. Eventually, he'd worked his brain around to accepting that it was perfectly nor-mal to be attracted to a smart, funny, beautiful woman. Even one who was too young for him. He just needed to admire her and appreciate her from afar like one would a movie star or a model in a magazine.

He realized Bering was waiting for him to

elaborate. "Iris has applied at different government agencies in DC and a few independent think tanks. She wasn't super specific. I'm not sure she knows what she wants."

Bering stretched an arm toward the middle of the banner and secured it there. "I swear, nothing would surprise me where she's concerned."

"Me, either. I just want her to be happy." Of all his siblings, he worried about Iris the most. She didn't seem to have the same innate contentedness that the rest of them possessed. Even with her academic success and innumerable accolades, she seemed to be constantly searching for some elusive element.

Bering added a couple more tacks. "Jack is stopping by later. Did I tell you that?"

"No, you didn't." Tag wondered why the senator was coming here.

"He's in town, and he wants to talk to us. He's bringing Randall."

Randall Fincher was the state senator serving in their district. He'd been in the legislature for eleven years and had committed to assisting Tag when he retired and the time came for Tag to run.

"Huh. Okay, well, I'm curious."

"Yeah, me, too." Bering climbed down the ladder.

They both stepped back to admire their handiwork. Bering nodded, and in tandem they picked up their ladders, folded them and carried them to Bering's shop. After stowing them away, they headed back toward the house where Shay and Hannah were preparing the picnic tables scattered around the grassy yard. Shay smoothed out a tablecloth while Hannah tacked it down so it would stay put in the breeze.

Shay said, "Hey, just the guys we were looking for."

"Oh, yeah?" Tag nabbed a chip out of the bowl Hannah placed on the table.

"Yeah." Hannah grabbed a handful of chips for herself and leaned a hip against the table. "A kind of weird thing happened to me a couple of days ago, and I was sharing it with Shay, who then told me that a kind of weird thing happened to her, too. And when taken together, these two things seem big weird." She held her hands apart for emphasis before biting off half a chip.

"Big weird, huh?"

"Yep." She grinned. "Lucas and I were outside playing catch a few days ago when these two women pulled up in this fancy rented SUV. I figured they were probably lost until they asked for me by name. Then they asked about buying the house." Lucas was Tate's nephew. Hannah and her husband, Tate, had adopted him. They lived in the largest, most luxurious home in Rankins. With the real estate market improving as it had been lately, Tag wasn't all that surprised, although it would take someone with pretty deep pockets to buy their place.

"Don't tell me you guys are going to sell?" Hannah adored the house. Not only had it been built by one of her close friends, but it also had an atrium with a large pond, where Hannah's treasured koi lived.

"Of course not. I haven't finished my story. They made an offer on the spot—almost double what the house is worth."

"Wow." Bering was shaking his head. "Double?"

"I know, right?" Shay stepped forward. "Listen to mine—a woman and a man came into the inn late Wednesday morning. They strolled around for a long time, took a walk outside, snapped some photos and finally went for lunch in the restaurant. Adele was hostessing, the way she often does when it gets busy, and they asked her a bunch of questions, like did she know the owner and did she think the owner would be interested in selling. She texted me, and I came out to meet them."

Bering crossed his massive arms over his chest. "Were they serious?"

"Not only were they serious, they already knew everything about the Faraway Inn. I mean, everything a person can get a hold of through public records and internet searching. The offer they made was outrageous."

"That reminds me," Tag said, knowing he was about to deepen the mystery. "I stopped to see Mickey and Mrs. P. on my way home the other night, and you know that piece of property Park bought across the highway?"

Bering nodded. "Yeah, I saw the for-sale sign, too. I figured Park was just trying to make a buck."

"Me, too, but when I asked Mick about it, he told me Park was asking more than double what he paid for it."

"Which means Park probably knows something."

They all looked at Hannah, who huffed out a breath. "Which means I have to talk to Park?"

Tag grinned at his sister. "He loves you, Banana," he said, hoping to soften her up by using her childhood nickname.

"Yes, he does," Shay added with a chuckle.

"Ugh. Well, he does owe me for the pool lessons I've been giving him. Fine. If he knows something, I'll get it out of him."

ALLY SAT IN the passenger seat of Flynn's SUV and tried to enjoy the scenery as they traveled out of town. A difficult feat, what with her stomach feeling like a wind spinner on a breezy day. After several miles, they turned onto a gravel drive. An attractively carved and painted sign read James Guide & Outfitter Service.

Where the long driveway forked, Flynn took a left, away from the house, and parked among the other cars already scattered near some outbuildings. Removing a gift bag from the back seat, he climbed out of the car.

"Should I have brought something?"

A grin played at his lips. "No, this is a little joke between Iris and me."

"You guys are good friends, huh?"

"Um, sort of."

"Hey, that reminds me, you never told me she was a triplet."

"I didn't?" He cocked his head. "Huh. I guess… I don't think of her that way."

Ally gave him a curious look, but there was no time to ask questions because Flynn was already moving. They headed toward a growing crowd of people near the large house, some bunched under a gazebo, others congregating in clusters around the spacious yard. They passed the professional-looking basketball half-court Flynn had mentioned. Kids were bouncing balls and shooting baskets.

"Wow…" Ally gawked at the parklike setting.

"I know. It's pretty great, right? Bering and Emily love to entertain, and they've spent a lot of time on this place."

A cluster of people milled around a horseshoe pit. Off to one side, there was a badminton net where four teenagers were laughing and smacking at a birdie. Farther away, the white wickets of a croquet course had been set up, and Ally heard the distinctive thwack of croquet mallet against ball.

Ally recognized Iris as she broke away from a group near one of the picnic tables.

"There's Iris." She glanced at Flynn, only to discover that he'd already spotted her. His body tensed even as his smile brightened. He waved and headed in Iris's direction. Interesting.

Ally felt the back of her neck prickle. Her gaze swept across the sea of people and quickly latched onto Tag's. His knowing grin paired with a quirk of one brow suggested he'd been waiting for her to catch sight of him. A furnace blast of heat radiated from her core all the way out through her skin. She returned the smile, and the next thing she knew they were moving toward each other.

"Hey," he said, stopping in front of her. "Nice of you to come today."

"Thank you. Flynn actually invited me like a week ago. I didn't know any of you yet. I mean, you and I had *met*, but, well, I didn't know who you were. And anyway, you know… it will be more fun now than if the party had been last week."

She loved the deep sound of his laughter, the way it seemed to vibrate through her. "It sure will. Do you think we can find a few minutes to talk later?"

Ally wondered what about. She'd spent the previous evening trying to decide if she imagined the connection they'd forged and what to do about it. She wanted to explore it, spend time with him. But she had no idea how to go about it. She hadn't dated much and when she had, the guy had always done the asking. Should she invite him over for dinner or maybe see if he wanted to grab lunch one day soon?

"Yeah, sure. There's something I'd like to ask you, too. As long as you don't plan on beating this age thing to death?" she teased.

"Hey," he joked, "I'll have you know age is

not an issue with me. My pretend wife is years younger, and we are as happy as can be."

A fluttery feeling spread through her, because even though he said it in jest, it was exactly what she'd hoped to hear. "How nice for you that you'll have someone to push your wheelchair in your later years. Which obviously—" she waved a hand up and down the length of him "—is not too far off."

Glaring playfully, he said, "Yes, and I'm hoping that soon she'll be able to go to an R-rated movie without having to show her ID."

"Oh, well, I doubt she'd care about showing it for that. I know for a fact she loves movies. She grew up in a village in the middle of nowhere, so a movie theater is like a huge thrill for her and… This third-person thing is getting weird now, isn't it, because I'm talking about myself like some kind of sociopath?"

"A little," he teased. "But it's okay—the guy you're talking to likes it. He finds it cute."

They laughed, and Ally was still grinning when Iris and Flynn approached them.

"Ally, hi!" Iris said.

Tag greeted Flynn, then hugged his sister. "I'm going to go give Bering a hand with the grill. Don't forget we're talking later, okay, Ally?"

Iris beamed at her. "I'm so glad you could

make it. Now I feel like I have two people who came here just for me."

"I'm happy to be here, but it looks like you have a lot of people who came here for you. I'm not even sure I *know* this many people."

Iris frowned and looked around. "I know. It's a little ridiculous."

"What do you mean?"

"Most of these people aren't here for me. That sounds bad, doesn't it? I don't mean to sound ungrateful. I love my family, and now that you're a fake part of it…" she paused to wink at Ally "…you should know that they will use any excuse to throw a party. Like herd animals, they like to gather. And graze."

Ally wondered about her reference to "these people" and "they" instead of "we."

"I'm just going to say congratulations and that I think a party in your honor is well deserved. It's not every day a person earns a doctorate—right, Flynn?"

Gaze glued on Iris, he agreed, "Right."

With a breezy wave of her hand, Iris said, "I worked hard for it, that's true. Let's not talk about the fact that a doctorate in economics doesn't have quite the same cachet as a medical degree."

She was obviously joking, but Flynn seemed a little irritated by the self-deprecating comment.

"Iris, seriously," he said. "Ask twenty people here about asymmetric shock and reserve currency and see what answers you get."

Iris furrowed her brow and looked like she was going to argue.

Ally pitched her expression to serious and jumped in before Iris could speak. "Plus, I'm very familiar with Flynn's work. Trust me—his job is not that hard. Everyone knows it's the nurses and the paramedics who do all the work."

Iris laughed and linked an arm through one of Ally's. Tilting her head toward the gazebo, she said, "Come on. Let's get you introduced to some people."

AFTER LUNCH, EMILY announced it was time for all basketball players to gather on the court. Janie read off the teams and went over the rules.

"We're doing three on three to twenty points or twenty-five minutes' total game time. Because we've got five teams, we'll draw for the first game, and it will be loser out. The winning team will take the bracket spot and continue from there. My handsome husband, Aidan, has a bum shoulder, so he's going to be our referee." She then informed the crowd they had five minutes to find their teammates and discuss strategy before the first game began.

"You're with my cousin Gareth and his friend Cody." Ally turned to find Tag behind her. He waved toward the opposite side of the court. He pointed at Ally, and a tall teenager held up a finger in an "I'll be right there" motion.

"Cool. Thanks."

"So, you play basketball?"

She shrugged. "Yeah."

"Did you play in high school?"

"No. I didn't go to high school. I was home-schooled."

His forehead knitted like he was puzzling out her meaning.

"Something wrong?"

"No, uh…" He shifted from one foot to another. "Nothing. It's just that my family is extremely passionate about sports, basketball especially. We can be a little, um, intense and aggressive."

"I understand. I can be that way, too, about certain things." She added a chuckle, but he still wore a pained expression. "Wait, are you worried about me?"

"A little. Please don't call me a chauvinist but you're tiny, and if you haven't played much I'm afraid…"

At least he was honest. Ally placed a hand on his arm. "Don't be. I'll be fine. It's just a game, right?" His arm was so much bigger than hers. She might have let her touch linger a little longer than necessary, she realized, when she noticed him staring down at his forearm.

She removed her hand, but his expression only held more angst as he said, "No, Ally, that's my point. It's not just a game with us. It's…" His words faded away as his expression turned sheepish. He squeezed her shoulder. "Well, you'll see. And I apologize in advance for the over-the-top behavior you're about to witness."

"Oh-kay, I guess?"

"What I'm saying is that I can't let you win."

Sliding her gaze toward the hand still on her shoulder, she said, "Thanks for the warning. Better be careful, though. All this looking out for me and I'll wonder about your intentions."

He went hands up, palms out, eyes wide, like she'd just caught him robbing a bank. "No, no. I don't… I'm not thinking about you…like that. I promise."

An invisible pain hit her in the chest, so sudden and powerful that she brought a hand up and placed it there. She glanced away, forcing a smile that felt brittle enough to crack her face. How could she have been so stupid?

He could have any woman he wanted. Why in the world would he consider…whatever it was she'd been thinking?

"Of course not," she managed. "I was only… kidding." Liar. And she knew she sounded like one. She tried for eye contact, but her eyelids felt heavy, her vision blurred. Why had she flirted with him? It was all that pretend-wife talk and the looks and the touching. She had zero experience with flirting, and clearly she was not a natural.

"Hey," he said, but she still couldn't bring herself to meet his gaze. Her cheeks were flaming with embarrassment. Not until the very tips of his fingers found the tips of hers and squeezed, making her breath catch a little, did she look at him. He let go, but that deadly green glint was blazing in his eyes, and his voice held a desperate kind of urgency as he whispered, "That was a lie, Ally. I was lying. I shouldn't say this, but if you were a decade or so older, my intentions would be exactly what you implied. But you're not and so I promised myself I would let it go."

His eyes roamed over her, and it felt like a panicky hummingbird had been turned loose inside her chest, darting every which way. She wanted to argue, to convince him age didn't matter, but that would probably sound…desperate.

And maybe he was just being nice and letting
her down easy. But, no, the way he looked at her,
watched her, had her believing every word. She
couldn't keep her eyes off him, either. And when
they touched, the air went all heavy and thick
between them, like a thundercloud gathering.
She might not have much experience, but their
attraction was about as straightforward as it got.
And now he was admitting it only to assure her
he wouldn't act on it? Because of her age? She
didn't know how old he was and she didn't care.

A whistle blew, and she nearly jumped out
of her skin. Game time. Further ruining the
moment, Tag gave her a buddy-type pat on the
shoulder and said, "Don't worry. You should
do fine with Gareth on your team. He's really
good. Almost as good as me. Don't hate me
after." Walking backward, he tapped his chest
with one finger before pointing it at her. "You
young 'uns can learn something from us old
guys." Adding a cocky wink, he left to find
his teammates.

And that's when Ally's blood began to boil.
Why did he get to decide she was too young?
Or he was too old or…whatever? Why did he
get to give her advice and tell her how things
were done? Why could he assume that she
would be careless where her job was concerned or that she couldn't operate her seat

belt or that she hadn't played much basketball? Maybe it was time someone showed Tag James a thing or two, that the world wasn't always just as he saw it.

Maybe, Ally thought, she should be that someone. And perhaps she should start with a basketball game.

CHAPTER SEVEN

GARETH AND CODY jogged over to her, and both boys gave her hand a quick shake.

The taller one said, "I'm Gareth. Good to meet you."

"You, too. You're Tag's cousin, right?"

"Yep, my mom is Janie. My stepdad is Aidan." He hitched a thumb toward his companion. "This is my friend Cody. We play on the high school team together."

Cody smiled, and Gareth wasted no more time getting down to business. "I'm assuming you've played at least a little if you're willing to subject yourself to one of our family melees?"

"Some." She added a smile because he'd managed to figure this out and Tag hadn't.

"So, looking at the teams today, Tag, Freddie and Brittany are going be our main competition. It doesn't matter who Tag plays with—he almost always wins. But, with any luck, we won't be playing his team until the championship game, anyway."

He went on to give a quick rundown on the strengths and weaknesses of the best players.

Ally was impressed. "Got it."

"Do you think you can handle the ball? Dribbling and stuff? I mean, I was thinking since you're shorter maybe you could play point?"

Should she ease his mind and tell him she was more than a decent player or just wait and let him figure it out? As usual, she decided to let her actions do the talking. "I think I can handle it."

The teams drew straws to see who would be matched up for the initial loser-out match. Unfortunately, luck was not with their team, as Gareth and Tag both drew the short straws, meaning they would play Tag's team first.

They flipped a coin for first possession, and Tag's team won. His teammate, Freddie, began the game with the ball at the top of the court. Ally allowed him to pass it to Tag, who made a simple jump shot, putting his team up by two.

Ally started play for her team. She easily moved around Freddie to pass the ball to Cody. Brittany was all over him, and Tag was on Gareth. Ally got around Freddie, and Cody called out a play and passed it back to Ally. When Gareth moved around Tag, she fired the ball to him, and he put the ball through the hoop and tied the game.

They went on like this for a few minutes, with Tag's team scoring and theirs tying it up. Ally held back, assessing the skills of everyone on the court. Tag was just as good as Gareth said, probably better. Like her, she felt he was holding back. But, she suspected, not nearly as much as she was.

A few minutes in she could see it would eventually come down to an under-the-basket matchup between Tag and Gareth if she didn't do something. From what she'd seen so far, this wasn't a strong bunch of three-point shooters.

She called a time-out.

Gareth looked concerned. "Hey, what's up? You okay?"

"Yep, good."

"You can obviously handle the ball a little better than you let on, huh?"

"A bit." She added a grin. "I just need to know how bad you guys want to win?"

"What do you mean?"

"I mean, I've seen enough to know that we can win this game if you want to, or we can just keep playing, and you and Tag can duke it out under the basket and see who comes out on top."

Gareth peered at her and lowered his voice. "You're a three-pointer shooter."

It sounded like an accusation and Ally laughed. "I am. And I can handle Freddie. But what's going to happen is this—I'm going to sink a couple of threes before Tag figures out that I can play. He's going to call a time-out and then he's going to guard me. That will put Freddie on you and free you up under the basket. Then we can have some fun."

Cody stared at her, his face an expression of hope and disbelief. Then his mouth curved into a little grin as he seemed to catch up with the plan.

"Are you guys okay with this?"

Gareth put a hand over his mouth to hide his smile. "Heck, yeah."

TAG WATCHED ALLY fist-bump Gareth and Cody in their little huddle. It looked like she was giving them a pep talk. Cute. He was relieved to see that she could handle the ball pretty well. All in all, he thought their teams were pretty evenly matched with his having a slight advantage.

Aidan blew the whistle, indicating the time-out was at an end. Ally passed the ball to Cody. He faked a drive and threw it back to Ally, who had already moved around Freddie and was heading to the baseline corner. Tag spun around to guard Gareth, expecting her to pass the ball to him. Only when the crowd erupted with a cheer as the ball slapped loudly onto the court behind him did he realize she'd made a three-point shot.

Huh.

Their possession. But as Freddie passed the ball, Ally batted it away and Cody grabbed it.

Turnover.

This time when Ally darted around Freddie, she looked like a streak of lightning. She launched the ball from beyond the top of the key and scored another three points.

Just like that, they were down by four points, and he realized that Ally, the little con, could play basketball.

"Time-out!" Tag waited for his fellow players to approach. "Guys, what do you think?"

"I think the quick one is making me look like a doofus." Freddie chuckled and used his sleeve to wipe the sweat from his brow.

"Let's switch. I'll take her, and you go under the basket."

Freddie nodded. "Okay, but you know I won't be able to shut him down, right? If Gareth gets the ball, we're toast."

"Just do the best you can."

Tag had no intention of allowing that to

happen. Ally appeared calm and unflappable. Holding the ball against his right hip, he waited for Aidan to call the action. Narrowing his eyes, he gave Ally a menacing smirk. She responded with an amused smile, but kept her attention on Aidan.

As the whistle blew, Ally lunged, her right arm shooting forward and stripping Tag of the ball. Stunned with disbelief, he whirled to defend against her. Too late. She fired the ball to Cody.

He caught it. Brittany was glued to him as he pivoted toward the basket. Tag moved that way, planning to intercept the impending pass to Gareth. Cody fired the ball back to Ally, who promptly scored again.

"Three points!" Gareth lifted a fist skyward. "Way to go, Ally." More fist bumping. Not nearly as cute now, Tag silently acknowledged.

On the next play, he managed to pass the ball to Brittany. Barely, because Ally was like an irritating mosquito and he had to rely on his height advantage to throw it over her head.

"That's it, Brittany!" Tag called when she hit a jumper and scored two.

This time when Ally started play, Tag went tighter. She drove hard to her right, flipped a behind-the-back pass to Cody, who zipped it to Gareth. His nephew dunked it to the roar of the crowd.

Brittany groaned. Freddie shrugged.

Tag sighed and threw up his hands because that was the moment he knew: the game might not be over, but ultimately, he was going to have to accept defeat. And all because of Ally.

That didn't mean he wasn't reeling when, a few plays later, Gareth walked up to him, dribbling the ball from side to side, a cocky grin on his lips. "Good game. First time for everything, huh?"

"Apparently."

"So, when are you two getting married?" Gareth quipped, and Tag knew it wasn't the last he'd hear of that old family joke. He should probably warn Ally.

He couldn't help but grin. "We already are. Sort of."

THE CRUNCHING SOUND of feet treading on loose gravel alerted Ally that someone was approaching. Her team had gone on to win the next two games. After accepting the wows, congratulations and at least one confusing comment about marriage, Ally had departed with a slice of "winner's cake" and a cold drink to a relatively secluded bench next to the river where she'd been cooling off. She turned to find Tag approaching. Finally.

"Hey." He sank down onto the bench beside her. His gaze traveled over her and, although it was quick, Ally felt the same intense pull of attraction, boosting both her heart rate and her confidence.

"Hi."

"Congratulations."

"Thank you. It was fun."

"Why didn't you tell me you were a basketball prodigy?"

She chuckled. "*Prodigy* is a bit of an exaggeration. And I told you I played."

"Mmm-hmm. No, not like that you didn't. I asked if you played in school."

"And I said no. Because I didn't."

"Yeah, so I assumed—"

She interrupted, "You have an assuming problem, are you aware of that?"

He scratched his chin, looking uncomfortable, which made her laugh.

"We have a basketball court in my village. I didn't have a television or video games or a screen of any kind. Not until I was a teenager, and then the computer was only for learning. Basketball was what I did for fun."

"Wow. Flynn knew, didn't he?"

"Yep. We used to play when he'd visit. And

he stayed with us for a couple of summers when he was in high school to study with my grandpa."

"I'm impressed. And I'm not often impressed by someone else's skills. It's your strategy, too."

"Well, strategy is vital when you have a distinct and fixed disadvantage, right? All great military leaders know that no matter how great a weakness you have, if you can turn it to your advantage, you've got a chance."

"I have bad news, though."

"What's that?"

"Now we have to get married for real."

"What?" She laughed.

He was grinning. "I've always made this joke to my family that if I ever found a woman who could beat me at basketball I'd marry her. You're undoubtedly gonna hear some jokes about it, too, so I thought I better tell you."

"I heard one already, but I didn't get it."

"Although…" Leaning back, he stretched one leg out and Ally admired its lean, muscled length.

"Although?" she said without bothering to look away. But she didn't immediately meet his gaze, either. Instead, she let her eyes inch slowly up, pausing briefly on his mouth. Smiling slowly, she watched his eyes darken as his gaze flickered to her mouth and away again.

He blinked, nostrils flaring, chest expanding as he slowly inhaled a deep breath. Ha. His smoldering gaze landed on hers again like... like he couldn't help himself? Or didn't want to help himself? She waited, wondering if he was going to see past the years between them and acknowledge the attraction simmering here.

"I suppose I could adopt you, instead. You're a sweet kid."

A loud sigh accompanied her eye roll while he sat there looking satisfied with his stupid joke.

"Are you...serious with this?" Slipping an arm behind him to grip the back of the bench, she inched toward him, studying his reaction. "Do you really not...?"

She scooted closer. Desire and terror looked to be at war on his face. He stared at her lips and leaned away from her at the same time. She would have laughed if it wasn't so exasperating.

"Not what?" The question sounded strained. He swallowed, his Adam's apple bobbing in his throat.

Ally planned every beat of her next move because she wanted to catch him off guard, wanted to see the heat flare in his eyes, wanted to elicit a reaction without giving him time to think.

Crooking a finger as if she was going to tell him a secret, she whispered, "I'm confused, and I need to tell you…"

He leaned in. She went closer. And closer still, exhaling softly near his ear. When she heard the sharp exhale of his breath, a spike of joy shot through her because it helped cement the truth of what she was about to say.

"You don't look at me like you think I'm a kid." Then she kissed him.

THE WORDS SHE spoke didn't even penetrate Tag's brain, or maybe he wouldn't let them. But that thought would only occur to him later, because the sweetest lips he'd ever tasted were moving over his and he couldn't think past how incredibly good it felt. And right and… He twined one hand into her hair right next to her scalp, the other he curled around her shoulder so he could deepen the kiss.

He coaxed her lips apart, and she seemed to melt into him, her fingers digging into his shoulders. He groaned. She responded with a soft little moan of her own, unleashing a not-quite-identifiable emotion inside him. Almost like fury, but not quite, because while the air was charged around them, there was a lightness inside his chest. And he realized that he never wanted to let go. Pulling her closer, adjusting so that more of her body pressed against his, he moved his mouth over hers, fitting it closer because he couldn't seem to get enough...

He had no idea how much time had passed when she pulled away, just enough so that her mouth still hovered over his. She was breathing as hard as he was, and after a few seconds, her raspy chuckle worked into him like a caress. He would have kissed her again, but she was talking...

It took a moment for her next words to compute. "Stop worrying about my age and tell me how you really feel."

Bees were swarming through his thoughts. Slowly he tuned out the buzzing and focused on her lazy-lidded eyes and swollen lips. *Ally.* So, so beautiful. Wayward strands of her silky black hair stirred in the breeze. She looked thoroughly...kissed. No, it was worse than that. A sick feeling rushed in, dousing the heat that had been muddling his brain only seconds before. What had he done?

"Ally, we..." We what? Not we, *I.* How could he make things right? Apologize? She'd kissed him, yes, but he'd let her. He'd more than let her; he'd kissed her back without an ounce of restraint and precious little self-control. And that wasn't like him. He'd never lost his mind quite like this before, not even back in high school when he was young and reckless and… and she made him feel things he'd never felt before.

Languid brown eyes stared back at him without any regret or hesitation reflected there. Which made him feel about a million times worse.

"Oh, no…" Shifting, she sat up straighter. The fingers of one hand burned into him where they still clutched his shoulder. Her other hand rested on his forearm. "You're not going to say we shouldn't have done that, are you?"

Reaching up, he removed the hand on his shoulder so he could think. One deep breath later, he did the same with the other. Another breath and words still weren't coming to him, not rational ones, anyway.

He went with "Yes, I am. That's exactly what I'm going to say. Except it's I… *I* shouldn't have—"

She interrupted, "You mean *I* shouldn't have? *I* kissed *you*."

"No, I mean, I know you did. But I shouldn't have let you."

"Let me? You seemed to enjoy it. In fact,

you kinda took over there at the end. Which is no surprise. You're used to being in control, huh? To having things go your way?"

"No! I mean, yes, of course, I enjoyed... kissing you. Obviously. But we shouldn't have. And we're not going to do it again. I should have, I mean I shouldn't have...and, yes, I like being in control of...certain things. But what does that have to do with this? I don't even know what I'm saying..." Words lost, thoughts jumbled, he scraped a restless hand along the bench beside him.

Eyes sparkling, she watched him, her mouth a perfect, satisfied half grin, and he realized just how ridiculous he must seem.

He chuckled, but it sounded painful even to him. "You have this singular ability to leave me tongue-tied." It was this way she had of not saying anything and then finally saying exactly what she thought. And this complicated, intense, amazing, uncomfortable thing that had just happened between them wasn't helping.

She beamed. "You want me to untie it for you? Bring it here again, and I'll give it a shot."

Like that. He groaned. "Ally, please don't..." Her eyes were fixed on his mouth, and he wanted to kiss her again. And again. And forever, maybe. What was he thinking? He couldn't. This was insane. "You." A long moment stretched between them while he stared at her and tried to come up with words.

"Me?" she finally prompted him.

Beside him, his phone chimed. He snatched it up, grateful for the reprieve. Coward that he was. Reading the text, he practically leaped to his feet.

"I need to go. I told Bering I would meet… We'll talk about this later, okay?"

She reached over and patted his arm. "Okay, but just so you know, I'm going to hold you to that."

"You set a date yet?" Bering quipped when Tag joined him. They walked toward the house, where the senators were due to be arriving soon.

Tag chuckled because it was all the response he could manage. He needed to get a grip.

"Ally-oop!" Bering called and then took a moment to laugh at his joke. "Did not see that coming. She's barely over five feet tall. She played you like a violin."

"The woman is full of surprises." So many surprises and other perfect, interesting, irresistible qualities that had him wishing for things… A pain crimped his insides, worse than the stabs of loneliness, of reluctant bachelorhood, that plagued him these days. Except worse. So much worse. Like hot-knife-twisting-in-gut bad.

"It looked like she and Gareth have been playing together for years. Too bad she couldn't play point guard on the team next year, huh? With that three-point shot, they would be unbeatable across the entire state."

Tag groaned inwardly. Bering was right; watching her with Gareth and Cody only illuminated the fact that she was undoubtedly closer in age to his teenage cousin than she was to him. Reaching up, he squeezed the back of his neck in an attempt to ease the tension clutching him there.

He still couldn't believe it had happened. The chemistry between them was unlike anything he'd ever experienced except…except he had higher standards for himself than kissing a woman who was barely old enough to vote. That might be a slight exaggeration, but still, she was too young for him. The knot twisted tighter. He needed to think. He might need some ibuprofen. What should he do? He had to be straight with her. A task that would be so much easier if he didn't like her so much. And she just had to be a Mariners fan and a basketball player? It was like some kind of cosmic joke.

He briefly considered, and then discarded,

talking to Bering about it. He knew Bering wouldn't judge, but would he approve? He wasn't ready to admit what he'd done, to open himself to the taunting of a middle-aged cliché, however much he deserved it. What would the rest of his family think?

"Perfect timing. There's Jack." Bering slapped him on the shoulder as Senator Marsh's SUV pulled up to the house.

Senators Marsh and Fincher climbed out of the vehicle as Tag and Bering approached. Greetings and handshakes were exchanged. Bering offered refreshments, and they both requested coffee.

Tag volunteered to fetch it. "I'll get it. I was going to get myself a cup, anyway." He headed toward the beverage area, stalling to gather his wits, while Bering gestured at an empty picnic table and led the men across the yard.

Tag joined them with the coffee. Small talk bounced around the table for a few minutes until Senator Marsh lowered his cup and said, "So, word has reached Randall that Mammoth Tracks Mining has been sniffing around the valley. They're quietly trying to purchase mineral rights along the Opal River."

Bering and Tag exchanged glances and Tag said, "That might explain it." He told the two men about the inflated offers Hannah and Shay had received for their properties.

Senator Marsh nodded. "Yes, obviously word has leaked out. Usually, Mammoth uses a number of other companies to gobble up the outlying land. If they move in here, real estate prices will skyrocket. And I don't think we need to talk about what this will do to Rankins if they're successful."

Bering exhaled a frustrated breath. "And I thought Cam-Field was the biggest threat we'd face in my lifetime."

Senator Marsh gave his head a defeated shake. "If there's one thing I've learned in my years as a politician, it's that there's always a bigger monster waiting to take the place of the one just slain."

"What can we do?"

"We'll fight it legislatively, of course, as much as we can at the national level. But that's the thing—we're going to need strength at the state level. Which is what we're here about."

"Okay." Bering nodded.

Tag tensed at the senator's expression, anxiety zinging through him like a fishing line gone taut.

Senator Marsh went on, "Circumstances have arisen in Randall's personal life, and he's going to have to retire at the end of his term. Tag, we need you to run in the upcoming election."

"Can we be ready by then?" Bering asked. "When will I have to start campaigning?"

"We will be," Senator Marsh answered Bering. "We can be. Nothing alarming in that background check and our research has told us that we've got strong financial backing coming Tag's way."

He turned to Tag. "Campaigning will have to begin immediately, I'm afraid. We've got a lot to do in a very short time. If you agree to commit to this, I'd like you both to fly to Juneau next weekend so we can get the ball rolling. Randall and I have ideas about hiring your staff. My assistant, Maura, is looking at some potential campaign managers. There's a dinner Friday night that I'd like you to attend—lots of potential donors and numerous important people to introduce you to."

CHAPTER EIGHT

TAG KNEW HE needed to talk to Ally.

He'd half-expected to hear from her the day after the party. Normally, he took Sundays off—well, off in the sense that he used the day to catch up on his personal to-do list, which usually included household chores, before meeting his parents and siblings at church. And he rarely missed Sunday dinner with his family.

Yesterday, he'd taken the opportunity to announce the new campaign plans to them. Not surprisingly, they'd been enthusiastic and supportive, if slightly concerned about timing and logistics. Tag had a few reservations about those, too, but hopefully the trip to Juneau the following weekend would allay many of them.

No word from Ally all day Monday, either. Not one to leave matters unresolved in any aspect of his life, Tag decided to drop by her cottage that evening after work. He knew the owner, Kenny Bitzle, a retired commercial fisherman who now lived in the lower forty-eight and rented the place out. It was an excellent location, within easy walking distance of the hospital and Rankins's small cluster of businesses generally referred to as "downtown."

After meeting his friend and fellow pilot Cricket Blackburn for an early dinner and a game of darts at the Cozy Caribou, he decided to walk to Ally's.

He tried to ignore the eager hammering of his pulse as he neared the house. Surely they could remain friends after they talked this through. It had just been a kiss. Several, technically, maybe? There had been a lot of lip contact in a short span of time, but regardless, after analyzing the situation, she was probably regretting the whole thing as much as he was.

As he stepped into the street to cross, a car turned the corner. Waving at Mrs. Keller behind the wheel, he waited for her to pass. Back on track, he started to move again but immediately froze because there was a guy standing on Ally's porch. His back was to Tag, but even from this distance he could see Ally smiling. A burning sensation flared inside him. Was this why she hadn't called? Was she seeing someone else? Not that she was seeing him, but...

The guy took a few steps backward, and the movement immediately struck him as familiar.

Confusion, anger and finally disbelief tumbled through him as he watched his teenaged cousin pivot, basketball in hand, and saunter down the steps in that easy, loose-limbed way Gareth had of moving.

Tag instantly recognized his deep voice calling out, "Thanks, Ally. I'll see you Thursday." The thudding sound of a ball bouncing, one, two, three times, rang in the air before Gareth climbed into the vehicle, his mom's SUV, and drove off down the street.

Tag considered walking away, but Ally had spotted him. Waving, she motioned him over, and he found himself plodding toward her, his legs heavy and weak.

"Tag, hi." Her voice was cocoa warm and just as sweet, and if she felt awkward about anything it didn't show.

A sharp pain in his jaw alerted him to the fact that he was clenching his teeth. He tried to relax, but it was difficult with a million questions piercing his brain. Gareth had just turned eighteen, old enough to date a woman in her early twenties. Had she kissed him, too? Was Tag even now being compared to his teenaged cousin? Dating an older woman would be a sign of prestige for Gareth, whereas Tag would be viewed as a walking midlife crisis.

But he wasn't middle-aged yet, was he? It was slightly depressing that he even had to wonder.

"What are you doing? I was just thinking about you."

Brown eyes shining with what looked like happiness matched her smile, and despite his cartwheeling emotions, his heart climbed into his throat. She always looked so…together and unaffected. Why was that, when he was the older one? Wasn't that supposed to make him wiser? More evolved? Okay, maybe not that last one, seeing how jealousy was stewing hotly within him at the moment.

"Do you want to come in?"

"I do." A few steps carried him inside. She shut the door, and he spun to face her. "Ally, I, uh, I need to know what's going on."

A little furrow formed between her brows. "With what?"

"Technically, he's old enough for you, but you know he's still in high school, right? Gareth, my cousin?"

Her lips parted with a little gasp of surprise. It made a nice change, Tag thought, seeing that display of emotion, as brief as it was. In a millisecond, confusion morphed to her go-to unreadable expression. How could he have ever believed it indicated indifference? Because as he studied her carefully, he realized that while her face was stoic, her eyes were flashing. And just that fast he knew he'd screwed up.

When she spoke, her voice held a calm, edge-of-cheerful tone. "Surely, you're not implying that I would throw myself at you and then make a play for your teenaged cousin?"

Wow. That sounded bad, even though that's pretty much what he'd been doing. It was painful to admit it. "Uh, not…really." What in the world had gotten into him? He should be encouraging her to see someone else. Not Gareth. But…someone. He swallowed the bitter, metallic taste on his tongue.

She stared at him. "You sure about that?"

Cringing under her doubt-filled scrutiny, he confessed, "Okay, yes." He muttered an expletive and raked a hand across his jaw. "I'm sorry. I…don't know what came over me. I didn't know it was Gareth, at first. I just saw this guy standing on your porch, and I lost my mind for a minute…" How was this honesty helping matters?

"Wait. You're jealous?"

"Apparently."

One corner of her mouth ticked up. "That's a relief, I think. I didn't hear from you yesterday, and I didn't call or text because I was trying to give you time to process what happened, maybe miss me a little."

Mission accomplished. And in a manner that was making him look and feel worse by the second.

"Today, when I still didn't hear from you, I started to worry. Then I saw you outside just now, and my heart did this nice little somersault because I thought you were coming to see me. But when you got closer, looking all broody and serious, I was afraid you were coming over to let me down easy. I didn't see a jealousy thing happening, but I think that bodes well, as far as feelings go."

"Yeah, I'll admit this isn't how this was supposed to happen. I'm sorry. I was totally out of line. You can date whoever you want. Although his mom, my cousin Janie, might not be thrilled."

Cocking her head slowly to one side, she said, "Or—wait… *Did* you stop by to let me down?"

"I, uh, I was hoping to do it with a lot more finesse."

She froze.

So did he. Then he sighed because what he wanted to do was pull her close and wrap his arms around her.

"Look, Ally, I'm the one who is let down. I like you, obviously. I've already told you that. And I'm beyond flattered that you would even entertain the thought of being interested in me."

She stepped toward him, right into his comfort zone, and his pulse took off like a helicopter rotor at full speed.

"How could any woman not be interested in you?" Her voice was all soft, like she was about to tell him a secret, and his blood went hot as he remembered what happened last time she'd gotten this close. He stared at her full, beyond-tempting lips, now curling up at the corners, and told himself he should take a step back. This perfectly rational message sent from his brain was refused delivery by the rest of his body. Wrenching his gaze upward, he found her brown eyes full of teasing humor.

"I know for a fact that they all are, Mr. Most Eligible Bachelor. And you can count me right there among them."

He made a growling sound, part desire, part frustration. "*You* shouldn't be. I am too old for you and…" The rest of his words were lost, lodged in his throat like dry oatmeal, because she'd brought her hands up to touch his chest. They were toe to toe, and with her palms flat she slid her hands slowly up while he watched, fascinated, until they disappeared from his line of sight to wind around his neck.

Because she was so much shorter, she had

to stretch to accomplish the task, and the move left only a fraction of space between them. One deep breath and she'd be flush against him... With a gentle pull, she urged his head to bow toward hers. She must have risen onto her toes at the same time because that last bit of space between them disappeared and their lips made contact.

Closing his eyes, he kissed her back, but only lightly, allowing himself this final goodbye. See, he could do this. One soft, sweet, goodbye kiss...

Then she made a little noise and went all boneless against him, her fingers biting into his shoulders. His arms tightened around her. Sliding the fingers of one hand up to the back of her neck, he curved the other around her hip and kissed her with everything he had.

Like it was the last time.

Because it was, he realized when she whispered his name. He had to stop this. He pulled away slightly. Her fingers bunched the fabric of his shirt and she laid her cheek against his chest. Tag rested his chin on the top of her head while he waited for his breathing to slow.

A long moment passed before she let out a soft chuckle and said, "Too tall, maybe. But definitely not too old."

Taking one of her hands, he tucked it in

his and pulled her toward the sofa, urging her down next to him. He had to let her go even as he wondered how it could possibly hurt this much when he barely knew her. But he knew enough. And if she was older, then he would learn everything. But she wasn't.

"Surely you're not still going to give me the speech? After that?"

He allowed himself a final moment to enjoy the sensation of her skin against his before he released her. "Yes, I am. Because the fact is that you are closer in age to Gareth and every other senior in high school than you are to me."

"I don't care. I don't even know how old you are."

"Great." His head fell back on the sofa. "That does not make it better."

"Forty?" she guessed.

"Close."

"Forty-five?"

"Seriously? I look forty-five to you?"

She shrugged. "No, but from the way you're acting I figured it had to be higher."

"That would for sure mean a midlife crisis," he muttered.

"What?" she asked with a laugh.

"Nothing. I'm thirty-eight."

She brightened. "See? Not even forty. It's all good!"

"No, it's not. It is not good at all. This is not going to happen."

"Well, I've got news for you, Grandpa, something already did. Twice. And I, for one, can't wait to do it again."

"Ally…" Her name came out like a groan. "Okay, I'll admit we've got a… I don't even know what to call this." He gestured helplessly between them. "But physical attraction isn't a basis for a relationship."

She looked offended. "I know that. I'm not attracted to you because of the way you look or because we happen to have some killer chemistry here, although you are gorgeous and this—" she gestured happily between them "—is pretty fun."

"You're not?" And it wasn't fun. Not to him. At least, not in a good way. Because it just made everything even more difficult and somehow increased his guilt exponentially.

"No, and that's not why you like me, either. We didn't feel anything the first couple times we met, did we? Except for irritation. I didn't even remember who you were at one point and you thought I was a crackpot. Maybe still do, a bit."

This was true, mostly. "Crackpot is kind of a strong term."

She chuckled. "Don't start pulling the political correctness card on me now. I know what you thought of me. And I thought you were just another arrogant know-it-all. I'm attracted to you because you're *not* those things. You are confident and smart and incredibly thoughtful and kind. You love your family, and from what I've seen you're extra good to them all, especially your sisters. You're also a paramedic, a decent basketball player and an excellent pilot, and I'll admit I find that particular skill set highly attractive."

Toast. He was toast. How was he supposed to resist this—her? He was 100 percent certain he'd never been tested this way in his entire life. And he'd thought running for the senate was going to be his biggest challenge.

She shifted on the sofa, curling one leg under her. "Let's talk about why this is an issue for you, the age thing. Do you even know how old I am?"

"Twenty-three or -four? Please say twenty-four. And twenty-five would absolutely make my day."

"Twenty-two." Her free hand shot forward. "Don't freak out. I've lived a lot—you know that. My childhood was unique, to say the least. I grew up fast in some ways. A little sheltered in others, but mostly in good ways,

I think. I've already served in the Army and been to college and traveled the world."

"But—"

"Tag, it's just time, days and hours that have passed. And when you think about it, it's a drop in the bucket."

He scoffed. "In a geological context, maybe."

She brought a hand up to cover her mouth, but laughter sputtered through her fingers. "Did you just call yourself a fossil?"

"This isn't funny." He fought a smile and lost. "Okay, that was a little funny, but the rest of this is not."

"It is, too." She choked out the words, trying to hold in another laugh. "Especially the way you set me up there."

He shook his head. "You make it hard for me to think clearly. This situation has me panicky in a way I've never experienced before."

Reaching over, she picked up his hand. And he let her. Because he was a weak, weak man. And he wanted to believe her. He wanted these years and days and hours between them not to matter. It was that simple. Turning his hand, she placed it on her knee. With her index finger, she traced the lines on his palm.

Serious now, she said, "This line right here, your lifeline, is strong and deep. It tells me you are healthy with excellent stamina and vitality. That's all I need to know." Shrugging like it was a done deal, she brought her gaze up to meet his. Gorgeous brown eyes, wide and sincere, and when she turned their full force on him like this, he feared he might not be able to deny her anything.

"Did I mention that in addition to having an interest in alternative medicine I'm also psychic?"

What? His stomach dipped nervously as her words sank in. Perfect. Maybe now she'd tell him he was going to die soon in a fiery plane crash.

"No, uh…you didn't. I don't know…"

She busted out laughing. "I'm kidding! I have no idea what any of these lines mean. I just like holding your hand." She began to massage the intricate muscles of his palm.

He chuckled. "You are a brat. But that feels heavenly, whatever you're doing."

"Pressure points I do know. You're very tense, by the way. I wonder why?"

"Yeah, I wonder, too," he said drily.

Grinning, she linked her fingers through his and squeezed. "But, seriously, why does a few extra years matter to you so much?"

Despite his anxiety, he felt a kind of soul-deep rightness seeping into him. Why *did* it matter? She was watching him, waiting for an answer. It seemed years ago that he'd been twenty-two. And yet, maybe not that long ago, after all. He couldn't remember when his feelings had ever confused him like this.

He sighed and said the first thing that came to his mind. "What would people think? You're younger than my little sisters."

"And you're older than my car."

"That doesn't even make sense."

"Exactly. Who cares what people think? Are you committed to someone else?"

"No."

"Good." She heaved out a breath. "I was worried because the way you bolted after I kissed you at the picnic, I figured maybe you were feeling guilty because there was already someone in your life. Same goes for me. And other than going to the prom with your cousin, I'm free to date whenever and whoever I want."

"Also not funny."

"I know. But you deserve it for even thinking that I would look at him in that way."

Tag laid his head back against the sofa and realized that since they'd been to Anchorage together, in fact the last time they'd been alone together, he felt relaxed and...? Himself. Happy. Right now, there wasn't anywhere else on the entire planet he'd rather be.

"Look, is it possible for you to let go of your…ageism," she teased, "long enough to just have some fun? I'm not looking for marriage here or kids or even a relationship. I like you, Tag. I haven't liked anyone as much as I like you in…a really long time."

And that was the heart of the problem: Tag *was* looking, he wanted all of those things. They were at very different points in their lives. He *needed* to look if he was going to get married and have a family. Did he have the time to waste on dating when he knew it couldn't go anywhere? And even if they did head in that direction, Ally was too young to make a decision about the rest of her life. He certainly couldn't have made that kind of commitment at twenty-two, or at any time in his twenties, if he was honest. And by the time she was ready, he would be way older than he wanted to be when he started a family.

Not that he even had time to think about that now, with the election bearing down on him. Although, she'd just said that she wasn't interested in a serious relationship. It was the only reason, he told himself, he would even consider dating her; they couldn't get serious.

That's when it occurred to him: their age difference could be the very thing that allowed him to date her. It would be a buffer of sorts, the justification for keeping the relationship casual.

He'd need to be straight with her about this campaign business before he even considered going out with her. Was he considering it?

"Maybe. But first, there's something I need to tell you."

ALLY LISTENED TO Tag outline the Senator Project. Concern for Rankins, the community and the surrounding environment welled within her.

"Almost every person in my family and most of my friends rely on the pristine beauty of this valley for their livelihoods," explained Tag.

His reasons made sense, and she respected his commitment, but as he went on, an unsettled feeling crept over her. She couldn't quite put her finger on what was bothering her. She was glad that he seemed more amenable to the idea of their spending time together, but what had made him change his mind so quickly?

"I want to make sure you understand that, if we start…dating, I won't be as available as I'd like. The campaign will be demanding. I'm going to have to travel and spend a lot of time in Juneau." He shrugged. "It could get crazy."

"I see. But why you?"

"What do you mean?"

"This all started with your cousin Bering, right? Why doesn't he run? Or your dad or one of your sisters?"

"They all have businesses to manage."

"So do you."

A flash of what looked a lot like uncertainty passed across his face and Ally's heart went out to him. She'd wanted to shake that ironclad confidence of his at the basketball game, but running for office was different, serious and more significant. He would need every bit of self-assurance he could muster.

"They all have families, except the triplets. Any of them could do it, but it makes the most sense for me to do it. I'm the one with the most time and the least to lose."

"Hmm." The most time? From what she'd seen and heard, that worked a lot more to their advantage than his. Helping people seemed to be his thing, but who, she wondered, helped him?

"You have to promise me that if we do start dating, we'll keep it casual, like you said. See other people, I mean, you can see other people and…you should."

She laughed. "I'm not interested in seeing anyone else. But just so you know, I am going to see Gareth again. I told him I'd help him with his outside shooting. That's what he was doing here."

"Oh. That's nice of you."

"So, we're really going to try this?" Ally glanced up at the wall. Tag followed her gaze up to the fish clock he suspected Kenny had left there. "You and me? And you're fine with people knowing?"

"Yep."

Leaning forward, she brushed her lips against his, liking the way his eyelids fluttered closed, like he was all-in. "Good, because your sister is going to be here any minute."

"Iris?"

"No, Hannah. We're having dinner." Hannah had approached Ally on Saturday when she and Flynn were leaving the party and asked if they could have that discussion about her leg Ally had offered before. But she wasn't going to tell Tag that part. Best to tackle one issue at a time.

CHAPTER NINE

"WORD HAS REACHED ME, Ms. Mowak, that you are encouraging patients to smoke marijuana."

"Excuse me?" Ally said to buy some time and get a handle on the situation. She wasn't surprised that she'd been summoned by Dr. Boyd again. It was the timing that caught her off guard. She'd met with Ginger a week ago. Clearly, his spy was slacking.

"I don't believe it's a difficult question. Did you or did you not recommend the use of marijuana to the patient?"

"I did not."

"That's not the way I heard it."

Careful to keep her voice calm and even she said, "With all due respect, Dr. Boyd, if you're going to ask me a question and then dispute my response, what's the point in asking?" *You condescending, unpleasant prig*, she silently added.

"I would advise you not to take that tone with me. You are already skating on very thin ice here."

Incredible how often the complete lack of emotion in her voice got her accused of the opposite. "I apologize if that sounded glib or facetious to you, sir, but I am rather confused. Medical marijuana is not only a scientifically proven effective treatment for the alleviation of pain and other cancer symptoms, but it is also now legal in the state of Alaska. Doctors are sanctioning its use for numerous diseases and medical conditions."

"Not in my hospital, they're not! I know you're used to watching your grandfather run around doing whatever he wants, but that's not the way it works around here."

"I see." Ally knew that continuing this conversation was only going to incite Dr. Boyd further. "You asked me if I recommended the use of medical marijuana to the patient and I told you I did not. There were plenty of witnesses in the room who can attest to the fact that the patient broached the subject. Did the patient or her family complain?"

"No."

"I've studied the handbook like you suggested, and there's nothing there or in my job description about not discussing the proper use of a legal drug with a patient. Perhaps if I missed it, and it is there, you could highlight those portions for me, as well?"

Ally watched Dr. Boyd and imagined that he was trying to gauge her level of sincerity.

"Did you tell her you would help her secure the marijuana?"

Fixing her eyes on his neatly trimmed cap of white hair helped her keep herself in check. It was like he was intimating that she'd agreed to buy weed for a teenager bent on a weekend party binge instead of counseling a terminally ill cancer patient.

"Not exactly. After inquiring if the patient had applied for a medical marijuana card I told her I could recommend experts to help her choose the right strain for her condition."

Blue eyes flashed with anger. Disproportionate and misplaced anger, because could he truly be this upset about a conversation regarding the use of cannabis as a medical treatment? Ally almost felt sorry for the guy. Almost, that is, until he started speaking again.

His jaw went taut, teeth bared like he was biting into a piece of tough steak. "This is unacceptable."

Ally waited while uncomfortably long moments dragged by. The tick-tock-ticking of a clock high on the wall behind her sounded through the room like a cartoon time bomb.

Folding his fingers on the desktop in front

of him, he leaned in. Ally resisted the urge to lean back.

"I am going to remind you of a few things, Ms. Mowak. The most important of which is that in this hospital we only practice modern medicine. You will adhere to that practice and behave professionally. And despite your innocent act here, I think you know exactly what I mean by that. But if you do have even one iota of doubt about what that might entail, you will ask."

"Of course."

He pointed one long spidery finger at her. "Watch yourself, Ms. Mowak, and comport yourself accordingly. That includes reining in your unorthodox opinions. Yes, I've heard you're spreading those around, too."

As if she had a disease and was trying to infect the population. Ally didn't bother to respond. If he thought he could silence her when she was off the clock, he was sorely mistaken. The whole point of her existence, her purpose in life, was to share her knowledge. Unfortunately, she reminded herself, there was also the matter of keeping this job.

"GREAT NEWS." Bering checked the brakes on one of the two ATVs in front of them. "Jack said your list of endorsements is already a mile long."

"That is good news." Tag wiggled the seat on the other ATV to make sure it was snug. His cousin Janie's six-year-old twins, Gabe and Finn, were going to be riding the matching vehicles. "Dr. Boyd has already reached out, too. He's setting up a meeting with some colleagues."

"That's awesome. Between my connections with wildlife organizations and your involvement in all the pilot and paramedic associations over the years, we seem to have made a lot of friends. Are you ready for our trip next weekend?"

"I will be. My biggest challenge is to find a tux before then. Senator Marsh's assistant emailed me a list of stuff to bring, and I guess I need one for that party we're going to. I haven't worn a tux since our senior prom. She said I should go ahead and buy one because I'll need it a few times in the next year. What a pain."

"I've got two," Bering said. Tag wasn't surprised. Bering and Emily sometimes attended formal affairs in the lower forty-eight with Emily's wealthy family. "Too bad we're not the same size. Juneau should be nice, though. Are you going to see Kendall? You should ask her to the party. You two always looked good together. And she probably knows a ton of people."

Tag's last, and only, serious girlfriend, Kendall, lived in Juneau. They might have looked good, but they hadn't been a good match. Besides the age-old issue of the city girl and country boy who can't meet in the middle, there hadn't been much of a spark.

Unlike with Ally. That strong pulse of electricity seemed to vibrate between them without any effort whatsoever. Kendall had managed to find that with someone else. The fact that she'd done so while they were still dating had also been a problem.

"Her fiancé might not appreciate that."

"She's engaged? Already?"

"That's what I heard. And we broke up a year ago. But since we're talking about women, can I ask you a question?"

"A year? Really? That seems unbelievable. Time goes by so fast now that we're oldies, huh? And, yes, you can ask me anything, you know that. But if it's about women I highly doubt I'll be able to help. Emily vexes me on a daily basis."

Tag forced out a laugh. His cousin just had to make a crack about age. "Your lack of confidence on this subject is disheartening, considering the fact you've been married for years now. But lucky for you, this isn't about their behavior in general. I'm just asking for an opinion."

"You know I'm always up for giving one of those."

"Do you think I'm too old to date a twenty-two-year-old?"

Bering's head snapped up. He looked at Tag, curiosity stamped all over his face. "My gut reaction to that question is probably yes, that seems young. But, since I'm guessing this is a personal concern, I will follow it up with a firm I think it would depend on the twenty-two-year-old."

Tag nodded. Ally was most definitely not a typical twenty-two-year-old.

"And what you're looking to get out of the relationship. If you're just wanting someone to hang out with and…wait, are we talking about Ally? Is she only twenty-two?"

"How did you know?"

"Dang. Dude, you could have given me a heads-up. I just lost the next three date-night choices to my wife. Emily said after the basketball game that you two were into each other."

"That sounds like a real hardship. And Emily is too perceptive for her own good."

Bering chuckled. "Fair enough. And tell me about it, she reads me like a book. But if this means I'm watching the cooking channel for the next three weeks in a row, I will never forgive you."

"If date night includes watching the cooking channel, you have more serious problems than not forgiving me."

"Just wait until you have kids. Trust me—an hour together of uninterrupted TV is a date."

This time the jab to his chest was even sharper than normal. With the election bearing down on him, it felt like he might never know. Dating Ally wasn't going to get him any closer to a family, either, and yet he was beginning to feel like he couldn't *not* spend time with her. He couldn't even be in the same room with her and keep his hands to himself. And they'd agreed to keep it casual. How he was going to manage that he had no idea.

"Seriously, though, the fact that you asked my opinion tells me you like her."

Tag felt himself smiling. He couldn't remember the last time just talking about a woman made him feel like this. "I do. She's..." He didn't even have words to describe how cool she was. "I can't..."

Bering was studying him, grin as wide as the entire state. "Uh-oh." He clapped Tag on the shoulder. "I get it, my friend. And I say go for it."

At that moment Emily appeared, Brady on her shoulders and Violet skipping along beside them.

"Tag!" Violet yelled and waved. She galloped toward him, clutching a plastic bag in her tiny hands.

"Hey, wildflower." He bent and scooped her up into his arms.

"I made you cookies." Chubby cheeks glowing with a smile, she pressed the bag of partially crumbled treats into his hand. "Snickerdoodles because they're your favorite."

"Thank you, Vi, but you're wrong about that. *You're* my favorite."

Tag loved how her entire body shook when she laughed. "I mean favorite *cookie*," she cried.

"Oh, of course. Yes, they sure are."

He kissed her cheek, his heart melting like it always did where Violet was concerned. Sticky fingers wrapped around his neck and just like that it reminded him how much care he needed to take with what life had dealt him. It might not be in the cards for him to have kids of his own, but nothing was more important than protecting the family that he did have. And to protect them, he needed to keep Rankins safe. Ensuring the security and happiness of his family and friends was worth way more than the sacrifice that political office would demand.

"CRIKEY, HE REALLY has it in for you, doesn't he? What are you going to do?" Flynn sat across from Ally at a table in the hospital cafeteria. She'd just finished relaying the details of her latest meeting with Dr. Boyd.

"Nothing."

"How did I know you were going to say that?" He stuffed another bite of cheeseburger into his mouth. "I wonder who his spy is? There's no way Boyd could have heard about what happened unless someone told him, right? The conversation wasn't documented?"

"No, not the specifics. What about that nurse, Nicki?"

"I don't know…" Flynn tapped a finger on the table and stared out the cafeteria window. "That seems too obvious. And if it was her, why wouldn't he have summoned you sooner? I feel like it almost had to have wound through the rumor mill."

"Good thought. But any of the family could have innocently repeated snippets of the conversation, too."

"True. But I don't think so. What are you

doing this weekend? You wanna go fishing or hiking or something? I need to get out of here for a while."

"Sure, but that depends on when and where. I have plans on Saturday."

"Something fun?"

"Hope so." She waggled her eyebrows at him. "Date."

"You haven't even been here two weeks, and you already have a date? I want a date."

"Yeah, and you're not going to believe who it's with so I'm just going to tell you it's Tag James."

Flynn brought his chin up like she'd smacked him in the jaw. "Really? I thought you didn't like him."

"Turns out I was a little bit wrong about that."

"Wow. Ally… Do you know how old he is?"

"Oh, no… Not you, too? He's all twisted up about it. Thinks I'm too young for him."

"Well, what is he, like, forty?"

"Thirty-eight. You think he's too old for me?"

"I don't know… I'm feeling all kind of big brotherly here or whatever."

"Aw, Flynn." Ally put a hand over her heart. "I am so touched, but it's not like we're engaged. It's just a date." Even though thinking about him, talking about him, looking forward to seeing him made her jittery in a way she'd never felt before. *Anticipation* didn't seem accurate here. It was more like excitement on steroids.

"But it's not just a date, Al. Every time we choose to spend time with another person in a romantic way it means something. Unless you're, um, focused solely on the physical, it's like an interview for a life partner. And you need to be sure an age difference like this wouldn't get in the way of what you want, or what he wants, for that matter."

"Whoa. Hold on there, my quasi–big brother. It's not that much of an age difference. And, besides, I don't agree. I think you can spend time with someone just because you enjoy their company."

"That's because you're only twenty-two. And sixteen years isn't that much to you?"

"No, it's not." Was it? She tried to ignore the niggle of doubt sprouting inside her. She couldn't help but wish for a mom to talk to, or a grandmother, a sister, an aunt. A bubble of sadness expanded inside her. People said you couldn't miss what you'd never had, but Ally knew they were wrong about that. She'd always pined for a feminine connection of some kind. Not that she wanted it to replace her relationship with Abe, just supplement it a little.

Right now, she'd settle for a girlfriend. She thought of Iris, felt like maybe they were headed toward that. Disappointing that she was Tag's sister. That seemed to preclude any advice seeking.

"You do realize you're breaking the half plus seven rule, right?"

"The what?"

"You know, the relationship rule that says you shouldn't date anyone younger than half your age plus seven years."

"That's ridiculous. Where did you hear that?"

He pointed a french fry at her. "Hey, I didn't make it up. It's a thing. Don't you read *Cosmo*?"

"*Cosmo?* Of course not. I read medical journals and *National Geographic*. Besides, he's not looking for a relationship. And I told him the same." Which was only sort of a lie. She had told him that, but she didn't know if she really meant it.

The problem, as Flynn had just inadvertently pointed out, was that she didn't know much of anything where relationships were concerned. She made a mental note to pick up a few of those magazines.

THE WOMAN WAS sitting on her porch when Ally got home that evening after work. She bolted to her feet as Ally approached. Tall and thin as a willow switch, she had sharp symmetrical features to match. Everything about her appeared lovely but fragile, like a piece of finely spun sugar. Bluish smudges beneath her eyes suggested she was also exhausted.

"Hi, Ally? Ally Mowak?"

"Yes, hello."

She reached out a hand. "Cami Hughes. It's wonderful to meet you."

Ally shook it and noted the cold clamminess of her firm grip.

"Thank you. You, too."

The woman nodded, her gaze roving over Ally like she was trying to make a decision.

Ally offered a gentle smile. "I love meeting new people. But why is it nice to meet me, exactly?"

"Oh." Cami's eyes widened for a split second before she let out a short laugh. "I'm sorry. I've heard that your grandfather is Abe Mowak, the Native doctor healer guy?"

"Yes."

Cami cast furtive glances up and down the street before blowing out a breath. "I was wondering if you might be able to help me with, um, alternative medical treatments? I can pay you cash."

"I see. Why don't we go inside and talk about it?"

Ally unlocked her door, and they both went inside. Ally set her bag down and flipped on the light.

"Please, have a seat. Can I get you anything to drink?"

"No, thank you. I'm good."

Cami settled on the sofa and Ally sat across from her in an overstuffed chair.

"What's bothering you, Cami?"

"It's my thyroid. I've been diagnosed with hyperthyroidism. Mood swings, fatigue, insomnia, weight loss, my hair… But it's the fatigue that's killing me." Her eyes filled with tears. "I have no energy. I'm so tired of feeling like I'm going to drop at any moment. Please, I hope you can help me. I'm sorry…" She wiped at her cheeks and pressed one fisted hand to her pursed lips.

Ally's throat went tight as sympathy welled within her. How could she not try and help? She plucked a tissue from the box on the end table and passed it to Cami.

"Cami, before we talk about this further I need to make a few things very clear. I'm not a medical doctor like my grandfather. I am a paramedic with the highest certification, and I served four years in the Army as a medic. Like my grandfather, I believe in a holistic approach to medicine, and that means a combination of what we call the old ways and the new, traditional and modern. Whatever works, in other words. The best approach for the condition."

Cami nodded. "I understand. How much do you charge?"

"That's another thing—I don't charge. I don't have a practice or a medical license to practice. I don't treat patients. What I can do is give you some ideas about where you can go and who you can see to possibly get treatment. And this discussion I give freely. But in doing so, I might also suggest that you see a naturopath, an osteopath, an acupuncturist, a physician who's a specialist or some other professional if I suspect your condition warrants it."

"I've been dealing with this for almost two years now. I can't do this anymore, one medication after another, so many side effects. Now the doctor is giving me more medicine to treat the side effects. Nothing is working."

"I understand. And if, after hearing my history and qualifications and lack thereof, you're still comfortable talking to me about this, we'll see what we can do."

"I am. I promise, I am. I have a husband and two little kids and I can't…" She choked on a sob. "I want to be able to take care of them and right now I can't."

CHAPTER TEN

ALLY OPENED THE door to her date on Saturday afternoon and paused to absorb two facts: she'd never been so conscious of the beat of her own heart, and she'd never seen a man look better in a pair of gently worn jeans.

"Hey." Tag greeted her with a lazy smile and not a hint of the nervousness plaguing her.

"Hi, come in," she said, waving him inside. A few strides and he was standing in the middle of her living room. A dark green knit shirt showed beneath his brown leather jacket, and she was fascinated by the way the combination matched the color of his eyes.

She realized she was staring only when he asked, "Is something wrong? Am I too early? I know I'm not late."

"Um, no. I was just admiring your…you, to be honest. Your eyes change colors, sometimes green, sometimes brown. You're so…"

Right before her, his eyes darkened, and he made a sound, part chuckle, part incomprehensible mutter while grasping the back of his neck in that way he did when he was uncomfortable. He took a step toward her. Her heart jumped toward him. She wondered if he was going to kiss her. That would be a nice change, since she'd been the one making all the moves up to this point. Which was funny, now that she thought about it, because she'd never kissed anyone first. Ever. Until him.

Her breath stalled while his gaze skimmed her neck and then lingered for a bit on her mouth.

"I'm sure 'so' must be a good thing," he said, his voice a ragged whisper. A warm shiver skittered across her skin.

"Pretty good," she managed.

"Grab a jacket." She felt his voice like a warm breeze. "We need to get out of here."

"Why?"

"Because I promised myself I would keep my hands, and my mouth, off you until we get to know each other better. And that's not going to happen if you keep talking and…looking at me like that."

"Okay…" she wheezed, because her heart seemed to have expanded to fill all the space in her chest, leaving no room for much-needed oxygen. She wanted to know him, too. So much.

Flynn's words flashed through her mind.

Maybe he was right that dating was like an interview. She'd just never realized it, because she'd never thought of anyone in those terms before or wanted them to think of her like that. She'd never wanted the interview, so to speak. She did now. Ally turned around and picked up her bag and the jacket she'd placed on top of it earlier and wondered how she was going to manage slow and casual.

After they were settled in his pickup, he pulled it onto the road and asked, "Do you mind if we make a quick stop on the way out of town?"

"Nope. I'll trust that we're not going to be late for...whatever. I don't even know where we're going, remember?"

"Ah, that." He glanced her way, a proud-of-himself smile on his face. "I was thinking maybe dinner and a movie?"

Joy swamped her so thoroughly she couldn't have stopped her goofy grin even if she'd wanted to. He'd remembered. She could count on one hand how many times she'd seen a movie in the theater. Three times when she'd been a kid and had traveled to Anchorage with her grandfather, once in the Army, and then again last year when she'd been going to paramedic school in Michigan.

"Sound good?"

"You have no idea. Well, that's not true, because you obviously figured it out."

"Well, you pretty much told me." Tag flashed her a grin. "And I'll admit to paying attention when I'm interested."

Yikes. What a perfect thing to say. Already this was the best date she'd ever had.

The pickup veered onto the road leading up to the Faraway Inn while Tag explained that his sister Shay had asked him to pick up some parts for one of the inn's hot tub pumps while he was in Glacier City. Ally understood completely. It was standard procedure when you grew up in a remote place to run errands and shop for family and friends whenever you headed to the city.

"This won't take long." He pulled the pickup into a visitor space in the lot.

They walked inside and turned down the first hallway. An office door was open and female voices and laughter drifted toward them. Tag strode in without knocking. Ally followed. Conversation halted. Three pairs of curious-sister eyes fixed on them—Shay's, Hannah's and Iris's.

Hannah seemed to recover the quickest. "Hey, Tag. Ally, hi!"

"You guys know Ally," Tag said, with a gentle touch to her elbow. "Obviously."

Shay's eyes narrowed. "Are you two here…" She gestured between them. "Together?" Then she focused on Ally and asked in a cool tone, "Or is there something I can help you with, Ally?"

Tag answered for them both, "If by *together* you're trying to ask if Ally and I are on a social outing the answer is yes."

Shay opened her mouth to speak, then closed it in a tight-lipped scowl.

Ally felt encouraged by the reactions of the other two women; Hannah appeared happily surprised while Iris's knowing smile gave the impression she was downright thrilled.

Hannah said, "Ally, I'm glad you're here. I was going to stop by and talk to you today. It's working! Between the tea and the acupuncture, I haven't felt this good in so long. Not ever, I think—definitely not since the accident. Thank you."

Tag swiveled his head to look at her, adding another pair of curious eyes to the mix.

"You're welcome. I'm glad I could help, but truly, I'm just the messenger." Ally had given Hannah the name of an acupuncturist she knew who had a practice in Glacier City. And the tea was an herbal mix her grandfather made that helped with inflammation. Normally she wouldn't pass it on, but her grandfather had given her permission, and she'd explained to Hannah that it was only something she'd do for family or friends.

Hannah asked, "Um, did someone else call you, by any chance? She's sort of a friend of a friend."

"She stopped by."

"Already? Well, that's good, but I was going to ask you first if it was okay."

Ally gave her an encouraging smile she hoped conveyed more than she could say. "It's fine. It was nice to meet her."

"Awesome." Hannah's face split with a wide grin. "I hope you can help her, too."

Shay stood. "Tag, I'll show you the part I need so you guys can get going on your…outing."

TAG FOLLOWED SHAY out of the office, trying not to feel concerned by the conversation he'd just witnessed. They walked through the inn until they exited out a set of doors. They kept going across the property to an outbuilding that housed supplies and tools.

Inside, Shay flipped on the lights and then whirled toward him, her face radiating tension and anger. "Are you dating her?"

"I'm going on a date with Ally, yes. And simultaneously doing a favor for my sister."

Shay dipped her head and pinched the bridge

of her nose for a few seconds before accosting him with another scowl. "How much do you like her?"

He shrugged. "I don't know yet. This is our first date."

That answer seemed to appease her, even though she was obviously under the mistaken impression that he hadn't formed an opinion yet when the fact was that he just didn't know how hard he'd fallen.

"Good. There's still time. How old is she?"

"Why does that matter?" Why was he being defensive when he had his own concerns about the age difference?

"Because…it just does. Does Bering approve of this?"

He scoffed. "Why would I need his permission?"

Shay sighed. "I'm talking about your campaign. Did you run this by him and Senator Marsh? How do you think it will look to people if you're dating a twenty-year-old? Especially one who already has a reputation."

"She's twenty-two. And what reputation?"

"Well, thank goodness she's at least old enough to legally drink a beer. People are talking about her, Tag. About the clay and the marijuana she gave to Ginger. And now she's *helping* Hannah—and others, too, apparently."

"She didn't give Ginger marijuana."

"That's not what I heard."

"Before you start repeating gossip, let me assure you that I know what I'm talking about. I was there, Shay, when the conversation with Ginger took place."

"Oh. But that doesn't—"

"I understand your concern about the medical advice, but Ally is a very intelligent woman." Despite his defense of her, he couldn't help but hope she was using that intelligence wisely where this subject was concerned. "She knows what the laws are."

"I'm not worried about *her*, Tag! She can practice voodoo and get arrested and sent to the gallows for all I care. I care about you."

"Voodoo is more of a religion," a voice said from behind them. "And while I believe in a holistic approach to health, it doesn't include animal sacrifice or zombies. Although, as a Native American, I do sympathize with the sensationalism and misunderstandings where the voodoo belief system is concerned."

Ally stood in the doorway, and Tag marveled at how unruffled she appeared. Like she was recounting a pleasant weather forecast and not defending herself against his sister's insulting comments. Shay, on the other hand, had enough grace to look embarrassed.

Ally pointed out the door. "Your sisters had to go so I thought I'd see if I could help."

"Ally, I'm sorry you heard that," Shay said, sounding anything but. "It wasn't personal. I was just trying to make a point."

Ally nodded. "Well done, then. Tag, I'll wait for you in the pickup."

"I'll be right there." He hoped his smile communicated some of the admiration he felt for her. Shay wasn't an easy person to combat.

They watched her walk away. Tag frowned at Shay. "I don't think who I date is anyone's business but mine."

"That's very noble, but also impossibly idealistic. Because, unfortunately for you, when you committed to this campaign, your life became the public's business whether you like it or not. It's also your family's business because we care about you. And dating Ally Mowak is going to imply things about you."

"Shay—"

"No, listen." She stepped toward him. "I'm sorry that just happened, but maybe it's a good thing. She should think about this, too."

"How can you be so—"

"I know—" she interrupted. Blowing out a breath, she continued more calmly, "I know I can sound harsh. I know I'm opinionated. Everyone agrees about that. Especially lately because I'm super stressed out, Tag, I'm…" She paused for a few long seconds. "Never mind. That doesn't matter right now. I'm not sure you understand how difficult running for office can be. I don't imagine Ally does, either."

"Shay, it's state senator, not king of the world. And to ease your mind where Ally is concerned, it's not serious, and it won't get that way. We're just…hanging out."

"Come on, Tag. You are so…good. Do you know that?" Her features softened, reminding him of the sister he used to know before the disappointments of life had so cruelly sharpened her bitter edges. "That's one of the reasons I think you're going to win. But I'm also scared for you. You're not used to people not liking you."

Tag sighed. "Shay, relax. Senator Marsh has done background checks and hired an investigator to find dirt on me. There's nothing. My *goodness*, as you so derisively refer to it, happens to be an asset in this case."

"Tag, what I'm trying to tell you is that these days you don't have to have any dirt for it to be flung on you."

Shay reached out and took his hand, her golden-brown eyes wide and beseeching. His anger dissipated because, despite his sister's approach, he knew her concern came from a place of love.

"You're my brother, but you're also the best man I know. Along with Jonah, there's not a man on this planet that I care about more than you. And, just like you, I'm protective of the people I love. When Jonah came back to town, you were afraid he was going to hurt me, and you went into attack mode. Remember?"

Tag chuckled, remembering how he'd fretted and stewed before warning Jonah not to break Shay's heart again. "Yes, I remember. Are you saying you're afraid Ally is going to hurt me?"

"Maybe not on purpose. But any way I turn this, I don't see your *hanging out* with her being good for you." She paused, her expression a mix of concern and thoughtfulness. "Or for her, for that matter."

TWENTY MINUTES LATER Tag and Ally were back on the road, and Tag was mulling over the conversation with Shay. His sister could be a little dramatic, but she made a good point.

"I'm sorry about that. My sister can be… intense."

"It's fine. I get it. She loves you. You don't need to apologize for her, and she already apologized for herself. I'm not sure how sorry she was, but either way, it's not on you."

"Ally, there is one thing that Shay brought up that I'd like to talk about."

"Sure."

"I know you're helping Hannah with her arthritis and that's great."

Ally nodded, her face a marble slab. But he could feel her gaze burning into him. He was glad he was driving so he didn't have to make eye contact. "My, uh, concern is that, well, she implied that you might be seeing other patients—people," he quickly amended. "And, apparently, other people are talking."

"Gossiping you mean?" She shrugged a shoulder. "I don't care."

"Okay." He paused, trying to decide whether he should drop it. But the fact was that he cared about her—and himself, too, where the election was concerned. "But Shay pointed out that people—the community—might scrutinize you even more because of the election, because of your involvement with me. I mean, assuming this date goes well and we keep…" He glanced at her.

"I understand," she said. Her tone was serious, but her lips were curling up a little at the corners.

"And that doesn't bother you?"

"No."

Did she mean that? Tag wasn't sure she understood what being the focus of town gossip could be like. In addition to being young, growing up in such a rural setting meant she'd been sheltered in certain ways.

"I think the real question is whether it bothers you," she said.

Did it? People talked in Rankins, just like they did in every other small town, but Ally hadn't committed a crime or done anything terrible. He couldn't imagine his reputation suffering because of his association with her. So long as her actions didn't hurt anyone, it didn't matter. No, his concern was that she was going to hurt herself, and he had a sinking feeling there wasn't much he could do about that.

"I've already voiced my reservations to you, which are about you and the security of your job."

"Okay then."

"Okay then," he agreed. He wasn't going to allow Shay's outburst or this topic to ruin their day.

"Moose!" Ally cried and pointed. Tag didn't see it but slowed the pickup to a crawl. A cow with twin calves stepped out from the brush onto the road. The trio sauntered across and disappeared into the trees along the other side.

"Nice catch."

She smiled. "My grandfather trained me well. Growing up, I used to go out on house calls with him. As I'm sure you can imagine, that entailed miles of very bad, very remote roads."

"Teeming with wildlife."

"Yep. One time when I was a little girl I asked him why wild animals seemed attracted to the road. They had miles and miles of wilderness they could travel on, and the road was so dangerous. He said, 'Remember, Alsoomse, in some ways animals aren't so different than people. It's always tempting to take the easy path, even when we know it might not be the best path.'"

"Alsoomse?"

"Oh, yeah, that's my name. It means *independent* in Algonquin."

"Are you Algonquin?"

"My grandmother was half. She spoke the language."

"Huh. Wow. It's a beautiful name." Tag chuckled appreciatively. "And it couldn't be more perfect, could it?"

She grinned. "My grandfather has always worked very hard to make me live up to it, believe me. But what about Tag? That's un-usual, too."

"It's short for Taggart, which is my mom's maiden name. Taggart Henry James."

"Hmm. I like that. And the concept, keep-ing a part of your identity in your child. It's a nice way to honor your heritage. I'd like to name a baby after my grandfather someday."

A shockingly painful cramp of longing fol-lowed as an image of Ally with a tiny black-haired baby cuddled on her lap materialized before him. His baby fantasies had never been quite so specific, and he reminded himself that Ally's "someday" was probably a good decade away. Way too far away for him.

Supposed to be having fun, he told him-self, casual and fun. "One time, a cow moose chased a guest into the koi pond at the Far-away Inn."

"No way!" Ally said, laughing.

"True. It wouldn't be as funny if the guy hadn't been such a jerk or if he'd gotten hurt. But it couldn't have happened to a more de-serving person. These teenagers filmed the whole thing. Hannah was working for Shay back then, and she somehow got a hold of the video. It's hilarious."

They continued to exchange stories, and by the time they reached Glacier City, he realized that for the first time in his life he'd met a woman who'd had as many outdoor adventures as he had, maybe more. Lots of firsts with Ally. Funny how the years between them seemed to be dissolving with every second he spent with her.

Tag pulled the pickup into the parking lot of the restaurant and turned off the engine.

"We're here already?" Ally asked.

"I know. Shortest drive to Glacier City ever." Time, he thought, had never meant so much to him as it did since he'd met Ally.

CHAPTER ELEVEN

ACCESSIBLE ONLY BY boat or plane and with a population of just over thirty thousand, Alaska's capital city of Juneau was the best option if Tag had to spend time in an urban setting. Situated at the base of a three-thousand-foot-high mountain and bordered by the ocean, Juneau offered everything an outdoor-loving city dweller could want. On paper, it should have been enough for him.

In reality, it was a point on which he and Kendall had not been able to agree. She wanted to live in Juneau, he didn't and she couldn't understand why. Tag didn't want to leave his family or relocate his business, nor did he want to be in a city, even one as small and charming as Juneau.

But Kendall hadn't felt that Rankins held enough opportunities to advance her career as an attorney. Tag agreed that, for the ambitious Kendall, it did not. They tried the long-distance thing for a while, but when visits from each direction grew less and less frequent, he felt the inevitable looming. And he was right; Kendall had met someone else and moved on. Tag had thought, and believed still, that if they'd loved each other enough they would have been able to work it out.

He hadn't been to Juneau since the breakup, and he'd wondered how he would feel when he returned, if Kendall memories would stir any regrets in him. But now, landing and docking his floatplane at Senator Marsh's waterfront home, all he felt was relief.

That wasn't entirely true, he realized as he and Bering fetched their bags from the plane and started across the dock where Jack and his wife, Gwen, were waiting. There was a surprisingly strong longing-type ache mixed in there, too—he already missed Ally.

In a weak moment, he'd nearly asked her to come with him. He'd talked himself out of it because he was afraid it would violate the ground rules he'd set. If they were going to keep things casual, he needed to act casual. Not an easy feat where she was concerned. He was counting on this weekend to provide some distance and possibly a bit of perspective. He told himself that focusing on the campaign would serve as a much-needed reminder that he couldn't let himself get too attached.

The Marshes greeted them on the dock. Jack

said, "Tag, beautiful landing, son, as usual. It's going to be darn convenient for you, when you're elected, to be able to fly in and out whenever you fancy."

Tag smiled. "Thank you, Jack, I appreciate your confidence."

"Welcome," Gwen said, hugging each of them in turn. "I'm so glad you guys could make it."

Tag said, "Thank you for having us, Gwen. Are you sure it's not too much of an inconvenience if we stay here at the house?"

"Positive," Gwen assured them. "Look at this place." She pointed at the mansion behind her. "We have to justify all this space somehow."

Jack agreed. "She's right. The party starts at seven, which gives us plenty of time to get changed. We'll show you to your rooms. You guys can freshen up or take a rest or wander around the estate. We'll meet out on the deck as soon as you're ready. That way, we can discuss a few matters and have a drink before we head out."

Jack's phone rang, so Gwen showed them to the second floor, where they had side-by-side suites overlooking the water. Tag entered his and headed over to the window. Discarding his earlier thoughts about distance and perspec-

tive, he pondered texting Ally. Maybe she'd
texted him. That would give him all the impe-
tus he needed to call and hear her voice. Pat-
ting his pockets, he realized his phone wasn't
there. He checked his backpack and tried to
remember the last time he'd had it.

Last night, for sure, because he and Ally
had taken a walk along the bay. He'd snapped
a photo of her with his phone; the wind had
been tossing silky strands of her long black
hair while she laughed and struggled to gather
them up.

He didn't think he could ever get tired of
looking at her. He could speak to her right now
if he had his phone. He rummaged through his
suitcase, thinking about how he'd pulled her
close after the photo and kissed her for the first
time. The first time *he'd* kissed her. The first
time since he'd established the hands-off rule.

Every time they were together seemed better
than the last, and all week he'd waited for her
to cave and kiss him again. It had been a blast
spending time with her and letting the attraction simmer right along with their friendship.

But last night, the idea of going away for
the weekend without kissing her had been out
of the question. And even though he'd prepared, braced himself for it, as soon as his lips
touched hers that fire had ignited in him all

over again, even stronger, fueled now by an almost overwhelming affection that seemed to grow bigger with every second they spent together.

Checking the time, he decided to get ready so he could head down to the dock and fetch his phone from the plane where he must have left it. After a quick shower, he brushed his teeth and donned his tux. He knocked on Bering's door and told him he'd meet him downstairs.

Once at the plane, he executed a thorough search but didn't find his phone. Nor did he see it on the dock or along the path as he made his way back to the house, where he found Bering visiting with Gwen and Jack and a few other men who'd come to discuss the campaign. He officially reported that he'd lost his phone.

"I'll text Milt at your office," Bering said. "Then I'll call Shay and have her let your mom know if there's an emergency they can call me."

"That would be great, Bering. Thanks." He wanted to add Ally to the list but felt awkward saying so in front of the crowd. He'd borrow his cousin's phone later and contact her himself.

They discussed Tag's campaign staffing needs and political strategies until it was time to depart. It was a short ride to the venue and Tag decided that at least half the population of Juneau must be in attendance. He met one person after another, members of Congress, judges, business people, professionals of all sorts.

Things went smoothly for the first hour, right up until he saw Senator Marsh approaching with a curvy blonde by his side. They first appeared in his peripheral vision, and his initial thought was that a woman was in attendance who was only a few inches shorter than he was when she was wearing heels, a trait he would have found attractive a couple of weeks ago. Everything, it seemed, no matter how circuitous, came back to Ally. But when the senator and the blonde stepped into full view, it took every bit of his self-control to keep up his smile as he focused on the face of his ex, Kendall Meade.

"Hello, Tag," Kendall said.

Beside her, Jack said, "Kendall was telling me you two are friends. I didn't realize."

"We are. Hello, Kendall. How are you?"

"And you have mutual acquaintances in Rankins?"

Before Tag could answer, Kendall said, "We do, sir. I know Tag's brother-in-law, Jonah Cedar. We serve on the Coalition of Alaska

Attorneys together. We're going to join forces and work on securing some endorsements and contributions for Tag."

Tag groaned inwardly. He was not aware of this connection. Jonah had mentioned that he planned to approach the powerful legal lobby, but he'd skipped over Kendall's involvement.

A photographer had been wandering around snapping photos, and now he appeared before them. "May I?" he asked, gesturing in their direction.

"Of course," Kendall said. She took a step closer to Tag and curled her arm through his, pressing her soft curves familiarly against his side and twisting so she was standing way too close. It caught Tag off guard, and he looked at her only to find her face mere inches from his. One of those slow-motion moments unfolded, the kind where the edges of reality blur and time stretches out uncomfortably. Kendall's blue eyes were wide and earnest, her lips curved up like they used to back when she'd always seemed pleased with him. Before she'd cheated and their already fractured relationship had collapsed.

Tag turned toward the photographer and smiled as prompted even as a sinking feeling spread through him, much the way a burn did after you'd already scorched your skin. The damage done, all you could do was wait for the pain that you knew would soon follow.

Jack waved to someone and excused himself. "I'm going to let you two catch up." Tag took a step backward.

Kendall asked, "How've you been, Tag?"

"Fine. Good. How's, uh…Pete?"

"Pete and I broke up."

"Oh, I'm sorry to hear that, Kendall." And he was. He wanted Kendall to be happy.

"I'm not." Clutching his elbow with an urgency that felt off, she said, "Tag, I'm so glad you're here. I've been thinking about you, wanting to call. You wouldn't believe how many times I've picked up the phone. But this feels like, I don't know, fate?"

"Fate?"

"Yes. When Jack contacted me about consulting for your campaign, I knew it was meant to be for our paths to cross again."

MADDENING WAS THE word that came to mind for this tight schedule. Tag was no stranger to working hard, but it felt completely different when his time was his own. They hadn't gotten back to Senator Marsh's house until after midnight Friday night. Too late to borrow a phone to call Ally, Tag had decided, but now that he was up and around he'd find a way.

They were going on a fishing trip with a small group of potential campaign donors, and Tag knew they'd likely be out of cell phone range most of the day.

According to the schedule, they'd have just enough time to return to the house to shower and change before another dinner party tonight. He hoped Kendall wasn't invited. He needed to figure out exactly how he was going to handle her zealous greeting and confession. He'd tried to put her off gently, explained that he was seeing someone, but the news hadn't seemed to faze her.

Especially when she'd asked if it was serious and he'd had to say, "No."

She frowned as if she was puzzling over a difficult concept. "So, you can't have been seeing her for long, right?"

"No, not long," he'd answered simply, evasively, because how could he tell the woman he'd dated for a year that the feelings he had for Ally surpassed those he'd ever had for Kendall, and in a fraction of the time, and yet they weren't serious?

"Good, then we don't have to worry."

"About what?"

"About me working with your campaign and...stuff." She'd added a wink and a meaningful look.

Before he could ask for clarification of "stuff" they'd been swept up by the crowd.

Kendall working on his campaign? He didn't know what to think about that. He didn't want to think about it. He didn't want to think about any of it. He just wanted to call Ally.

Dressed in a pair of comfortable jeans and two layers of shirts, he grabbed his boots and pack, and headed to Bering's room. He would borrow his phone and call Ally when Bering headed down for breakfast.

Bering opened the door and waved Tag inside. "I'm almost ready. It's going to be weird going on a fishing trip and not being the guide. Don't let me try to take over," he joked.

"I'll make sure you don't." Tag took a seat in one of two oddly shaped, spindly legged chairs situated in the corner near the window while Bering rummaged through his bag.

After pulling out a pair of thick socks, he picked up his boots, crossed the room and lowered his muscled frame into the chair across from Tag. The chair protested with an ominous creak. Bering froze, socks and boots still in hand.

"Why would anyone even make a chair this small and stupid?" he whispered.

Tag laughed. "Don't break it. It probably costs as much as your new jet boat."

"No kidding." Gingerly Bering rose and settled on the edge of the bed. "I'm glad you stopped by here because there's something I need to talk to you about."

"Ready," Tag said with feigned enthusiasm, expecting more campaign talk.

"I called Shay last night about your phone, like I told you I would."

"Yeah?"

"I hate saying this to you, especially after I encouraged you." Bering heaved out a sigh that sounded as painful as his expression appeared. "But she expressed some concerns."

Tag shook his head, a mix of irritation and anger at his sister coursing through him. "This is about Ally?"

"Yes. I'm sorry. According to Shay, people are *talking*..." he paused to add an eye roll and air quotes "...and she's worried about how it will look for you 'being associated' with her. Younger woman, possible midlife crisis, her medical...opinions. Shay is afraid people in town—voters—will turn on you."

"Are you worried?"

"No, I'm not. I trust you, buddy. I know protecting Rankins is as important to you as it is to the rest of us and that you'd never do anything to jeopardize this campaign."

He tilted his head back as if to study the

ceiling and muttered some unintelligible words before fixing his gaze back on Tag. "I can't believe I just said that. It sounds like I'm trying to use some sort of reverse psychology on you. And you know how I hate that kind of stuff. I wish I hadn't even brought it up now, but she made me promise and you know Shay."

Tag wanted to believe him, but he knew his cousin almost as well as he knew himself. Better in some ways. Next to his family, his town was his life. Tag knew the sacrifices and the efforts Bering had once made for Rankins. Winning this election was beyond important to him. It was Tag's turn to step up to the plate. They'd already agreed on that, and the last thing Tag would ever do was let Bering, the rest of their family or his community down.

"But you told me it's not serious, right?"

Tag nodded. "That's right," he said, irritation and disappointment curdling his gut. No way would he ask to borrow Bering's phone now.

SUNDAY MORNING, ALLY stared at her phone and told herself everything was fine. It was good. It had been only two days. No calls. No texts. Completely and totally incommunicado. But it wasn't like he'd told her he'd text or that he'd call. They were keeping it casual.

Stupidly, she realized now, she'd told him she wasn't looking for a relationship. That had seemed like a selling point at the time to get him over the age-difference hurdle. Now it felt like its own hurdle. An invisible one that she was afraid to talk about for fear it would put them back at the start line.

And that kiss the night before he'd left had been anything but casual. It had felt... What was the opposite of casual? Serious? Real? Intense? All of the above. Had it all been one-sided?

Only one more day to go before he got back. All would be well when she saw him again. Her insecurities slipped away when they were together. In the meantime, he was probably super busy doing important political things. Surely she'd hear from him that evening when he returned. Of course she would. Unless...? Unless he was so busy he hadn't had time to think about her? Ouch. She didn't want to go there.

She tried to remember the last thing he'd said before leaving her on Thursday night: "I'll see you next week."

Hmm. Apparently, he'd meant that in a very literal way.

Her phone chimed, making her jump. Her heart answered with a thump so hard it seemed to echo inside her head. Hands shaking, she swiped at the screen; it was a text from Flynn. He was coming over later after an unexpected shift at the hospital, so without reading it she set her phone down, disappointed.

"What am I, in middle school now?" she asked her empty living room.

At least she assumed this was how an infatuated middle-school girl might act about a boy she liked.

"I wish I'd gone to middle school. Ha." She barked out a bitter laugh. "I bet no one who went to middle school ever says that." There'd only been a handful of guys around her age in Saltdove, and they'd felt more like family.

She'd only ever dated in the Army. And not much, and never one guy long enough to consider him a boyfriend. Admittedly, she hadn't tried very hard. She'd been busy, focused on her goals. At paramedic school in Michigan she'd been so intent on her studies and nervous about her grades that she'd turned down any requests beyond friendly group gatherings or study sessions.

Not that Tag was her boyfriend. Was he?

"Either way, I'm being ridiculous." Standing up, she grabbed her jacket and headed out the door. She was just hungry. A donut would help, or two. She'd walk to the Donut Den because that way she could do the preemptive calorie burn. Or at least wear off the frosting. Okay, fine, some of the frosting.

Mr. Most Eligible Bachelor obviously had plenty of experience. She needed advice. Once again, she found herself wishing for a girlfriend to talk to. Not that Flynn wasn't great. He was, but from the way he'd acted when she'd told him about Tag, she didn't think she was going to get a lot of help from that quarter.

Ally pushed through the door of the bakery and instantly began to relax. The smell alone could count as aromatherapy. The soothing combination of yeast and maple and vanilla stirred into her, and just the promise of sugar was added comfort.

A teenaged girl with deep dimples and a long French braid smiled at her from behind the counter. The name embroidered across the top of her bubblegum-pink apron was Molly.

"Good morning," she said. "What can I get for you today?"

"Hey, Molly. I'll take one maple bar, one of the half-chocolate, half-maple bars, two cinnamon twisties, two apple fritters and one of those cream-filled things. Oh, and, mmm... two...*Emilys*? How many is that, nine?"

"Yep, nine."

"Might as well make it a dozen, then, huh? That's probably cheaper at this point, right?" Ally stared up at the board and tried to calculate the cost per donut versus a dozen.

Molly grinned. Ally figured she probably got this a lot, people losing their ability to count and do math in the presence of fresh-baked pastries.

"It is cheaper. What would you like for your last four?"

"Four? I thought you said I had nine in the box."

"Yep, you do. But our dozen is a baker's dozen. If you buy twelve, you get one free."

"Wow. Does anyone ever get this close and not buy twelve or thirteen or whatever?"

Molly giggled. "Not really."

"Brilliant. Just surprise me. Anything will do." It was too many donuts. She'd give some to Flynn tonight, stash the rest in the fridge and take them into the hospital tomorrow morning. That would help her popularity. She'd eat all the chocolate-covered ones to stave off any mud jokes still floating around.

"I'll have a cup of coffee, too, please. The big one, and I don't need room for cream."

"You got it."

Ally settled in at a table in the corner facing

the door. Three donuts and half a cup of coffee later she was already feeling better. She'd just pulled up Flynn's message when a voice floated over to her.

"Look at our Tag. He's always been such a good-looking boy, but I swear, he just gets more handsome as time goes by, doesn't he? Made to be photographed. Like one of those underwear models, but with clothes. Which is too bad, now that I think about it."

"Bernice! He could be your grandson."

"But he's not, Erma, is he? I'm not dead yet."

Ally homed in on the two older women standing next to a nearby table where a newspaper lay open. "I suppose you're right. He's going to be a wonderful senator. They sure make a striking couple. Who is that woman, though? She's a pretty thing, isn't she? And so tall…"

"Call who?" Bernice asked.

"Not call, Bernice, *tall*," her companion shouted. "I said the woman is tall."

"Oh…she sure is. It's partly because of those shoes. Those are real *beauts*, Jimmy Chows, probably. Do you think I could pull off a pair of shoes like that?"

"Not without aggravating your gout."

Behind the counter, Molly giggled, and said, "I think it's Choo, Jimmy Choos."

"I know they're shoes, sweetie, that's what we're talking about."

They continued discussing the topic of Tag and his beautiful companion and her shoes while one of them paid and the other took the box of donuts. Finally they left the bakery, bickering all the way. It would have been cute if Ally hadn't felt compelled to see that paper. Standing, she walked over to the table and then stared down at the nightmare plastered across the page.

The photo was big and bright and clear and featured a truly stunning shot of Tag looking elegant and perfect in a tux and so out of Ally's league it made her heart ache with equal parts pride and anguish.

He was looking at a gorgeous blonde, right into her eyes, their faces only inches apart. A mile of leg stretched from beneath her tight dress, ending at feet encased in a pair of tall, sexy heels. Ally had never worn heels in her life.

"She probably has bunions the size of Denali," she muttered. But the thought didn't give her much satisfaction because it was the way they were standing that had her regretting that third donut. Hot frosting burned like acid in her stomach as she stared at the image. One of the woman's arms was twisted tightly through Tag's, the other stretched across his chest to playfully tug on his lapel. *Snuggling* was the word that came to mind, and only in a way that someone who knew him very, very well would do.

The first few lines of the article jumped out at her:

Alaska's newest political power couple? Local businessman Tag James, of Copper Crossing Air Transport, with companion, attorney Kendall Meade, at the Wayfarer Political Fundraising dinner in Juneau. Sources say this hot couple used to be a regular sight around Juneau as recently as a year ago. With rumors flying about the handsome pilot's entrance into the upcoming Alaska state senate race, and Ms. Meade's connections, one can't help but wonder if we're seeing the beginning (continuation?) of a beautiful friendship?

Ally flinched as the phone now gripped in her hand chimed again. She looked at the screen, where three messages from Flynn seemed to pulse and vibrate. Swiping the screen, she read:

Have you seen the newspaper today?

Call me.

Where are you?

With trembling fingers, she tapped out an answer. Yes. Help. On my way home.

I'll be there as soon as I can.

CHAPTER TWELVE

"KENDALL MEADE SUPPORTING your campaign? Score. What type of role is she going to take?" Bering asked Sunday morning while he and Tag sipped coffee in a restaurant in downtown Juneau. They were waiting for their breakfast companions to arrive, Sally and Tom Meade and daughter, Kendall.

"Consultant or adviser. Not sure yet." Tag didn't want Kendall taking any role at all, but how could he refuse? She was a perfect asset—intelligent, wealthy, connected, personality galore. And, if last night was any indication, she also believed in him. Which should make him happy but instead left him feeling unsettled.

Bering had also set up meetings with officials from a number of outdoor organizations. The two of them were headed out to talk with them after this chat with the Meades. Time to start soliciting contributions, a chore Tag already knew he was going to find uncomfortable, if not distasteful. He reminded himself that no one ever said running for office was easy.

"What do you think of the campaign manager candidates so far?"

"They all seem fine to me. I'm going to let Maura sift through them and make a recommendation."

"You okay? You look a little out of it."

"I'm fine," Tag lied. "Tired. So much to think about."

Ally was what he was thinking about, worrying about, wishing for. Two days without talking to her was taking a toll. Late the night before, he'd made up a believable excuse to borrow Bering's phone and duck out of the party for a few minutes to call her, but realized he didn't know her number.

The cell phone paradox at its finest: she'd texted him first, and he'd added her to his contacts without memorizing the number. Now it was nearly 11:00 p.m. Aside from Iris or Hannah, he couldn't think of anyone other than Flynn who would have her number. Iris was the only one he felt comfortable contacting so late, and she hadn't answered.

So here he was, stuck again. Between this breakfast meeting and the ensuing appointments, he would have to wait until he got back home. Besides, he told himself, even though it seemed like an eternity, he'd been away less than forty-eight hours. Maybe this was fate's way of forcing him to get that distance he'd been seeking.

Either way, they were flying back this afternoon, and by tonight all would be well. The day couldn't pass soon enough for him. And not just because of Ally. He needed some peace, time to reflect, to regroup, to prepare for this campaign battle. Bottom line, he wasn't used to feeling overwhelmed. He didn't like it.

"Don't Kendall's folks have, like, a billion dollars?"

"I have no idea. They are very wealthy. Her dad comes from money. Kendall has a trust fund. But it's her mom who is responsible for taking them to the next level. She's an investment genius or something like that."

"Do they like you?"

Tag smiled. "They do. Sally came to visit me in Rankins after we broke up. She cried." He shook his head, remembering how glad he was that Kendall had been the one to break it off. "Asked me to give Kendall another chance. When I pointed out that she was dating someone else, Sally told me she could snap her fingers and make him go away, whatever that meant."

"So, we're looking at a hefty contribution?"

"Kendall alluded to as much last night. Said

Sally and Tom are 'beyond thrilled' that I'm running."

Bering shook his head. "Seriously, you've got to be the only guy I know who can break up with a woman and keep the parents. There she is."

Heads turned as Kendall strode through the door of the restaurant. Appearing oblivious to the attention, she glided toward their table. Tag had commented on it once, her seeming lack of awareness of her eye-catching beauty, to which she'd responded, "No, not oblivious, sweetie. Not at all. But if you pretend you don't notice, it makes you even more noticeable."

He'd been impressed by the statement at the time, awed by her confidence. Now, though, he saw things, and her, a little differently, and as she neared the table he purposely kept his eyes averted.

WHEN ALLY ARRIVED HOME, she discovered she had a visitor, but it wasn't Flynn. One of Tag's sisters was sitting on her porch swing.

"Hi, Ally. I hope this isn't a bad time."

It's not exactly a good time was what she wanted to say, because unfortunately, this wasn't a James sister she was eager to see.

"Hello, Shay. Tag's not here if you're looking for him."

"I know he's not. He's still in Juneau. He'll be back late this afternoon."

"Mmm-hmm." Ally didn't want to confess that she wasn't privy to his estimated return time.

"Have you heard from him?"

The sinking feeling she'd been battling won out, further plummeting her spirits. She didn't want to confess, but she also wasn't going to lie. "No," she said.

"I understand you giving me the cold shoulder here. I deserve it. But I came over because I thought you might not know that Tag lost his phone."

Ally's knees went weak with relief. "No, I didn't," she said calmly, careful to keep her expression blank. She wasn't going to give away even a fraction of how she felt about Tag to his sister, not when Shay didn't approve of Ally or her traditional healing techniques. She had every right to disapprove of their relationship, but Ally wasn't going to give her the satisfaction of seeing Ally's insecurity.

Shay gave her head a wry shake. "You're a cucumber. I'll give you that much."

"I don't know what that means, but if you're here to insult me again, I really would rather you hurried it along."

"No, you know that expression—cool as a

cucumber? We just say 'cucumber' in our family. It's a compliment."

"I see."

"Kinda the opposite of me, especially lately."

Ally had no idea what to say to that.

Shay went on, "Anyway, so, yeah… Tag lost his phone. Bering called on Friday night to tell me. I didn't think to let you know. It was Iris who mentioned it. She was gone this weekend and stopped by the inn on her way home. She said you guys were dating, and I realized you might not have heard from him. It was thoughtless of me not to tell you."

Apparently, Shay wasn't finished tormenting her.

"The woman in the photo is his ex-girlfriend."

This time Ally didn't have to think about the blank stare. It was either that or cry, but Ally didn't cry. Almost never. And definitely not in front of strangers.

"But I want you to know that my brother would never cheat on you. If he told you that you're exclusive, he means it."

The final, threadbare piece of hope she'd been holding on to frayed and broke at those words, because that was just the thing. He'd never told her they were exclusive. The opposite, in fact. He'd specifically said she should see other people.

When she'd asked him if he was *committed* to anyone, he'd said no. At the time, she hadn't thought to ask if *he* was *dating* anyone else. Still, she hadn't seen it coming. Maybe she was, if not too young for Tag, then too inexperienced.

Shay was here to tell her he'd lost his phone, but Ally couldn't see how that mattered now. If he'd wanted to contact her, he could have. But what difference would that have made? If he'd had his phone, would he have called to tell her he was going to a fancy party with a tall, model-gorgeous, sexy-high-heel-wearing blonde? *Hey, Ally, don't worry when you see my photo in the* Rankins Press *snuggled up with a hottie. It's just my ex.*

It didn't matter, because she would have just been crushed that much sooner. She was glad she didn't have experience if this was what it felt like to really care about a man and then have him tear your heart in two, especially when she didn't even know if she had a right to be feeling this way. She might be young, but she was clearly old-school when it came to this sort of thing.

Sounds from next door drew their attention. Little Mason Hatch bounded out of the house with younger sister, Liza, hot on his heels.

Mom, DeAnne, followed, carrying the baby, Albert, on her hip.

"Mason!" she called, to no avail. "Liza!"

The little boy sprinted into Ally's yard, across the grassy expanse and up the porch steps, where he climbed into the swing next to Shay. Liza stopped and waited for her mother.

"Hey, Mason!" Shay greeted him with a warm smile and slipped an arm around him. "What's up?"

"Oh, not much. I'm going to get in trouble when Mommy comes. But I saw you over here, and I just started running because I wanted to see you close up. I like seeing you close-up, Shay."

"That's so nice, buddy. I like seeing you close-up, too."

Sure enough, DeAnne was only seconds behind him. Ally often marveled at the speed at which toddler-wielding moms could move. "Shay, Ally, hi." Scaling the porch, she shook her head at her son. "Mason, I'm speechless. How many times do I have to tell you not to run out of my sight?"

"But I'm in your sight, Mom. I know because you followed me real easy."

Ally could see that Shay was trying not to smile. She did an admirable job until DeAnne lost it and then both women laughed hard. Ally couldn't quite bring herself to join in, but she managed a smile while DeAnne tried to explain the intricacies of "in sight."

The women proceeded to visit for a few minutes until Liza toddled off across the yard. DeAnne began to fidget when she neared the road.

"Do you want me to take him?" Shay held out her arms for the baby. "So you can round her up?"

"Would you mind? I don't want to yell and wake my little peanut here."

Shay settled the sleeping baby in her arms while DeAnne went to fetch his sister. A lump formed in Ally's throat as she watched Shay with the baby. There was so much longing in her eyes that Ally could barely stand to watch her for the ache it caused in her own heart. Tag and Iris had both told her how much Shay wanted children.

DeAnne returned with Liza and a car seat for Albert. The little guy barely stirred when Shay buckled him in. DeAnne and the kids said their goodbyes, settled in the minivan and drove away.

Shay stood. "Well, I should get going…"

Ally had forgotten about the donut box inside the bag she held. Under normal circumstances, she would have offered donuts to the kids, but her state of mind was nowhere near normal. Now she held the bag aloft.

"I have donuts. Would you like to come in?"

"You know what? I think I will."

They went inside and Ally made tea. For some reason, she felt more kindly disposed toward Shay when the woman wolfed down a donut in short order and took two bites of another before setting it on the plate Ally provided.

"This donut—" she pointed at the maple-glazed pastry that Ally had already decided was her favorite "—the Emily? It's named after Bering's wife."

Ally had to smile. "Seriously?"

"Yep. You'd never know it by looking at her, but she's a semireformed junk-food addict. When she first came here, that's pretty much all she ate. She's since become an excellent cook, but back then she spent a lot of time at the Donut Den."

Shay took a sip of her tea. "This is really good. What is it?"

"An herbal mix I make myself. Don't worry—there's no dried chicken feet or buffalo tongue in it."

Shay cringed and cleaned her fingertips with a napkin. "I'm sorry about that voodoo comment. It was incredibly insensitive."

"Yes, it was. But I'm sorry, too."

"What? Why?"

Ally sighed and explained, her heart heavy. "Because I'm purposefully throwing it back at you to make you feel uncomfortable. Which makes me just as bad in my own mind."

Shay gaped at her. "You are so…mature for your age, do you know that? Shoot, does that sound condescending?"

"No. Honesty rarely does."

"Good, because I'm going to be brutally honest right now. I know we got off on the wrong foot. At first, I didn't care because I was only thinking about Tag. But I want to explain myself. This election is very important to him, to me, to our entire extended family, to our community—the whole state, for that matter. I don't know how much he's told you, but he's been considering it the last few years. We just didn't think he'd be running so soon, but circumstances have evolved and he has to now. I'm just worried that he doesn't… That he's not prepared."

Has to? Ally needed to think about this. She probably needed to know Tag better before she commented on something that had been troubling her almost since she'd met him. Instead, she said, "Your love and concern for your brother is admirable."

"He's truly the best man I know. That might sound odd. You're probably thinking I should name my husband or my dad. They're both right up there, but Tag is… He's special to almost everyone who meets him."

Ally nodded. She could believe that.

"I'm not saying he's perfect. He's got plenty of faults—he's conceited and proud and thinks he's invincible and plenty of other things that you'll discover soon enough." Shay chuckled a little before adding, "I guess what I'm saying is that if you're special to him, you must be worth it."

"Worth it?"

"Yes. Worth the controversy his involvement with you is causing and will continue to cause. He can't see it yet. My sisters don't see it. But, as you've probably figured out, I'm generally considered the cynical one in the family. I prefer *realist*, but we can't always control the opinions of others, can we? And before you take offense, please know that if, after considering what I've said, you and Tag choose to pursue a relationship I'll back you a hundred percent. Like my brother, I'm also very loyal. Family means everything to me."

Ally knew she was expected to respond at this point, but nothing she could say would help matters. She wanted someone to talk to, sure, but not Tag's sister. She didn't trust Shay. Not to mention, she didn't even know where she and Tag stood at this point. Instead, she took the opening Shay had just given her to change the subject.

"I can see that about your family. You don't have any children of your own yet?" She knew the answer but hoped the question would prompt Shay to talk about herself.

Shay looked a little stricken by the question. "No, um, not...yet. I don't know if I can have children."

Squelching the prickle of guilt for raising the subject, she asked, "So, it's not a medical certainty?"

Shay stared back at her, indecision stamped across her face. Ally sensed that she wanted to talk about it and so she waited.

Shay inhaled a deep breath, blew it out and answered, "No, I can get pregnant. It's the carrying the baby that hasn't worked out. But...sometimes I think it would be easier if I couldn't..." Her voice cracked, tears welling in her eyes. Ally felt her heart twist with sympathy. "Because that tiny kernel of hope is slowly destroying me. It shouldn't be, I know. And right now, I should be thrilled..." She paused to swallow a sob.

Ally slowly absorbed the implication of her words. "Are you…pregnant?"

Nodding, Shay wiped at her tears with her shirt sleeve. "I'm sorry, that just slipped out. I'm so emotional right now. I'm… Stressed out doesn't even begin to cover how I'm feeling. Please, don't tell Tag or anyone. No one knows, except Jonah. I'm only a couple of months along and I've been here so many times and then…lost it. Every day, every waking moment I worry about losing this one, too. Pregnancy is supposed to be a happy experience, but for me, it's not. It's more like a nightmare and… And I can't bear the thought of facing anymore pity."

Ally wondered if Shay's family, her husband or anyone knew the true depths of her misery and fear? And at that moment, she didn't see Shay as her adversary, the sister who didn't approve of her brother's relationship with an eccentric, younger woman. She saw her as a person who needed help. And Ally wanted to help her if she could.

Ally nodded. "I won't say a word, Shay, I promise. It's your secret to share."

TAG COULD BARELY think straight, so crowded was his brain with information about polls, PACs, endorsements and finances, not to mention a myriad of complicated and hot-button issues, all of which he needed to wrap his brain around. But above everything was this aching need to see Ally.

By the time he and Bering returned to Rankins late Sunday afternoon, Tag wished, right or wrong, that he could flip a switch and turn it all off, except for the part about Ally. Because all he wanted to do was relax with a cold beer and have Ally snuggled by his side. His phone, unfortunately, was not at the hangar/office where he kept his planes or in his pickup.

At home, he dropped his bag in the bedroom, changed his clothes and brushed his teeth. No phone. Had Ally worried when she hadn't heard from him? Why hadn't that thought occurred to him sooner? Surely, Iris would have told her he lost his phone. Would Ally be as happy to see him as he would be to see her? If he'd spent even a fraction of the time in her thoughts that she'd spent in his, all would be well. He was even beginning to wonder how he was going to manage future campaign events if he missed her this much over a weekend.

The thought flickered through his mind that he should check the newspaper, because Bering told him that Laurel had texted to say the *Rankins Press* had picked up an article from the newspaper in Juneau. Later, he decided, climbing back into his pickup and heading to Ally's house.

"So, HE LOST his phone, and that's why you didn't hear from him *all* weekend?"

Flynn stood in Ally's kitchen, where less than an hour earlier she'd comforted and counseled poor Shay to the best of her ability. They'd made plans to meet again. Flynn held the newspaper in one hand and both his expression and tone conveyed the same skepticism Ally felt.

"Yep."

"She also told you this woman is his ex?" He gave the newspaper a shake and Ally secretly wished it could be that easy to dislodge the blonde from the page.

"Yes."

"Ally, I'm sorry, but if I was away for the weekend and I lost my phone, I would find a way to contact the person I was dating."

"I know. Me, too."

"What do you think?"

"I don't know. Flynn, you're the closest thing to a girlfriend I have, and I was counting on you to tell me what you think. You know I don't have any experience here, right? Where men are concerned, I mean?"

He grinned. "Oddly, I'm honored to be your quasi-girlfriend. I just wish I had the wisdom of a woman to give you here."

"I've never thought a lack of experience was a bad thing, until now."

"It's not a bad thing, Ally. Not at all. Does Tag know this? That you haven't…dated much?"

"Yes, but I'm not sure he gets just how little I've dated. We've only been seeing each other a couple of weeks. Granted, we've managed to pack a lot in there if I add up the hours, but still… You know how I am about this girl stuff, sharing or whatever."

"I love how you say it like it's profanity. *Sharing*," he repeated and chuckled.

The impersonation made her smile, and she appreciated the fact that he managed to bring it out in her. "Yeah, well, I'm not all girly like you are."

"True. A lot of women like that, though."

"Do they?" she asked skeptically.

He chuckled. "So glad I've always resisted falling for you. You'd be so bad for my self-esteem. You need to talk about this—to Tag, I mean."

"Wouldn't that seem needy and desperate? We're supposed to be keeping it casual."

"You can be casual and still communicate.

In fact, you have to, so you know you're on the same page, so one of you doesn't end up more attached than the other."

Too late, she thought, her stomach gripped with a new bout of despair. "What do I do about the photo?"

"He'll have an explanation. You just have to decide whether you believe it. You don't want him to think you're jealous."

"I don't?"

"No way. Guys abhor jealousy."

"Abhor? Really?"

"Yes. Trust me. On this one, I have experience."

Huh. Ally had kind of enjoyed it when Tag was jealous. Wouldn't a little jealousy show him that she liked him?

This was all so confusing.

"But—"

A knock sounded on the door. Ally jumped, her heart taking a tumble. "That's him."

They headed into the living room together. Ally opened the door to a smiling Tag, who didn't look at all like he'd been cuddling with another woman all weekend. But what did that look like? Aside from the photographic evidence, she wasn't sure.

"Hey."

The sound of Flynn shuffling behind her drew his attention. His smile faltered. "Oh, hey, Flynn."

"Tag," Flynn answered flatly. "Looks like you had a good time in Juneau."

Tag's brow creased. "It was productive."

"Ha. Yeah. No doubt." Sarcasm dripped from his tone and Ally felt a surge of fondness for her good friend. It felt nice for someone to have her back. Stopping in front of her, Flynn brushed a kiss across her forehead and took a moment to look her in the eye. "See you later, Ally. Call me."

"Bye, Flynn. Thanks. I will."

He gave her hand a little squeeze and left.

Tag's face wore a scowl as he came inside and shut the door behind him. "I want to say something smart-alecky about how touchy-feely he is with you. But I won't. I know you're just friends."

Ally stared. *Because you're an expert on touchy-feely, huh?* The sarcastic retort tickled the end of her tongue. He couldn't possibly mean that, could he? Unless…? Was there a chance he hadn't seen the photo? Or was she making a bigger deal out of this than it was?

Despite her efforts to remain unreadable, he must have seen something in her expression because he said, "Ally, what is it? What's the matter?"

"Have you seen this morning's newspaper?"

CHAPTER THIRTEEN

TAG STUDIED THE PHOTO, remembering the un-settled feeling that had swept through him in that exact moment and willing his brain to compute how the photographer had managed to capture something that had never existed. Kendall had snaked her arms around him so quickly he hadn't registered what was happening until it was too late. He'd been confused by her actions, but that didn't show in the photo. No, it depicted a different scene entirely: warmth, intimacy, romance, a couple totally into each other.

Nausea churned his stomach, and his head felt like it was filled with cold helium. He looked at Ally, watching for a clue as to how she might feel about this. He knew how he'd feel. And it wasn't good.

"I need to ask you something, Tag. Are you seeing other people? I know you told me I could, but I'm not, and I don't plan to, but if you are, then it will change this conversation."

Regret pierced his insides even as a bubble

of joy welled up to soothe the pain. He liked that she didn't want to see anyone else.

"No, I'm not. And this isn't what it looks like."

"Okay… Then, what *should* it look like?"

Opening his mouth to the rush of words already gathering, he closed it as the cleverness of the question caught up with him. He needed to get this right.

"It *should* look like two old friends meeting after a long time. I mean, factually, she is an ex-girlfriend, but I wish it didn't look like that."

The slightest lift of her brows was enough to tell him he was already veering off course.

"Wait." Tamping down his panic and desperate to make her understand, he inhaled a breath. "Starting over now… It *should* look like two old friends, exes, meeting after not seeing each other for a while. One—the woman—is greeting the other—me—way too enthusiastically. In my surprise, I glanced at her to see what the heck she was doing wrapping herself around me like an octopus. When I did, I discovered her face was much too close to mine, also catching me off guard. A little shock and dismay mixed with a bit of fear are what the shot *should* show. I realize that it doesn't, and I regret that more than I can ever express."

Tag realized he was getting better at this, at reading her. The left side of her mouth twitched like it did when she thought he was funny but didn't want to give him the satisfaction of letting him know.

"That's not bad."

He felt like it was enough encouragement to continue. "Immediately after the unfortunate nanosecond that this quick-drawing freak of a photographer captured, I stepped to one side and several more photos were taken. Normal ones." He flicked his gaze back down to the picture and shook his head. "How he managed this…completely inaccurate representation I will forever wonder about. And why he used it, I don't…? Anyway, her name is Kendall Meade, and we dated for about a year. It was mostly long-distance and, after she cheated on me, we broke up."

He searched her beautiful, curious, wary brown gaze, hoping his conveyed the truth of the situation. He didn't care if it hinted at the depth of his feelings for her if it meant they could get past this.

"Ally, I know that last part could imply that I was heartbroken but I promise I was not. The relationship was already headed for the end. Kendall just pushed it over the cliff faster.

Sure, maybe my pride was bruised, but mostly, I was relieved.

"This morning, before we left, Bering and I had breakfast with her and her parents, Sally and Tom Meade, because they are interested in making a major contribution to my campaign. I had—have—an excellent relationship with them." He didn't see the point in mentioning that Kendall might be consulting on his campaign. It wasn't as if she'd be working with him directly.

Her composure was unnerving. "Ally, please, say something."

"I don't know what to say."

"Just say what you're thinking."

She blinked and then nodded once. "Okay."

When she didn't elaborate, he asked, "Okay? That's it? In that brilliant and incredible brain of yours, that's the only word forming?"

"Yes. I'm choosing to believe you."

Tag shifted on his feet, trying not to let his doubt show. She was taking this awfully well. He'd never dated a woman who wouldn't be at least a little jealous about this photo. Even in the early days of their relationship, Kendall would have come unglued. Truthfully, he'd be jealous to see a photo of Ally like this. Without cause, he'd been jealous of his eighteen-year-old cousin. Not to mention Flynn, who'd never acted like more than a big brother to her from what Tag had seen.

And then it hit him, knocking the wind out of him like a solid blow to the solar plexus. This just proved what he already knew; he was more into her than she was him. Sure, she'd told him she didn't want to see other people, but that didn't mean her feelings matched the ones he had for her. Asking how she felt about him would only lead to a conversation about how much he liked her. And that was a place he didn't want to go, couldn't go. His heart sank a little more.

If he'd been hoping for some perspective on their relationship, he'd certainly succeeded. This photo and a weekend of no communication had inadvertently cemented his feelings. And it had revealed hers, too. Or, more to the point, it highlighted the disparity between them. But this was a good thing, he assured himself. Exactly the way he'd wanted, the way he needed, for this to evolve.

He'd examine the repercussions to his psyche and the damage to his heart later. Right now, he wanted to think about what he wanted, and what he wanted was Ally, as much of her as he could get.

He stepped toward her. "Thank you. You're amazing. I missed you."

She graced him with a full-blown smile. Finally. "I missed you, too," she said. The pressure in his chest immediately began to ease.

Reaching out, he pulled her into his arms. Relief flooded through him as she hugged him tightly. She might not like him as much as he liked her, but she definitely liked him. Because he couldn't wait for another second, he dipped his head and kissed her.

When he pulled away, she gripped his shoulders and held on. "I didn't like not hearing from you."

"Yeah, that was no good for me, either. I lost my phone."

"I heard."

"You did?"

"Yes, Shay told me."

"Shay? I'm surprised she would bother."

"I was, too, and I only heard this morning, so you're not off the hook. In all of Juneau, you couldn't find a phone to call me?"

He smiled at the irritation in her tone, not because he'd caused it but because of what it might mean. Twining a hand into her hair, he asked, "You were worried, or you missed me?"

"Both."

"Good."

"Good? It didn't feel good."

"So, you're saying you'd like to hear from me every day?"

"Yes. Or, at the very least, I'd like to know that I wasn't going to hear from you."

That felt promising. Sweeping her against him, Tag took a moment to enjoy the fact that finally, he was right where he wanted to be. "If it makes you feel better, this is where I wished I was all weekend." He didn't add that, had he been in possession of this information when he left town, he would have stolen a phone.

WITH IVY STILL on bereavement leave, Tag was ready to pull his hair out until Iris volunteered to fill in. He was incredibly grateful for her help and impressed with both her business sense and her efficiency. Iris spent the first few days trying to figure out how to adjust his business schedule for the upcoming year of campaigning.

"When are you hiring a campaign manager?" she asked one morning as they studied an email from Maura encouraging him to hold a rally to officially announce his candidacy. They were waiting for Bering and Emily and the kids to show up along with Hannah, Tate and Lucas. Tag was flying them all to Anchorage, where they were meeting Emily's mom and stepdad for a visit and a trip to the zoo.

"Soon. By the end of the month, for sure."

He was going to have to hire a pilot to take some of his flights. His friend Cricket, who was Hannah's partner at JB Heli-Ski, was the obvious choice. If he was this busy now, he couldn't imagine how his life would be once the campaigning officially began. He was grateful for the near-constant reminders that fueled his ambition and helped to keep his eye on the prize.

Like the increase in real estate listings and transactions in Rankins and the surrounding area, further proof of Mammoth Tracks' intentions to move into the valley. Hannah had had confirmed it via Park Lowell, and Bering's source in the borough's government office had revealed that a major retail chain had inquired about the permit process to build a huge discount store between Rankins and Glacier City. Evidence was mounting quickly, and it worried them all.

"I'll be glad when this election is over," he said absently. He looked up to find Iris scowling at him. "What?" he asked.

"You do realize that it hasn't even officially begun, right? And when you're elected, then you have to be a senator."

"Yeah, I'm… I think it's just the campaign part that has me out of sorts. The not knowing what to expect and the logistics are getting to me. I'm used to being able to handle things on my own, you know? I'm sure it'll get better once we have a campaign manager."

"Sure, it will," she said. "For now, let's tackle this email. Maura says you should hold the rally here in Rankins. Since we don't have a campaign manager, we'll need to hire someone to plan it, but we can at least set the date and stuff. Maybe we could hire an event planner?"

"An event planner? For what?" Emily said, walking into the office, the baby on her hip. Hannah, Tate and Lucas filed in behind her. Bering and Violet followed.

With all gathered around, Iris read Maura's email aloud.

"How exciting!" Hannah clapped her hands. "I can't wait."

"I'll do it," Emily said. "You don't need an event planner. I'll organize it. It will save the campaign a ton of money."

"I'll help," Hannah said.

"Emily, are you sure?" Tag asked.

"Absolutely. I'd love to do it. A rally is a great idea. It needs to be a big deal with the entire community invited. Generate some grassroots support."

"Like the waterfront? Memorial Day weekend!" Hannah suggested.

"Yes, brilliant, Hannah! It's a little later than Maura recommends, but I think it works because the turnout and the momentum will more than compensate for the later date. The crowds will already be here because of the craft fair. We'll do it Friday afternoon to kick off the event." Emily already had her phone out, making notes.

Hannah's eyes were shining. "This is going to be awesome. I wonder if we could get some fireworks?"

"I love that idea."

Tag said, "Emily, I wouldn't even know how to thank you."

Gray-blue eyes snapped up to meet his. "That's easy," Emily said. "Win."

He grinned. "I'll do my best." A different kind of tightness clutched his chest, one that was becoming all too familiar. They didn't call it campaign pressure for nothing, he thought wryly.

Hannah's stepson, Lucas, who had been silently listening to the exchange, scrunched his face. "Do I have to call you Senator James?"

Hannah laughed. "He heard Tate and me talking the other day. We're all so proud of you, Tag. I think this is the greatest thing anyone in our family has ever done."

"Thank you, Hannah, but I need to get

through the election first." He turned to Lucas. "You don't want to call me Senator James?"

"No." He gave his head a somber shake. "I just want you to be Uncle Tag."

"Me, too," Violet chirped.

"I'll always be Uncle Tag to you guys."

"Don't worry, guys," Hannah chimed in. "Uncle Tag can be both. Uncle Tag can be everything."

He could only pray that she was right.

CHAPTER FOURTEEN

"So, LAUREL TALKED you into doing the article, huh?" Tag asked Ally as they strolled along the waterfront through the park. They were meeting Tag's family and some friends at the Cozy Caribou to have dinner and watch the Mariners game.

Fluffy clouds rushed across the sky, changing the landscape from light to dark and back again like they were making a game out of turning the sun off and on. Dampness hung in the air and they'd both worn jackets to fend off the breeze threatening to bring rain.

"I kind of don't have a choice. My grandpa agreed, and she already went to Saltdove to interview him." Laurel had presented the article as a human-interest piece outlining her grandfather's career and Ally's decision to follow in his footsteps.

"That sounds like our Laurel."

"I don't trust newspapers." She glanced at him, and Tag knew she was thinking about the photo of him and Kendall.

In the days after its publication, Tag had faced a fair amount of speculation about the resurrection of his relationship with Kendall. A few people had asked him about it outright, twice in front of Ally. She'd braved it like she did everything, with composure, grace and a quiet humor that she mostly reserved for him and, to a steadily growing degree, his family. Hannah and Iris adored her. Ally and Iris had already cemented a friendship. Relations between Ally and Shay seemed to be improving, as well.

Kendall had called him and emailed him several times since that weekend. Her communication always started out campaign related, asking him about attending one event or another or informing him that she'd met with some important person in her ongoing effort to secure contributions and endorsements. Tag appreciated it, but inevitably, talk turned personal, often in the form of an invitation for them to spend time together. That's when he would find a reason to end the call.

"You'll like Laurel," he assured her.

"I hope so," she said.

They stopped in front of the *Rankins Press* office. Laurel lived in an apartment above the newspaper's office, and Ally had agreed to meet her there before they joined the crowd at the Caribou.

"Wish me luck. I'm nervous."

"Good luck. Just be yourself, and Laurel will fall in love with you…" He froze, because he'd almost added the word *too* to the end of that sentence.

And, just that fast, he could no longer ignore what his heart had been telling him; he was in love with Ally. He loved her, and the realization left him equal parts stunned and terrified. And disappointed in himself because, despite the logic he'd employed and all the safeguards he'd constructed around his heart, it was too late to stop it now. It would be like trying to turn off the northern lights or halt a storm. It would be funny if it didn't hurt so much; he'd finally fallen in love, and everything about it was wrong.

Instead, he kissed her. Because if he couldn't say how he felt, he was going to show her. A long, sweet moment passed before he pulled away to watch her face. He loved doing that because it was one of the few times her expression was unguarded.

Her eyelids fluttered open, and when she smiled up at him, his heart swelled. The sensation felt different now, even stronger, and sweeter because he'd acknowledged what it was. Almost immediately that annoying, persistent ache clawed its way back in, scratching at the sweetness. He loved her, and he found that he desperately wanted to say it and he wanted…he wanted more. But he couldn't have more, and he couldn't tell her how he felt. It wouldn't be fair to lay his feelings on her when they'd agreed on the parameters from the beginning.

She squeezed his hand and said, "I'll meet you at the Caribou." He watched her walk inside the building and across the floor until she disappeared up the stairs.

AT THE CARIBOU, Mack had the big screen fired up and the first pitch of the game was about to be thrown and viewed in all its high-definition glory. Emily had reserved two tables up close and personal to the action. Family and friends were filing in and filling chairs. Appetizers had been ordered, and the fragrant scents of garlic and cheese had his mouth watering.

Tag settled in with a cold frosty beer, Jonah on one side of him and Iris, who was saving the seat between them for Ally, on the other. RJ Filson threw the first pitch for the Mariners. Strike. A fastball and a slider came in quick succession, and the Mariners had their first out. The waitress delivered a plate of nachos to the table. Tag relaxed, determined to enjoy a no-stress, campaign-free evening with his family and the woman he loved. Even the thought of his eventual, inevitable heartbreak wasn't going to ruin it for him.

Shay leaned around Jonah and said, "Um, Tag?"

"Yep?"

"Isn't that…?"

Following his sister's gaze toward the door, he froze, his mug halfway to his mouth.

"Hey," Iris said. "Is that Kendall? What is she doing here?"

Tag didn't answer because Kendall had already spotted him and was moving toward the table.

"Kendall, hi!" Shay rose from her seat and greeted his ex with a hug. They had gotten along well, undoubtedly the attorney connection between Jonah and Kendall providing common ground.

Ever polite, the rest of his family, sans Iris, chimed in with greetings, even though none of them had been impressed with the way Kendall had ended things. Iris glared openly at Kendall.

Tag stood. Iris joined him. Kendall moved closer. Iris and Shay were flanking him.

Kendall reached out and touched his forearm. "Hey, handsome. Are you surprised? I told you I'd see you soon."

"Hello, Kendall. Yes, very surprised. I'd assumed you meant the next time I was in Juneau."

"Lucky us, we didn't have to wait that long." She curled the fingers of one hand around his biceps. "Right?"

He wished she'd stop touching him. Most of the table, and at least half the restaurant, now appeared more interested in them than the game. Stepping back, out of her reach, he crossed his arms casually over his chest. "What brings you to town?"

"I had a meeting with a client here so I thought I'd stop in and see how you're doing."

"You have a client in Rankins who can afford for you to make a legal house call?" Iris asked, doubt coloring her tone.

Kendall shifted a speculative gaze toward Iris. Tone dripping with warmth, she said, "Iris, right? Tag's little sister? The self-described misfit who hasn't been home in ages? I don't think we've ever met."

"Yes, that's me. And you're Kendall, the 'best-dressed attorney' in all of Juneau who cheated on my brother and made him feel like it was his fault."

Kendall gave her a condescending smile. "Spoken like a devoted baby sister."

Tag knew Kendall hated that "best dressed" distinction, given to her by the Juneau Jester, a hip, wildly popular lifestyle blog known for its scathing assessment of the city's social elite. How in the world Iris had known this would get to Kendall, he had no clue. But he had to give his sister credit for pulling this card.

Despite Kendall's smile, which never wavered, her eyes were firing bullets. "You have to spend all your hard-earned money on something, right? What are you doing for work these days, Iris?"

Iris's eyes were shooting laser beams. Tag realized he'd made a mistake in telling Kendall that Iris was working for him temporarily while she looked for a job. But Iris was answering his phone, and how was he to know these two would get along like a pair of cranky cats? He decided they could both learn a thing or two from Ally about keeping their emotions at bay.

Thankfully, Bering chose that moment to join them, greeting Kendall with a handshake and a "Nice to see you again."

"You, too, Bering."

"Is everything okay?" he asked.

Shifting into soft and gentle Kendall, she

said, "Yes, Bering, I hope so." Then she fo-cused on Tag. "Tag, my parents are here with me, and we were hoping you might be able to join us? Mom would really like to talk to you. She has some ideas about the campaign."

The woman knew how to get what she wanted; he'd give her that. It was about the only thing she could have said that would have torn him away. Across the room, near the door, he saw Sally and Tom Meade visiting with the hostess. It was all he could do not to groan out loud. Maura's words of warning came to him about never alienating a possible donor. He glanced at Bering, whose enthusiastic expres-sion made the decision a no-brainer, as pain-ful as it would be for him.

"Sure. Of course. I'd love to see your par-ents."

"He'll meet you at your table," Iris told her in a dismissive tone. "As his personal assis-tant and unofficial campaign manager, I need to have a word with him first."

"You know, my first job was working for family, too. Nepotism isn't so bad when you're desperate, is it, Iris?"

"I suppose you'd know, huh, Kendall? See-ing as how you've taken desperate to a whole new level."

Kendall's smile flickered, her nostrils flaring in anger as she looked at Iris. Tag was a little afraid of what she might do.

Before she could respond, Iris took Tag by the elbow and led him away from the crowd. "What are you doing? You have plans with your family and Ally is going to be here any minute."

With a helpless shrug, he said, "I know, and I'm not thrilled about it, but the Meades are very important supporters of mine. You know the campaign has to come first right now. I have to do this."

"Before Ally?"

"Iris, what are you getting at?"

"Ally will see you with her."

Ignoring the twinge of doubt spreading through him, he said, "Ally won't mind."

"Okay, Tag, I didn't say anything before because it seemed to blow over, but that photo of you and Kendall—"

"Iris, Ally and I talked about it. I explained everything and she understands how it is."

"Understands what, exactly? I don't understand, and I'm only your sister. Kendall calls you every day. Does Ally know that?"

"Not every day. Ally knows how it is with Kendall and me." Sort of, he added silently, because he hadn't told her how much Kendall had been calling. "She knows that photo was a…mistake. She understands how important this campaign is to…everyone. Besides, Ally's not jealous."

Iris lifted a hand and pressed a thumb hard to her temple. Silently, she stared over his shoulder for a few seconds before shifting her gaze back to him.

"It's not about being jealous, Tag. Not exactly. It's about…a lot of things, actually. But right now, it's about this woman trying to get her hooks back into you. She knows what she's doing. She's obviously done her homework, and she's trying to use this campaign to get close to you."

Even if what Iris said was true, it didn't matter. He couldn't allow it to matter. "I can handle it."

"Fine, go. But that woman is trouble and don't say I didn't warn you."

"NOT ONLY IS your grandfather one of the most fascinating people I've ever met, but he could also charm the skin right off a snake."

Ally smiled at the reporter. "I still can't believe you traveled all the way to Saltdove to meet him."

Laurel shrugged. "Worth every second. I'm not a fan of these interviews that are done through email these days. I can't get to the essence of a person without meeting them. And in this case, I have to confess, Ally—I'm a little in love with Abe Mowak. I'd go out with him if we lived closer to each other. If he accepted my invitation, that is."

Ally chuckled. "I have no doubt he would."

She loved to hear people talk about her grandfather this way. Either people seemed to get him or they thought he was totally off base. Much like they did her, she was discovering. At least her grandfather didn't have to concern himself with all the minute details of living his life, the way Ally did. Because of the nature of her job, she had to be careful about balancing one foot in the old ways and one in the new, while Abe just did what he thought was best without explaining himself. Laurel obviously got him.

"So, like you and Tag, a little age difference wouldn't get in his way? You'd be okay calling me Grandma?"

Ally sobered, wondering if Laurel had a complaint about her relationship with Tag. Ally knew Laurel was a close friend of the family, especially of Shay, Emily and Janie. Janie wrote a column for the paper and Emily was a regular contributor.

"Ally, I'm teasing."

"Oh…"

"Unlike my dear friend Shay, I don't think you and Tag should concern yourself with your age difference. Not that you seem to care what people think."

This was where she was supposed to reveal the status of her relationship with Tag. Even if she'd known what it was, Ally wasn't about to bite, but she had to admit the woman was a skilled interviewer. "I care what Tag thinks."

Laurel laughed. "You are so much like your grandfather—wise, intelligent, grounded, capable, well-rounded. With a bit of mysterious thrown in to keep things interesting."

"Thank you. That's kind of you to say. He has a way of keeping my priorities in the right place. I can only hope to have his wisdom one day. And I don't know about the mysterious part—it's not a quality I strive for."

"Yeah, well, I don't think it's one you can create. You just have it. You come off as very intriguing."

Laurel asked more questions and soon announced she had all she needed. For Ally, the experience was more like hanging out with a friend than being interviewed. She supposed that's why Laurel had the excellent reputation she did.

Together, they walked to the Cozy Caribou to find that the place was hopping. It was easy for Ally to spot the pushed-together tables full of James family members and friends in front of the big screen. But she didn't see Tag. Laurel waved and moved toward an empty chair near Shay. Iris appeared by her side and took her elbow.

"Ally!" she said loudly, a too-wide smile on her face. "Thank goodness you're here. I have those samples to show you."

"Samples?"

"Those paint samples." Iris steered her to the window and began digging through her bag. Fake smile in place, she pulled out a handful of paint chips and fanned them out. Lowering her voice, she said, "This is just a diversion so I could warn you that Tag got kidnapped by his man-eating dragon of an ex and her parents. They are sitting at that table in the far corner right next to the bear carving. Please don't worry about it, though, okay? I saw it happen and he wasn't pleased. The only reason he agreed to join them is because of all this campaign…garbage."

Ally glanced across the restaurant, her gaze zeroing in on him immediately. "Garbage?" she repeated, hating the way the tumble of emotions colliding inside her made her voice go hoarse.

Tone fired with annoyance, Iris said, "Yes, I

think all of this campaign crap is over the top. I don't understand why he's even doing it. But who am I, right? I don't live here anymore, and I don't plan to stay for much longer."

Ally forced her attention back to the paint chips that Iris was moving in her hands, but she knew Tag had spotted her. She could feel him watching her. With a marching band playing in her rib cage, she lifted her gaze, and it locked into place with his. Silently, he seemed to plead for understanding. Ally tried to muster it. Knew she failed miserably. And then she wished she could disappear.

"Ally, stop looking at my dumb brother. I know you want to run right now and I don't blame you."

Ally swallowed a lump of emotion but couldn't seem to look away.

Until Iris tapped her arm with the paint chips, and said, "Hey, eyes here and smile, okay? So people don't suspect this is upsetting you. Especially not that smug witch he's sitting with."

Ally did as Iris instructed and all the feelings of friendship that had been building between them seemed to coalesce at that moment, swirling around and then encasing them in an invisible cocoon. The sensation settled into her, and Ally felt a peace like she hadn't known since she'd started this crazy journey with Tag. Finally, someone seemed to understand what she was going through.

Iris asked her, "The question is, do you want to stick around here and pretend you're fine or do you want to leave with me right now? If I were you, I would leave. Not in a huff, of course. Just in a…" She plucked one of the paint chips out of the group, lifted it higher, pretended to analyze it. "I have somewhere else to be right now kind of way."

"Okay." Ally pointed to the sample. "I wouldn't know how to leave in a huff if I tried. And the baseball game is on. Everyone knows I love the Mariners. I feel like if I leave, it will be obvious that it bothers me that he's with her."

Iris paused, lowering the paint sample and giving Ally an assessing, satisfied smirk. "I knew it," she whispered.

"Knew what?"

"Nothing."

Tapping the color with her finger, Ally read the name Melancholy Blue. How fitting.

Iris nodded, shifting all the cards back into a neat pile. "You're right. I would be too… emotional. It's possible I would punch him. No, her. No, both of them. First her for trying to steal him and then him for not seeing it. Do you want me to just do it for you?"

And, despite it all, Ally laughed. Because no matter what happened between her and Tag, she knew she officially had her first girlfriend.

"Atta girl," Iris said with her own happy grin. "I have no doubt you can pull this off. Let's go sit."

CHAPTER FIFTEEN

"ALLY, I'M SO SORRY. I had no idea she was coming," Tag told her later when they left the Caribou and walked toward Ally's house.

"I know. Iris told me."

From her vantage point during the game, Ally had been able to see him as he talked and ate with the Meades, all the while enduring what felt like the slow torture of being roasted on a spit over an open flame. Kendall touched him at regular intervals, and while he didn't respond in kind, he didn't move away, either. That stupid newspaper photo kept pushing its way to the front of her mind. Iris's offer to punch Kendall played out in various fantasies and gave her a small measure of relief.

Kendall and her parents had finally left sometime during the sixth inning, and Tag had joined the others at the table. She'd done her best to play it cool and hoped she'd succeeded.

"I knew this campaign was going to demand sacrifices, but it's difficult to imagine how hard it will be until you're faced with it."

This managed to diminish some of her despair and disappointment. Sacrifices she understood. Just like she knew how important this senate seat was to him.

She felt his gaze traveling over her. "You're sure you're okay?"

"Yep. Good." Reaching toward him, she found his hand and entwined her fingers with his. The little whooshing sound of his relieved breath managed to further loosen the sting of being displaced tonight.

"I feel like I'm going to miss out on a lot."

She nodded. She needed to get used to this, to taking a back seat to the campaign. And to Kendall, to his family, work, neighbors, friends and the million other demands that were thrown at him on a daily basis. A combination of sympathy and frustration and affection followed because she didn't think anyone else could manage it all as well as he did. Qualities to be appreciated and admired. Except, did she want to be in a relationship where she had to take a back seat? What choice did she have, though? This Tag was better than no Tag, at least for now.

She made a silent vow not to add herself to his growing column of negatives. If this was how it had to be, then she would learn to deal with it.

She slid a smile his way. "Yeah, and not to make it worse, but tonight you missed a great game. Lucky for you, you've got me to fill you in…"

"ALLY, THANK GOODNESS I found you. Can you tell me the natural way to treat a urinary tract infection?"

Ally looked up from her clam chowder and garlic bread to find Gareth's friend Kyla standing in front of the table at the hospital cafeteria where she and Tag were having lunch. Ally had played basketball with her and some of Gareth's friends. No makeup, long brown hair pulled back. Her unnaturally pale face held the tension lines of someone in pain. A tattered backpack hung from her shoulder. The fingers of one hand were fidgeting with a cuticle on the other.

"Kyla, hi."

"Hi. Oh, wow. I'm so sorry. I shouldn't have blurted it out like that. I was practicing all the way here from school, and then I saw you, and I was so relieved, it just came out."

"It's okay. You know Tag, right?"

"Yeah, hi, Tag. How are you?"

"Hey, Kyla," Tag greeted her. "Better than you, sounds like."

Ally asked, "Do you want to have a seat?"

"I'm totally interrupting your lunch."

"Please, sit." Ally gestured at the chair beside her.

Kyla nodded and shrugged off her pack. It hit the ground with a thud. She melted down into the chair beside it.

"Have you been diagnosed with a urinary tract infection by a doctor?"

Kyla shook her head. "No. But I've had one before. I'm sure that's what it is. My friend Sydney told me that you can cure them with cranberry juice, and I've downed like a gallon in the last day, but it's not working. Gareth showed me that article in the paper. He said that you helped his cousin."

Ally had been pleased with the article. Laurel had done a wonderful job of describing her grandfather and his efforts, and of singing Ally's praises, as well. She hoped it would help bolster her reputation in town. But even though Laurel had made it clear that Ally didn't see patients, she feared it would increase the incidence of people coming to her for help. Apparently, she'd been right about that.

"You know what? I think I'll go, uh…wash my hands?" Tag stood, and Ally loved him for the obviously contrived gesture.

"Listen, Kyla," Ally said when Tag was out of earshot. "You need to see a doctor right away. Forget about the cranberry juice for now. You need an antibiotic. UTIs can be very serious if left untreated. Sometimes it can feel very similar to a kidney infection, so you need a test to be sure."

"But I don't…"

"It's a simple urine test."

"I know. It's not that. I don't want my parents to know."

"Oh. How old are you?"

"Eighteen. I'm a senior."

"Well, that's easy. They don't have to know."

"But I still live with them. At least until I go to college this fall…"

"That doesn't matter. By law, your medical care is private. You don't even have to tell them you saw a doctor."

"Right." A frustrated scoff followed. "I don't think I can see a doctor without my parents knowing. Not in this town. Maybe in Glacier City."

"I have an idea. Wait here a sec, okay?"

Ally stood, walked into the hall and called Flynn, who she knew was working at his grandfather's office that day. A brief explanation and he offered to see the teen as soon as she could get there.

Back at the table, she said, "Okay, you're all set. Dr. Ramsey is going to see you."

"Doc?" Kyla squeaked, eyes wide with panic. "But he knows my dad."

"This is Doc Ramsey's grandson, Dr. Flynn Ramsey. Same office, but Doc is retiring and the younger Dr. Ramsey is taking over."

"I'm scared. What if he tells them?"

"Kyla, it's against the law for any doctor to disclose your medical records to anyone without your permission. Neither Doc nor Dr. Ramsey would ever tell your parents without your consent."

"Ohh…" Head shaking, she said, "Last time I had one, the doctor told my dad. This is super embarrassing… My dad went ballistic because he thought it meant my boyfriend and I were having sex. We weren't. We're not, I swear. But the doctor made it sound like it was probably why I got it. So now I'm afraid to say anything because of what my dad will think." Tears pooled in her eyes. "But I'm in so much pain I can barely even breathe. I don't know what to do…"

"Under the circumstances, your fear is perfectly valid," Ally said calmly, even as a hot flash of anger bolted through her, directed at both the doctor and the dad. "There are a lot of reasons why women get them."

"I know. I've googled it. But it was the way he said it. You know what I mean? He has this way of talking…" She trailed off with a shake of her head. "It was all my dad heard. I cannot wait to get out of this town."

"And you were eighteen at the time of that appointment, too?"

"Yeah, I turned eighteen in January, and this was right before spring break."

"Kyla, I promise you, Dr. Ramsey will keep this between you and him, okay? That's what doctors are supposed to do. I'm sure you've heard the term doctor-patient confidentiality?"

Kyla nodded, looking scared and hopeful at the same time.

"That confidential part is the law. When you reach the age of eighteen, it is illegal for doctors to discuss your medical issues with anyone but you unless you give them consent. That doctor could get in huge trouble for what he did. Now get going. Dr. Ramsey the Younger is expecting you."

Kyla stood and gave her a quick hug. "Thank you so much. Gareth is so…cool. He said you would help me. I'm sorry again to bother you in the middle of your lunch."

"It's fine. I'm glad you did. Make sure you tell Dr. Ramsey that you're eighteen, okay? And that you don't wish to disclose your records to your parents." They quickly exchanged cell phone numbers before Kyla went on her way.

Tag returned to the table. "How did that go?"

She briefly outlined the conversation, but kept Kyla's privacy intact. "She's on her way to see Flynn."

"Good. That's good. What's wrong? It sounds like you handled it well, but you look upset."

"No, I don't."

"Yep, you do. You have a tell."

She responded with her best vacant stare.

He chuckled. "Sometimes you do. Mostly I see it when it involves someone else and not your own feelings, but I'm learning that's kind of a tell, too."

She grinned, liking that he'd figured this out and wondering if that should worry her.

"I'm right, aren't I? You are upset."

"Yes, you are. And it's not about me. Something a doctor did…said." She didn't want to betray Kyla's confidence. "So, I take it that the fact you left me alone to handle this means you weren't worried I'd encourage her to dance naked on a bed of hot coals or something?"

He laughed. "Nope. I've got you all figured out." His exaggerated confidence made her laugh.

"You do not."

"Maybe, though. I didn't realize your grand-father was a real doctor until I read Laurel's article."

She frowned. "A real doctor?"

"Yes, a board-certified medical doctor as opposed to a…someone who's not."

"He has a medical degree, but his practice is still very unconventional by modern stan-dards."

"Yeah, well, I agree with his overall ap-proach to health and disease prevention. I think preventative care is the future of medi-cine, or at least it should be. He's right about modern medicine too often treating the symp-toms and not the condition."

"Working backward, he calls it. Creating a healthy vessel so disease doesn't have a chance to grow."

"But when it does, then what?"

"Just like the article says, he's not opposed to using whatever means available to cure a patient. But even then, he relies on a mix of traditional and modern means. The relation-ship between the body and the mind is incred-ibly complex. The mind plays a huge role in healing the body and keeping the body healthy. There's a strong connection, and we believe in drawing on it whenever and however possible."

"I-think-I-can meets the placebo effect?"

She tried to smile. His voice held a teasing edge, but the question felt a little disparaging. This was her fundamental belief system, her identity and her life's work, not to mention her grandfather's. Their beliefs were unconventional; she knew that, and so she was used to people questioning them. Funny, the more she cared about Tag, the more she cared about what he thought.

"Tapping into the power of belief is a big part of it. Wellness is a balance of body and mind and science."

"Hmm."

Ally tried not to let his noncommittal response bother her. "I didn't intend for this to happen, by the way, people coming to me with their medical problems. My plan was to lie low and settle into the community gradually. But fate had other plans. And I can't turn people away who need help."

JAMES FAMILY SUNDAY dinner was more than tradition, more than the fulfilling of duty or seeing to an obligation. The entire family looked forward to it all week. It was a time to regroup, recharge, rekindle, make plans and remember what they liked about each other—and maybe be reminded about what they didn't, too. No matter what, there was always plenty of laughter, lots of teasing, the occasionally heated discussion, some cutthroat game playing, random tears and tons of delicious food.

Kendall had been the last woman Tag invited over to his parents' house for the occasion. Once had been enough. He could tell almost immediately that his mom didn't like Kendall, just like he could tell today that she did like Ally. It may have had something to do with the fact that Kendall never offered to help in the kitchen, brought a very expensive bottle of wine instead of the dessert she'd been assigned and shooed the cat away, declaring that her cashmere dress and cat hair "did not get along." The experience had been something of an eye-opener for Tag. Nothing like meeting the family to gauge the health of a relationship.

Ally had already helped Iris set up the buffet table, fetched the plates and silverware, and mixed a huge carafe of lemonade. Together, Ally and his mom chopped the fruit for a salad, and then Ally had thrown together the ingredients for Mom's poppy seed dressing while he'd helped Iris with the potatoes.

Tag had purposely arrived early with Ally, so Mom and Dad could get to know her a little before the rest of the James pack descended.

Although he hadn't quite anticipated this level of…acceptance. Now, kicked back on the love seat with Fanny the cat curled contentedly on her lap, Ally looked like part of the family. Gareth sprawled beside her, his dad sat in the adjacent recliner, and the three of them were talking basketball and fishing while his mom beamed in Ally's general direction.

Tag headed to the kitchen to refill his coffee mug and wasn't surprised when his mom, Margaret, followed.

"Tag, honey, I love Ally. She is just… enchanting. A keeper. You are keeping her, right? Please, tell me you're keeping her."

Pouring coffee into his mug, he said, "Well, Mom, I don't know. She's not a rescue cat."

His mom huffed and threw him an exasperated look. "Don't be a brat, Taggart."

He chuckled. "It's kind of just a casual thing." Maybe if he kept saying the words, they would get easier to accept.

"Ha. Liar," Iris scoffed, breezing into the kitchen and halting before the coffeepot. She nudged him out of the way with her elbow.

"Ouch, Iris. And don't call Mom names."

Margaret snickered.

"That's cute." Pulling a mug out of the cupboard, Iris dumped approximately half a carton of cream into it. "Stop deflecting."

"Why don't you add a splash of coffee to your cream there."

Iris pivoted to face them, a smug grin on her face. "See, you're doing it again. In all your many years of life and massive amount of dating, brother dear, do you realize—not including Ally—that you've only brought three women home to meet your family? Hannah and I were Skyping with Hazel in Mongolia last night, and we tallied it up. I mean, sure, some of us have met a few others here and there, but you've only made an effort to introduce us to three women." Ticking them off her fingers, she went on, "Holly, Amanda and the witch attorney. And I'm not sure Holly even counts because she was your high school girlfriend, so everyone already knew her. And, by the way, the witch was only here one time." She held the remaining finger aloft as if it were proof of something profound. "And no one liked her. Not even Mom. And she likes everyone."

"Shay got along with her."

"Why are you defending her?"

"I'm not."

"Besides." Iris flipped her hand dismissively through the air. "Shay just pretends to like her because of Jonah and their attorney club or whatever."

Their mom looked thoughtful. "Your sister is right."

"About what?" Tag heard his voice rise a couple of defensive octaves.

"You're a smart man…" Iris let her head fall to one side and added "…most of the time." With a grin, she lifted her cup for a sip. "I'm sure you can figure it out."

"Hey, everyone!" Shay chirped as she and Jonah came through the back door. Her hands were gripping a huge plastic container, but it was the aurora borealis–like smile on her face that caught him off guard.

"What happened to you?" he asked.

"Shay, honey, you look lovely," Margaret said at the same time.

Popping a hand over her mouth, Shay made a noise that sounded a lot like a giggle. She removed her hand, but the smile remained, so bright Tag wanted to flinch. And hug her. When was the last time he'd seen her looking this happy?

"Thanks, Mom. I feel lovely." Shay headed to the fridge and opened it to stow her container.

A side glance at Iris and her wide-eyed, brow-raised expression told him she was thinking along the same shocked lines. "Did she just giggle?" Iris whispered.

"She feels lovely?" Tag answered with a disbelieving shrug.

Shay spun around to face them again and asked, "Is Ally here?"

What was *this* about? "Uh, yeah, she's out in the living room with Dad and Gareth and Reagan."

"Awesome. I'll be back in a few minutes to help finish dinner, okay, Mom?"

"Sure, dear. But Iris and Tag already did the potatoes, Ally and I did the fruit salad, and the roast needs to cook for another half hour."

But Shay was already gone in a haze of happy sauce. Margaret trailed after her. Tag looked at his brother-in-law standing off to one side and realized he looked rather pleased, as well. There seemed to be a dash of dazed in his expression, but Tag couldn't blame him under the circumstances. His sister was definitely acting strangely.

Iris flashed him another "what the heck?" look and followed Shay and Margaret into the living room. Jonah stepped toward the coffee maker.

"Jonah, what happened to your wife?"

Lifting a shoulder, he answered with a simple "I'm not... I can't..." Words tapering away, he stared off into space. Finally, he focused on Tag. "But I will say one thing to you."

"Okay?" Tag prompted when Jonah didn't continue.

"Ally."

Tag waited, but Jonah just stared, his dark blue eyes filled with far more emotion than made Tag comfortable.

"Uh, what about Ally? Jonah, what is wrong with you? And Shay?"

"What I'm trying to say is… Ally happened." Another goofy grin split his face. "I am so grateful. I can't express how…fond I am of her. Tag, if you have half a brain in your head, you will never let that woman get away."

CHAPTER SIXTEEN

TAG SPENT THE next few days preparing for the rally, going over details with Emily and Hannah, corresponding with Maura, brushing up on the influential people and donors who'd been invited, and getting a handle on pertinent issues that might concern voters. Hannah had written him a fantastic speech and insisted that he spent practice it in front of her and Emily. She kept texting him pointers and suggestions.

But through it all, Tag couldn't stop thinking about Sunday's dinner, and Shay in particular. Something had changed, something profound. And while he knew this notion should bring him joy, he couldn't stop wondering about the cause.

Ally happened.

That's what Jonah had said in the kitchen. Looking back, he saw that the seed was planted at that moment. He'd assumed Jonah was trying to change the subject, take the focus off whatever was going on with him and Shay. But another part of the conversation kept surfacing, bumping around in his thoughts. Because why would Jonah be grateful? He'd thought Jonah meant he was happy for Tag and that it had come out as grateful. But what if he'd meant it literally?

Then there were the looks, suspicious in retrospect, that had passed between Shay and Jonah, and Shay and Ally, and among his sisters and Ally the entire afternoon. At one point, he'd seen Shay and Ally whispering and laughing outside like old friends. An idea, a theory, had started as a niggle and grown steadily, cold and insistent, the way ice creeps over a lake at winter's first hard freeze.

Thursday evening, he and Ally were eating sandwiches at Ally's house, and he was filling her in on the details of the next day's rally when her phone chimed on the table between them. Shay's name popped up on the screen. Ally picked it up, read the message, grinned and then typed out a quick response.

Watching this unfold, Tag felt all the misgivings and cold dread of preceding days reach critical mass.

"You and Shay are texting now?"

"Um, yeah. We've been…talking."

And that was the moment he knew. It felt as if he was standing on that frozen lake, knowing that if he delved into this subject he might fall through, yet he couldn't stop himself. He had to risk it in order to save his sister.

Tone level, he asked, "Ally, do you know what's going on with Shay?"

Just as he'd hoped, he could see the question caught her off guard. And for the first time, he found her enigmatic expression disturbing rather than alluring.

"What do you mean?"

"I mean she's been acting like a different person. And I suspect you know why. Please, don't pretend you don't know what I'm talking about. She openly disapproved of you and then, seemingly out of nowhere, last Sunday you two are like BFFs. I let it go then because I was just happy that she was happy and relieved to see you two getting along. But then Iris mentioned that you had lunch together and now you're texting. But neither of you has said a word about it to me. What is going on?"

"I can't tell you."

"Why can't you tell me?" he asked, fearing that no matter how she answered he already knew.

"You have to talk to Shay."

Tag had experienced very few moments in his life where he both wanted and didn't want to know certain information. The last time he could remember was years ago when Janie's first husband, Cal, had died in a logging accident. A fierce and inexplicable need to hear the details had battled with the desire to tuck the suffering and hurt and his own grief away and never have to face them. But, as painful as it was, he'd quickly reached the conclusion that he had to know. You couldn't solve a problem you didn't fully understand or fight an enemy you couldn't see. He'd wanted to help Janie and her boys then, just like he wanted to help his sister now.

"Ally, please don't tell me you've been discussing my sister's fertility issues with her."

Her expression, or lack thereof, gave him his answer. The one he'd feared and the one he suddenly despised. Anger fired to life inside him. His lungs constricted so tightly it hurt to breathe.

Pressing a fist to his forehead, he focused on reining in his temper. "How could you do this?"

"Do what?"

Opening his eyes, he forced his gaze to meet hers and wished he hadn't because he could clearly see the trepidation, the uncertainty in her expression.

"Tag?"

When he spoke, he could hear the disappointment in his voice, and he hoped she did, too. "Ally, it's one thing for you to give Hannah or Cami your pep talks and…herbal potions. Those are harmless, and I accept that the placebo effect is powerful. And it's fine to support Ginger's decision to forgo treatment. That was her decision. It's even fine for you to risk your job and possibly your career over beliefs that, frankly, I don't think are worth it. But that's *your* decision, and you're the one who is going to have to accept those consequences. But this…this is about someone's dreams, her deeply felt thoughts concerning her future. Shay wants a child more than anything in this world and what you've done is not only irresponsible, it's downright cruel."

Tag wouldn't have guessed that Ally could look so devastated. He would have felt like the worst kind of a jerk if he wasn't so utterly and completely heartsick himself. But this was about Shay. And Ally leading her to believe a baby was possible.

"Cruel? Tag, I would never do anything—"

"But it's obvious that you already have."

"Maybe. In a way."

The idea of his sister getting her spirit crushed once again… He wanted a family, too. So much so that at times it left his insides tangled and raw and he could barely stand it. And poor Shay had done everything right, everything she could do and it still wasn't enough. He could only imagine the longing, the despair and disappointment that she and Jonah lived with on a daily basis.

"I don't…" Every single thing he could think of to say was mean and horrible, and he didn't like himself very much for wanting to say them.

"But maybe what I have done is given her something really great. Tag, this placebo effect—as you refer to it—I think of as healing. The mind is so much more powerful than people give it credit for."

"Maybe, but it can also be incredibly destructive. Can't you see that?"

She seemed to be searching for words, and the thought crossed his mind that he should feel a sense of satisfaction at finally getting her to show what she was feeling. But, instead, he just felt hollow.

"When the mind and the body are in sync—"

"Stop." One hand shot up as if he could snatch her words out of the air. "Please, enough of this. You have no idea what you've done here, do you?"

Shock and sadness and confusion danced in her eyes. Her voice was whisper soft, filled with hurt. "What is it you think I've done, exactly?"

A part of him wanted to take her in his arms

and another part wanted to try and talk some more sense into her. Despite the doubts he now realized had never really dissipated, he'd been reassuring himself that she would use good judgment when practicing medicine. He'd seen her in action, told himself that she would allocate her beliefs appropriately. He'd made too much of the fact that Abe was a doctor and that she'd had a traditional education. She'd proven him wrong in the worst way imaginable. All those reservations he'd been tamping down now came rushing up like a geyser.

They were too far apart on this. Ally wanted him to understand her position, but she needed to understand his, too.

"Ally, you have no idea how… Shay has suffered so much. I've lost track of the number of miscarriages. They've been trying to adopt, and that isn't working, either. It's been one baby disappointment after another. If you have somehow given my sister false hope, I'm afraid of what it will do to her."

"False hope? How can you—"

"How can *you*? is the point, Ally. How could you?" The anger in his voice, the tension in his body, was too much. "I don't… I can't handle this. I can't do this. I need to get out of here." And with those final words, he walked out of her house.

TAG DROVE AROUND, took a walk by the river and then sat in his pickup for a while staring at a tree. Then he headed to the hangar intending to take care of some paperwork because he couldn't face the emptiness of his house. Since the first time he'd brought Ally there, he'd been harboring fantasies. Fantasies, he realized now, that had been pointless and possibly self-destructive. Pointless because they were never going to happen. Self-destructive in that they were only amplifying his disappointment and heartbreak.

He'd been fooling himself by thinking that their biggest obstacle was their age difference. He'd been so focused on it that he couldn't see that the bigger—the huge, giant, dinosaur-sized—problem was in their fundamental belief systems. Ally thought she could save the world. Tag just wanted to do what he could to make it a better, safer place for the people he loved. He knew his limitations. Ally didn't. She wasn't a miracle worker, and she needed to face that fact.

Iris's car was in the lot. What was she doing here this late? Not in the mood to see anyone, he considered leaving, but movement at the window suggested his presence had been noticed.

"Hey," she said when he came through the door. "I thought you were at Ally's?"

"I was. I just needed to catch up on some stuff. What are you doing here?"

"Same. Trying to get a handle on all this business that is going to have to be shifted when your campaign begins. You've got quite an empire, brother. I didn't realize."

"Well, what else have I had to do all these years?" He busied himself with a stack of mail because Iris was giving him an assessing look.

"Is everything okay?"

"Yeah, fine."

"Did you and Ally have a fight?"

How did she know these things? "Not exactly." Tag couldn't imagine Ally ever fighting.

"A disagreement?"

"Yes."

"What about?"

"None of your business."

"Ouch." She added a chuckle. "Not used to seeing you so testy."

"I'm not testy," he snapped, falling into her trap, which only made her laugh again.

"You know," she said, leaning back and throwing her sock-covered feet onto the desktop. "One thing that being away for so many years has given me is this weird objectivity and keen insight where my siblings are concerned. Or maybe I've always had it. I don't know."

"That's interesting," he muttered drily, hoping to give her the impression that it wasn't.

"Yeah, what I'm saying here is that this good-guy act that you're into doesn't fly with me. Aren't you exhausted?"

Yes, was his immediate gut reaction even though he wasn't sure what she was referring to, exactly. "Iris, what in the world are you talking about?"

"Well, Tag, the way I see it is this. Almost everything you do in life, you do for someone other than yourself. Running here and there and fixing this and that." Before he could respond, she held up a hand and began ticking items off finger by finger. "Helping. Fixing. Listening. Giving. Saving." Out of fingers, she threw up both her hands. "Animal trapping. Even babysitting! When are you going to start doing what you want? When are you going to take care of you?"

He shrugged. "I like babysitting."

"I know, and even though you're trying to deflect like you always do, you're making my point. You'd make such a great dad! Don't you want to settle down and have a family of your own?"

He paused. She might as well have jabbed

a hot poker into his chest, right into that perpetually raw spot. The way she was looking at him had him believing what she'd said about possessing that insight thing.

He jammed a frustrated hand into his hair. "It's not that easy, Iris. People can't just snap their fingers and have families. Look at Shay."

"At least our sister is trying."

With an uncharacteristic bite to his words, he said, "Yeah, well, I can't. In case you haven't noticed, I'm up to my eyeballs, here. I don't have time to try even if I wanted to."

Tag immediately felt guilty for taking out his frustration on her. She'd done nothing but try to help him. It was the fact that he was beyond help that had him cross. But mostly, it was the growing conclusion that he and Ally were never going to work. Well, they were never going to work long-term, anyway, but he'd hoped for a little more time.

"I'm sorry," he said. "I'm just… I don't even know what I'm doing…"

Removing her feet from the desk, his sister sat up straight in her chair. "You don't know what you're doing, or you don't know why you're doing it? If you—"

"Iris, I do know that I do not want to talk about this right now."

"Fine," she said. "I'll let it go. For now."

OVER THE COURSE of a restless, blanket-tangling night plagued with alternating bouts of bone-chilling despair, disappointment, confusion and dismay, with a few violent flurries of anger sprinkled throughout, a numbness finally seeped into Ally. She hadn't heard from Tag, had no idea if he'd broken up with her or even if he'd ever speak to her again. She thought about calling in sick but knew sitting at home would only make her feel worse.

Shortly after arriving at work, she proved herself wrong. Because if she hadn't come in, she never would have seen the email that was waiting for her. She was still staring at it, trying to decide how long this extended nightmare could possibly drag on, when Flynn came through the door, a large coffee in each hand.

"Hey, good morning. What time are you heading to the rally? You're supposed to help Iris with the food, right? We should…" He paused to look her over. "Wow, you look terrible. What's wrong?"

Lifting her hands helplessly, she said, "All I want to do is help, Flynn. That's all I try to do. All the time. Most of the time. Okay, I honestly almost always try to do the right thing. But sometimes it's so hard to know what the right thing is, isn't it? Do you ever feel that way?"

"I'm a doctor, Ally. I feel that way every single day. But listen, love," Flynn said, walking closer and handing her a coffee. "You sound funny. What are you talking about, specifically?"

Despite her angst, the gesture managed to produce a half smile. "Thank you for the coffee," she said gratefully, taking the cup. In her tired, emotionally overwrought state, the gesture nearly brought her to tears. "And thank you for being my friend. You're awesome."

"You're very welcome and very weird. You need to tell me what's going on because you are freaking me out."

"To start with, Dr. Boyd is trying to have me fired." *And Tag hates me for trying to help his sister*, she added silently. "I got an email from the hospital board secretary. There's a disciplinary hearing next week at which my presence is requested."

"What?" Flynn frowned and gestured at the monitor. "May I?"

"Of course."

He read the message over her shoulder. "He can't do this."

"Yes, he can. That's the problem. He warned me. He and his scary spider fingers told me his reach was far and wide."

Settling into the chair across from her desk, he said, "You have to fight."

She pulled one shoulder up into a shrug. "Of course I'll fight. I don't think it will do a lot of good. But I'll never stop fighting for what I believe in, Flynn. Even if it costs me everything. Even if it upsets people that I care about."

"Uh-oh. I know you don't care about upsetting Dr. Spider-Fingers. What else is going on here? Is this about Tag?"

The hot coffee scorched her mouth, and she was glad for it. It was a familiar pain, one she could identify and handle. "I think Tag and I are over."

Flynn eyed her warily. "What do you mean you think? Did he break up with you?"

"He didn't have to."

"Ally, talk to me. Tell me what's going on."

CHAPTER SEVENTEEN

THAT MORNING, THE day marking Tag's first official campaign event, broke with early summer temperatures predicted to reach a high of only fifty-five degrees. A light cloud cover hid the blue of the sky and tempered the sun, but most attendees, especially the James campaign volunteers, were feeling fortunate the forecasted thundershowers appeared to have bypassed Rankins.

For anyone complaining about the jacket weather, a reminder of their good fortune loomed off to the northeast where a storm was boiling, the horizon so thick with angry gray clouds the mountains weren't even visible. Hannah reported flakes were falling at Snowy Sky Resort.

The waterfront park in Rankins had long been a popular venue for community events. The last few years, under the guidance of Emily and the tourism bureau, the area had been expanded and transformed into a true gem. The brilliant landscaping included sidewalks and a boardwalk around a portion of the bay. Dotted here and there were unique benches and metal sculptures by local artist Kella Jakobs. The attractive timber-frame pavilion, large playground, basketball court, tennis courts, restrooms and the waterfront location ensured community use remained high.

Today, to encourage turnout of the possibly not quite so politically minded, Emily was providing entertainment. A miniconcert by Whiskey Cake, a popular country band from Anchorage, was slated to kick things off. Emmet Brummel, a comedian from Seattle, had been flown in to do a stand-up routine.

Tag's friend Ryder was going to deliver a Memorial Day address. Senators Fincher and Marsh would give short speeches that concluded with Marsh introducing Tag, who would then wrap the event up with the official announcement of his candidacy.

The atmosphere Emily had created around the pavilion fueled the festive occasion. Pots of red, white and blue flowers decorated the tables, and matching baskets suspended from attractive metal hangers outlined the perimeter. A raffle ensured that some lucky partygoers would win a display to take home to their patios and porches.

Tag approached the small crowd gathered

around two large grills, the smoky scent of Grizzly Quake brats drifting through the air. Bering, Jonah, Aidan, Gareth and Reagan were in charge of grilling. Hannah and her husband, Tate, were stringing a banner Reagan had made across the portable stage. Tag hoped Reagan's superbiodegradable paper wouldn't melt if it started raining.

"Weather is cooperating nicely," Bering said.

"How could it not with your wife in charge?" Jonah asked wryly. "Not even Mother Nature would be brave enough to cross Emily when she's in go-mode."

"True," Bering said, while laughter and agreement followed. "Although, I have to say, Hannah's enthusiasm is getting a little scary, too."

"Is Ally coming?" Gareth asked. "Kyla wanted to thank her for hooking her up with Dr. Ramsey."

Just hearing Ally's name made Tag feel as if there was an arrow lodged in his heart, and every mention, every thought of Ally wedged it a little deeper. They needed to talk, and he was dreading it with every fiber of his being.

"She's helping Iris with some of the food," Bering supplied before Tag had to admit he didn't know. He'd both hoped and feared that she'd show, but at hearing those words, a grateful riff of affection played inside him. Last night's conversation had left him frustrated and despondent. He wished he could put this rally on hold until he could figure things out. He'd barely slept the night before, and as the day broke, a disconcerting feeling threatened to overwhelm him. He'd written it off as a combination of a bad mood due to what happened with Ally and nerves.

But as the day wore on, he couldn't shake it. It was like a tidal wave was bearing down on him; he couldn't see it, but he could feel it—the force and rage rushing toward him, ready to sweep him away. And there was nothing he could do to stop it.

The crowd was outnumbering the seating provided. Tag was looking around and wondering what to do about it when Emily materialized by his side. "Don't worry. We're setting up more chairs. I was kind of hoping this would happen. It makes it look like you're even more popular than we anticipated."

Tag shook his head. "You're incredible. You know that?"

"Yes. But remember, I used to do this type of stuff for a living. My work with Cam-Field was a lot like organizing one campaign rally after another."

A tinny rasp bellowed from a nearby speaker. Emily frowned in the direction of the stage. "Uh-oh. That does not sound good." Without waiting for a response, she hustled off.

"Tag?" A voice called behind him, and he turned to find Maura, Senator Marsh's assistant, striding toward him.

"Hi, Maura. It's nice to see you. I didn't know you were coming."

She smiled. "Wouldn't have missed it. This is fantastic. Better than I could have imagined."

"Bering's wife, Emily, and my sister Hannah deserve most of the credit. With the rest of my vast and industrious family providing supporting roles."

"I can assure you that with support like this, the road you're embarking on here is going to be a whole lot smoother. Senator Marsh wanted me to clear a point with you before he goes onstage. He's planning to make an announcement, and I wanted to make sure—"

"There you are!" An anxious Shay appeared next to him with a grinning Laurel by her side. "Sorry to interrupt, but Kip Patton is here."

"Are you kidding me?" a wide-eyed Maura asked.

"Who?" Tag asked at the same time.

"Kip Patton, the billionaire computer app

guy," Shay explained. "Laurel has interviewed him, and he's a regular guest at the inn. He lives in Glacier City, and he wants to meet you."

"Oliver Patton," Maura explained. "Kip to his friends. He's on your endorsement list. A contribution would be a huge bonus. Go! Go and charm his socks off."

Oliver Patton—*that* name Tag recalled. Shay and Laurel set off. Tag had followed a few steps before he remembered Maura had a question, but when he turned, she was already gone. He rejoined the women, and Laurel performed the introduction.

"Hey, Tag. Thrilled to meet you." The hand extended in his direction belonged to a tall, skinny guy wearing worn blue jeans and sneakers with a hole in one toe where a snippet of yellow-plaid sock was visible. His uncombed hair looked too long, and he had a stain on his *Star Wars* T-shirt. Tag wanted to ask if he was trying to cement the computer geek stereotype or if it came naturally.

"Hi, Kip. Pleasure's mine. Thanks for coming today."

"You bet. I believe we have a mutual friend."

"Oh?"

"Yeah, Robert, um, Dr. Boyd? My company is working on some medical apps, and he's applied to do consulting for us. We've been conducting interviews. He and Laurel both encouraged me to come today."

They continued chatting, and Tag soon discovered that the questionable social skills portion of the computer geek stereotype did not extend to Kip Patton. Tag found they had a lot in common and he genuinely liked the guy.

Dr. Boyd joined them. "Ah, wonderful, I see you two have met."

"We have. Thank you, Dr. Boyd."

"I suspected you'd hit it off, with the piloting and all."

"Tag has about a gazillion more hours than me, and he's offered to teach me about gliders. We also share a love of basketball, and I think I might have him on that one."

Shay laughed. "He's not going to argue with you there. Last time he underestimated a basketball opponent, Ally took him to the cleaners."

"Ally, your wife?" Kip asked.

"No, girlfriend," Tag said, wondering if it could still be true.

"Ally Mowak," Shay explained. "She's our brilliant new hospital liaison here in Rankins."

"Any relation to Abe Mowak?" Kip asked.

Beside him, Tag felt Dr. Boyd tense. He stole a glance and was a little startled by the expression on his face. *Murderous* was the word that came to mind, and every fine hair on the back of Tag's neck stood up in agreement. Maybe Ally hadn't been exaggerating the man's opinion of her.

"Yes, granddaughter," Shay answered.

"Then I'm not surprised she's brilliant. Dr. Mowak is an awesome guy. I know him, too. We've been—"

Kip's phone chimed, and he brushed a thumb across the screen. Face erupting in a smile, he lifted a hand and waved across the expanse before looking back at them.

"I'm going to have to leave you guys to it for now. My wife needs some help with our kids. We have a two-year-old and a three-month-old."

Tag grinned, appreciating how that explained his disheveled appearance. Kip executed a quick goodbye. In the time they'd been talking, more chairs and tables had been arranged, and the people still milling around the perimeter appeared to be doing so out of choice.

Laurel had disappeared, no doubt gathering information for the story she was writing about the event for the paper. Shay looped an arm through the doctor's and said, "We should find our seats, Dr. Boyd."

They moved away, and seconds later Emily was stepping up on the stage. When the crowd quieted, she announced Whiskey Cake and the band began strumming a popular patriotic country tune that immediately had the crowd singing along.

The event ran like clockwork, and before he knew it, Senator Marsh was taking the stage. Tag had seen the senator speak many times and knew he was a gifted orator.

Hand raised in greeting, he said, "Thank you all again for coming out here today. As your United States senator, there's nothing I like more than talking about how much I love the state of Alaska. Because I know how much you all love it, too." The crowd erupted in cheers and applause.

"Once in a great, great while I meet someone who I think might love it even *more* than I do." More jubilant clapping. "I know, I know, I shouldn't say that, but it's important to be honest about this. Ladies and gentlemen, I'm happy to say that we're all here today to put our support behind that someone. And he is soon going to be representing your district in the state capital of Juneau…"

He went on to recite Tag's accomplishments and qualifications, and by the time he finished,

Tag almost felt worthy to represent this crowd of people he liked, admired and respected.

"And before I leave you, I have one more bit of exciting information to share. Now, I didn't intend to surprise Tag with this today. But I received the final confirmation from my assistant, Maura, just before I stepped up here. So I thought I'd share it with you all at the same time I share it with him. What do you say?"

The audience went wild. Like the angry clouds banking in the distance, that feeling of foreboding roiled more fiercely inside Tag. This was in addition to the already unpleasant sensations bombarding him: too-tight muscles in his neck and shoulders, jaw aching from smiling, and a tight, tension-filled chest. Campaign sickness, as he'd already begun referring to it in his mind.

Movement on the edge of the stage closest to him caught his eye. Before the figure even came into full view, he knew it was Kendall. And that's when he knew what Maura had been going to ask him, what the senator was going to say. A hot spike of anger knifed through him along with the realization that the tidal wave was about to hit and he wasn't sure he was going to survive.

Up until now, the rigors of this campaign had felt surmountable with Ally by his side.

He'd allowed Bering, Hannah, Maura, Emily and Iris to make decisions because he'd trusted that each one was in his best interests, or more specifically, the best interests of his campaign. But this was not in his best interests. More to the point, it was not in Ally's and certainly not in his and Ally's.

And he knew that Kendall wasn't doing this for him, not just for him, anyway. She was doing it for herself. She wanted something. Iris was right; she wanted him back. Now that Tag would be spending time in Juneau, rubbing elbows with the elite, she wanted to be by his side.

What would Ally think after Tag had assured her that Kendall was out of his life? Especially after what had happened last night. He'd all but broken up with her. But that wasn't what he wanted. Not at all. He wanted her even though he knew it couldn't work. And even though it couldn't work, he didn't want to hurt her. Frustration boiled inside him. Finally, he'd fallen in love, but instead of conquering all his problems it had created more.

His gaze homed in on Ally, who was sitting with Iris, Flynn, Hannah, Tate, Gareth, Kyla and Reagan at one of the picnic tables on the periphery. Already, she seemed ingrained in his life, in his family, and he wanted her there.

He had no idea how to make this right, how to reconcile the million different directions he felt pulled.

More alarmingly, he had no idea how to stop this avalanche of a problem now barreling down on him.

Ally, look at me...

She shifted in her seat, and Tag was struck with the feeling she could "hear" him but refused to look.

"We've been working hard to put the best team in place to lead us to victory next fall. So, you can imagine how honored we are to have this talented lady spearheading this campaign. She's put her life, her career on hold to lead this charge for Tag. Ladies and gentlemen, I'd like to introduce to you the Tag James for Senator campaign manager, Kendall Meade."

AS SENATOR MARSH listed Kendall Meade's education, accomplishments and qualifications, Ally watched the woman move toward the podium and marveled at how she managed to appear stunningly beautiful, powerful and demure all at the same time in her snug black pencil skirt and tailored pink button-down blouse. And not ridiculous in designer heels. White-blond hair shimmering around her shoulders, she positioned herself behind the podium and claimed ownership of the stage. Her commanding voice soothed the crowd into confident silence as she thanked the senator and Tag's supporters, and revealed what an honor it was to be chosen to work for the most "honest, honorable and downright sweet" man she'd ever known.

Ally felt like a wolverine had been turned loose inside her gut and was gnawing its way out. She'd told Tag that she understood the campaign had to come first. She'd thought she could handle being number two, at least for a while. But the deal had not included these non-stop Kendall surprises.

And that's when the realization hit her; he had to have known about this last night. Surely, he had the final say as to who his campaign manager would be. Was all that anger about Shay just a ruse to break up with her gently? Was Kendall the real reason and he hadn't wanted to tell her? But that didn't seem to add up. Tag didn't have it in him to be that cruel, did he? Then again, where this campaign stuff was concerned, all bets seemed to be off. Then there were his angry words about Shay. This was all too…much.

And regardless of Tag's intentions, she knew one thing: she couldn't do this. Ally tuned back in to Kendall's speech.

"Now, it is my great honor to introduce to you the next state senator, and the first from your fabulous little town of Rankins, Tag James."

Like a game show assistant, Kendall swept her arms toward Tag and stepped to one side. And even though every eye was probably glued to the stunning couple on stage, Ally felt like the entire town of Rankins was staring at her. Or, if not staring, then sneaking glances. Again. Still. Much like they had for the previous weeks. She imagined sympathy, curiosity, pity and a fair amount of glee were in the mix as the town's "witch doctor" was once again humiliated by Rankins's golden boy. Afraid that she'd hear it somewhere else, Gareth had reluctantly confided the nickname to Ally when he'd gotten wind of it floating around town.

And just when Ally had begun to think the gossip had died down to a dull roar, that maybe people were even getting used to the idea of the two of them together, Kendall had once again flounced onto the scene. As if to underscore the thought, a camera flashed in her periphery.

Tag gave his speech. When he finished, Kendall went to him, arms out wide. They embraced, she kissed him on the cheek. It was all Ally could do not to crawl under the table. Her lungs burned. She couldn't swallow because her tongue was a wad of wool in her dry mouth. Even her eyes felt scratchy. Her fingers ached from gripping the bench beneath her.

Beside her, Flynn said, "That's it. I'm going to kill him. I know he's your brother, Iris, but—"

Iris interrupted, "You don't need to worry about it, Flynn, because I'm going to get to him first."

Ally said nothing, just continued staring blankly at the stage as the crowd erupted in applause.

Flynn whispered, "We're getting out of here." He stood, and she felt his strong hand wrap around hers, urging her to her feet. His fingers were warm against her icy skin.

Ally rose, and keeping her close to his side, Flynn slowly threaded their way through the crowd. Iris stuck close to her on the other side. Between Flynn calling out greetings and Iris smiling and waving, there was a lot of commotion, but Ally focused on putting one foot in front of the other as they slowly wended through the crowds.

They almost made it. Ally heard the voice behind her and knew who it was even before Kendall Meade stepped into their path.

"Excuse me?" she asked. "Ally Mowak?"

"Yes." Ally felt like she was slowly sinking in quicksand.

The woman's gaze flicked down to Ally's and Flynn's still-joined hands, a smirk playing on her lips. Flynn gave Ally's fingers a reassuring squeeze.

Flattening a flawless hand just below her neck, she said, "I'm Kendall Meade. I understand you're a...friend of Tag's?"

"Yes, I am." The desire to say she was more than that was overwhelming. The fact that she didn't know if it was true felt like a knife to the heart.

"Huh. I just wanted to introduce myself to the competition. My goodness, you are a cute little thing, aren't you? I love how your generation is so...casual."

Ally was pretty sure the thorough eye trip up and down her blue-jeans-and-fleece-clad length was supposed to be intimidating. Ha. All it did was hint at the woman's own insecurity. And that's when Ally realized that it wasn't Kendall she was jealous of, not precisely. It was what she represented. What she couldn't have. Still, that didn't mean she cared about Tag any less.

"Competition?"

A practiced laugh followed, and Ally wanted

to roll her eyes. "Yes, competition for his time in the coming months. You're going to have to share him, you know? He'll be spending a lot of time in my neck of the woods now."

Ally knew in her soul that this woman would never love Tag the way she did. Okay, maybe she was a little jealous of Kendall. But the fact that Kendall was manipulative and downright mean was what prompted her to say, "Oh, I'm not worried. I'll be by his side every minute. After that fiasco with the photographer in Juneau, where you held on to him like a desperate barnacle? He's refused to ever visit there without me again." The lie rolled off her tongue like blueberry jelly on oven-fresh bread. She spread a dollop of warm, comfortable laughter on top for good measure.

A less perceptive person might have missed the woman's subtle reaction, but not Ally. Buoyed by the flash of uncertainty in Kendall's crystal-blue eyes, the muscle ticking in her neck, Ally knew she had Kendall right where she wanted her. And even though she and Tag might be finished, she wasn't about to let Kendall Meade believe she'd played any part in it.

"Oh, dear…" Screwing her face into a concerned expression, Ally took a step closer. Tilting her head, she lifted a hand and pointed at

Kendall's face. "Right there…on your cheek. It's hard to tell for sure with all that makeup you're wearing, but that rough patch on your skin with the discoloration? You should have that checked out."

Kendall paled and lifted a finger to touch the spot.

"You know what? Never mind. On second thought, it's probably just an age spot."

Beside her, Iris snorted with laughter.

Kendall opened her mouth, but no words came out.

Ally said, "We've gotta run. But it was nice to meet you, Kendall. See you in Juneau." Ally tugged Flynn's hand, and he and a chuckling Iris fell into step beside her as the three of them continued to Ally's house.

IF THE SOUND of the alarm from her phone hadn't been indicating the need for an emergency medical transport, Ally would have been relieved for the distraction. Okay, she was relieved, but her guilt was alleviated by the fact that her concern was far greater.

Flynn offered to drive her to the hospital, so they left Iris at Ally's house and took off in a hurry. Shifting into rescue mode would take her mind off Tag and give her a purpose. A quick call to dispatch indicated the emergency was in Killebrew and Ally wondered if she knew the patient. As the crow flies, Killebrew wasn't far from Saltdove.

Flynn pulled his SUV to the front of the hospital to drop her off just as her phone signaled again.

"Ally? It's Carla again, from dispatch. We've received word that the helicopter can't fly through the storm. It's too dangerous. We've got an airplane pilot ready to try. Are you still willing to go under these conditions?" It was the weekend, and Ally knew that most of the paramedics and the nurses trained in air transport were probably still at Tag's rally. Along with Tag.

"Yes! I'll go. I'm ready." She'd agree to fly to Mars right now if it meant getting out of here for a while.

"How soon can you get to the hangar out at Copper Crossing airfield?"

She relayed the information to Flynn, who was nodding that he could take her. He pulled away from the curb before she even had a chance to respond.

"I'm at the hospital, already in a vehicle, so as long as that takes."

Ally knew that small planes could more easily fly through inclement weather. Under the circumstances, it didn't surprise her to learn that Tag was allowing another pilot to use one of his planes. She'd met his friend Cricket Blackburn and hoped it was him.

Flynn turned the vehicle onto the drive leading to the hangar where the plane was waiting. Ally recognized Milt, one of Tag's employees, when she hopped out.

"Oh, Ally, hi. I wasn't sure who was coming. Carla didn't say. The plane is ready, and Tag is already onboard."

Tag? Ally's stomach did a flip. A part of her wanted to back out, send Flynn in her place. But she knew he was needed here. And she had experience with bad weather. She thanked Milt, hugged Flynn and ran toward the plane.

CHAPTER EIGHTEEN

IN THE ARMY, Ally had once flown through the ruins of a Syrian village in the immediate aftermath of a bombing, the smoke like a mass of viscous liquid creeping around the plane in a cloud so thick she couldn't tell which way was up. This fog reminded her of that day. The bone-jarring turbulence assured her that it was Alaska.

Tag was calm, completely confident at the controls as he maneuvered through one of the worst storms Ally had ever encountered. He would have made an excellent combat pilot.

Despite their meaning, Ally was relieved when Tag's words came through her headset. "This is going to be a rough landing. Hang on, okay?"

Ally knew he didn't really expect her to answer, so she just braced herself. The plane touched down and bumped hard along the runway. She was grateful for her restraints when they finally slowed, then skidded and lurched to a stop.

Tag muttered under his breath before looking her way. "You okay?"

Trying not to let the concern in his expression get to her, she mumbled a "Fine" and scrambled to unbuckle her seat belt.

They exited the aircraft. Tag walked around the plane as an SUV pulled close. Ally and Tag gathered their gear and climbed in, and the men introduced themselves to Tag. Ally already knew the local law enforcement officers, Dale Sandy and Max Courtright. Dale was medium height, heavily muscled with black curls fringing the edges of his knit cap. Max had close-cropped red hair and was nearly as tall as Tag but looked to be a good twenty pounds lighter.

Dale drove while Max updated them on the status of the patients injured in an ATV accident. Emergency responders had moved them to the pastor's home nearby, which served as a makeshift emergency medical clinic for the area.

"Thankfully, we were able to get to them fairly easily. For the life of me, I can't understand what they were thinking going out riding in this storm. If the girl hadn't been conscious, we never would have found them..."

Max went on to tell them that the young

woman had used her cell phone to call for help and was able to guide them to the scene.

"It was probably a blessing that the kid was unconscious. That compound fracture to his leg is real bad. We're awful grateful you guys could fly in. This storm isn't supposed to let up any time soon, and the reports say there's another one following on its heels. We need to get him to a hospital ASAP."

That's when Tag spoke up. "Unfortunately, we're not going to be able to fly out of here today, not in my plane."

Ally gave him a sharp look.

"What's that?" Dale didn't sound happy.

"I've got some faulty landing gear. I can't take the chance in this weather of taking off and landing again. I'm going to have to ask you guys to call around and see if anyone has a part for me." Tag went on to explain what he needed.

Dale asked, "What are we going to do about the patient? How are we going to get him out of here?"

Ally stared at Tag, her stomach cramping with fear. He hadn't said a word about it, but that explained the rough landing. No point in thinking about what could have happened. They were safe now. A rush of appreciation flowed through her for his experience and excellent piloting skills.

Dale steered the vehicle onto a side road, and they skidded slowly through the snow-covered turn. Ally held on, reminded of the more immediate problem. How were they going to get the patient out of here?

Dale stopped the SUV in front of a modest home at the end of the drive. The accumulation of snow had already obscured the path and softened the edges of the footprints dotted around.

Inside, she was relieved to find that the more severely injured patient, Zeke Laughlin, was conscious even though he was experiencing intense pain. She discovered his pupils were not dilated, so she ruled out brain trauma.

His girlfriend, Bonnie, informed them that they'd both been wearing helmets, and that the young couple had been on their way to deliver medication to her grandmother, not on a joy ride as had been reported. Ally was sure the helmets had saved their lives. Beyond some bruising and a twisted ankle, Bonnie appeared to be in good condition.

The first responders had done a fine job moving and stabilizing Zeke. His leg was the obvious problem, but there was something else troubling her. There was no way to know for sure unless they could get him to a hospital or… Ally had just finished checking his vitals again when Max poked his head into the room.

"Tag, no luck getting my hands on that part yet. Brandon Smith has one in Smiranov but I realize that doesn't do you any good right now."

Tag exhaled a deep breath. "Thanks for trying, Max."

"I'm not giving up. I'll keep calling, and there are a couple of places I'm waiting to hear back from yet."

Ally watched him go and then looked at Tag. "Can you step into the kitchen with me? I have an idea."

Nodding, he moved in that direction and Ally followed.

"My grandpa can do this surgery."

"Can he get here?"

"I'll call him, but I think we should transfer Zeke there. He's got the facilities and a nurse. By tomorrow morning we're going to be snowed in, and if the forecast is accurate, another front will be moving in right about the time this one lets up. Even if you get the part for the plane by morning, which I doubt, and we get shoveled out, will you have time to install it before the weather starts up again? That kid is lying in there in agony and…" Ally held back the rest of what she suspected.

"But transporting him in these conditions won't be easy, either. The roads are a mess and getting worse by the second."

Ally had seen her grandfather resort to the simplest solution too many times not to consider it now. "But the river's not. If we get him upriver as far as Clifton, it's a straight shot to my village across a good road. It won't be comfortable, but he's not comfortable now. We can be there in two hours, maybe less."

Tag nodded and gave her a tense smile. "I would ask where we are going to get a boat, but I'm guessing you have an answer for that, too."

She smiled, relieved that he'd already opened his mind enough to consider this a viable plan.

IF TAG HAD had any lingering doubts about Ally's medical proficiency, they would be gone now. She prepared the patient and supervised his transport, firmly but gently giving orders until they'd loaded him into the boat.

They thanked Dale and Max, and the men promised to keep Tag informed about the search for the plane part. The owner of the boat was a young man of Native descent with an intense gaze and eyes so brown Tag could barely distinguish the black of his pupils.

"Tag, this is my friend Coda. Coda, this is Tag. Coda and I go way back."

Coda gave him a quick "Hey" and a nod before narrowing his focus onto the boat's controls. Expertly, he maneuvered the vessel away from the shore and into the current. Snow was dumping so hard the river couldn't swallow it fast enough. It looked like the surface had been frosted and then dusted with powdered sugar. In this weather, Tag knew that navigating the waterway would be accomplished as much by habit as sight.

Ally remained huddled by the patient, monitoring his condition and holding his hand. Tag was already feeling she'd made the right decision. The trip was much smoother than it would have been by road, and within the hour Coda was informing them that they were nearing the marina in Clifton. Even faster than Ally had predicted.

The snow had let up a bit, and Tag could see that an SUV waited nearby. As they approached, two men emerged from the vehicle and Tag recognized Abe Mowak, Ally's grandfather, from the newspaper photo. He looked at least a decade younger than he was and Tag wondered how often people assumed that he was Ally's dad.

The other man was younger, short but wiry, with a cheerful smile and longish blond hair visible under a red knit cap. He introduced himself as Dave and helped Tag load Zeke into the vehicle. Ally gave Coda a quick hug and a thank-you. Tag shook his hand and added his appreciation. Abe climbed behind the wheel of the SUV. Tag joined Ally in the back and Dave climbed into the passenger seat.

Abe drove while Ally recited the details of Zeke's condition. Tag listened, silently agreeing, until she said, "I'm worried about his liver. I'm afraid he might have a small laceration."

Tag swung his head to look at her. She stared straight ahead, and Tag felt the dismissal like a punch to the gut. The expression reminded him of the Ally he'd first met, the closed-off, distrustful Ally. But how could he blame her for that now? He'd given her every reason to behave this way.

"Hmm. Blood work and the scan will let us know," Abe said. "Got our work cut out for us. Good thinking, calling Coda with the boat."

The next leg of the trip went as smoothly as the last, and soon the patient was housed inside Abe's clinic.

Ally had disappeared, so Tag took a seat in

the waiting room. Bright watercolor paintings adorned the pale gray walls, and sturdy hand-crafted furniture sat before a stone fireplace. A fire crackled on the hearth. The far corner of the room featured a kid-sized table and chairs. Neatly arranged books filled a bookcase, and a wooden toy chest overflowed. It felt more like a home than a medical clinic, although Tag had learned it wasn't far from that. The facility was right next door to Abe's residence, the two buildings linked by an enclosed breezeway.

Ally stepped through the doorway and exhaled a sharp breath. "Liver has a small laceration. They're doing surgery now. Do you want to come with me? I'll show you around so you can get settled in for the night."

Tag stood and followed her through a door and into the hall leading to the house. At the end of the passage, she opened a door and motioned him into an entryway. A few more steps and they were inside a cozy living room sporting floors of knotty pine. Oversize comfortable-looking furniture in neutral tones sat atop braided rugs in muted colors. Antiques and rustic decor filled the space, and as they headed past the stone fireplace, Tag noted an array of framed photos on the mantel. A smiling Ally featured prominently in most of the images, and Tag's chest went tight. It felt like days since he'd seen her smile.

Continuing through to another hallway, she pointed out the bathroom, passed a closed door that she identified as her room and then walked through the next doorway. Tag joined her inside.

"We keep this guest room ready, so sheets are clean. There's a spare toothbrush on the sink in the bathroom. I put some clothes on the chair there, in case. If you need anything else just let me know."

Tag lowered his pack to the floor and gestured at it. "Thanks, but I have an emergency bundle in here—toothbrush, T-shirt, socks, underwear."

Giving him a curt nod, she walked out the door and pointed down the hall. "The kitchen is that way. I left a sandwich on the table for you."

"Why didn't you tell me you were worried about Zeke's liver?"

"It was more of a feeling." She shrugged. "I didn't have any real proof beyond the pain in his abdomen."

"So, how did you know?"

One brow quirked up. "Not in any way that you'd approve of."

"Ally." Her name came out with an exhaled

breath of frustration. "I'm…sorry. I'm sorry things have reached this point between us."

Was he imagining the yearning in her eyes? She was so adept at hiding every emotion; he wondered if he was wishing it there now. He knew he wasn't when the whisper-soft "Me, too" passed her lips. It was all he could do not to step toward her and take her in his arms.

"I want to explain about Kendall, but it's this thing with Shay that still has me in knots. I can't concede my anger and my disappointment—"

She interrupted with a gentle "I know, and I understand. About Shay, I mean. But I can't be anyone other than who I am, either. I won't change for you, Tag. I won't change for anyone. I believe how I believe, and you believe how you do and I'm beginning to think that the two can't meet in the middle. I will always do what I feel is right for a patient, no matter the consequences."

With a tired sigh, he scrubbed a hand over his jaw. "I'm terrified that attitude is going to get you into real trouble one day. And when it does, I'm afraid there won't be anything I can do to stop it."

"I'm not asking you to. In fact, I'd rather you didn't."

Frustration coiled so fast and so tightly inside him, he couldn't contain it. "But I want to! Can't you see that I…" He wanted to say it, but telling her that he loved her would only make things worse at this point. Neither of them was willing to give where this issue was concerned. And they hadn't even addressed what had happened with Kendall yet.

"Tag, I've learned that my notion of trouble and yours are different. For me, it's worth it to give up something, even something very important to me, if it allows me to be who I am."

And there it was. He recoiled like he'd been slapped because it was clear to him that "something" was him. Still, the pain of hearing the words aloud cut hard and deep.

"Will you at least let me explain about Kendall?"

"I see your relationship with Kendall as a similar issue. You see it as something you have to do. It's something you're not willing to give up in order to be who you need to be—who you think you need to be. Right?"

A double punch. Right to the gut. "Ally, I…" What could he say? She was right on one level, but what choice did he have? "It's complicated."

She responded with a single firm nod, as if it was the answer she'd been expecting. "I need to check how things are going with the patient and then I'm off to bed. I'll see you in the morning." And with those final words, she walked away.

"ALLY, YOU WANT to check out my new baseball card?" Dave asked her the next morning.

"Sure, Dave," she said.

Tag watched Ally smile at the young doctor and felt his insides twist. That smile should be for him. Baseball card? How old was this guy, twelve?

Tag had awoken, if one could awaken from hours of blanket kicking and ceiling staring, and found his way to the kitchen. Coffee was in the pot, so he'd helped himself. Ally had joined him a few minutes later, and he'd barely had time to say good morning before Dave sauntered in, casting longing glances Ally's direction. It was obvious the guy had it bad for her. With his floppy blond hair and easy smile, Tag thought he looked like he belonged in a tweeny band instead of a remote medical clinic in the wilds of Alaska.

Tag itched with the desire to make it clear to Dr. Boy Band that Ally was off-limits. But that was the problem; she wasn't off-limits, was she? A funnel cloud of disappointment, frustration and jealousy whipped him up and out of his seat. The chair made a screeching sound on the hard tile floor and nearly toppled. He mumbled an "Oops" and stepped toward the coffeepot like he'd been headed there all along.

Dave went on, "Yeah, major score on eBay. It's a rookie card. Mint. Take a walk next door with me, and I'll show you."

Tag wanted to ask Dave to take a walk out into the foot of snow that had fallen overnight and then bolt the door behind him. He watched them disappear and had to admit they made a striking couple, not to mention they'd probably never disagree over medical practices. Dave would probably never disagree with her, period. Kneading the pain in the back of his neck, he realized Abe had walked into the kitchen and was watching him. No mistaking the curiosity stamped all over the man's face.

Hoping his smile didn't look as forced as it felt, Tag asked, "Anything I can help you with around here? If you've got a shovel, I can get started on that mess of snow outside." Anything would be better than watching the woman he loved frolicking around with a charming and engaging guy, younger than him and completely suitable for her.

THE SIGHT OF Tag outside shoveling snow off the drive made Ally irritable. Helping. Always helping. Seeing to everyone else's needs rather than his, or hers—or theirs, now that she thought about it. She felt like marching out there and demanding that he explain himself. Last night, she'd opened the door for him to clarify his onstage display with Kendall and he'd just stared back at her looking all wounded and confused.

The thought of that...that...dragon, to steal a term from Iris, directing his campaign, dictating his every move and sucking the life out of him filled her with absolute despair. And a fair amount of anger. And...

Oh, no, what would he do when Kendall told him what she'd said about being glued to his side? Humiliating to think about, considering they weren't even a couple anymore. Ally thought about how that superior, smug look had dissolved from Kendall's face and decided it had been worth it.

Could he not see what this campaign was going to do to him? Had done already? Was it worth it to sacrifice so much of yourself for a greater cause? And yet... A deep sigh escaped her as she realized that she was no better than he was. She was about to lose her job because of her beliefs. She had no room to talk.

If this was love, then she was glad she'd managed to avoid it for so long. Although, to be fair, she didn't see a path other than the one they were taking. Retreat. He didn't respect her beliefs, and worse, he didn't trust her to dispense them appropriately. And she wasn't sure she trusted him, not when it came to juggling his personal life with the campaign.

She needed to let him go before any further damage was done. As it was, she could barely breathe for wanting to run to him and confess all. Why did this in-love feeling, now that she'd acknowledged it, want out so desperately? She'd always wondered about that in books she'd read. Why did people feel compelled to spout off words of love without being sure they would be returned? Now she knew, and it was like trying to contain a herd of migrating caribou inside a corral made of twigs. Eventually, they would stampede their way out, so compelling was their need to get where they were going.

Turning away from the window, Ally headed down the hall, every step jarring her cracked and aching heart, and agitating those wayward caribou. She was glad Tag didn't know about the hospital board hearing next week, glad that he wouldn't be conflicted about coming to support her. It was better this way, she assured herself. The last thing she wanted was for her association with him to damage his chances in the election, and that would happen if she got fired. That senate seat meant everything to him. And deep down she knew it was selfish of her to want to mean more to him than it did.

When she walked through the door leading to the clinic, she discovered Abe in the reception office, his laptop open in front of him. She loved the way his eyes always lit when he noticed her. Even when she'd been a little girl getting in his way or into trouble, there had always been love in those eyes. She was extra grateful to see it there now.

"Hey, Als."

"Papa, hey. How's Zeke doing?"

"Good. Very good. Storm's supposed to ease tonight. We'll fly him to Rankins on Monday morning."

"You're taking him?"

"Yep, just arranged it. Eric from Flyway is available." Flyway was another company that operated medical transport in the region.

"You think he's going to be okay to travel?"

"Oh, yeah, no problem. Mainly, I'm going because I want to be with you at your hearing on Tuesday and there's a guy in Glacier City I need to meet with."

"Who is it?"

"A computer software developer. It's a business opportunity. I'll tell you about it later. Right now, I want to talk about you."

She winced. "You don't have to come to the hearing."

"Yes, I do, if that's what's troubling you."

"Why do you think something is troubling me?"

A quirk of his brow was all it took.

She sighed. "I'm fine. Just a little stressed."

"Because of the hearing?"

"Partly. I don't want to whine about it, though. I knew this job was going to be difficult."

"If you were going to whine, which I know you're not because I didn't raise a whiner, but if you were, what would you say right now?"

"That Dr. Boyd has it in for me. Part of the problem is that people in town seem to think I'm some sort of all-powerful healer, or that I think I am. Now I've got people seeking me out, and I'm afraid of making a mistake, afraid I'm going to say something that could get me into trouble. Maybe I already have." Tag had warned her, but Ally hadn't realized how much she feared it until now. She wouldn't change who she was, but facing the consequences still scared her.

"Ally, all you can do is the best you can do. It was unfortunate that you got started in

Rankins the way you did, with Louis and the clay. It made people *notice* you. But, as you mentioned, it also made people notice *you*. You've told me yourself—you've been able to guide several people who wouldn't have come into your path otherwise."

"I know. But I don't want to disappoint you. I know how much this job means to you."

"Me? You could never disappoint me. You've exceeded my hopes and expectations in every single way. If this job isn't meant to be, a different, better one is."

She managed a weak smile. "Wow. No pressure."

He chuckled. "Nope. None. That's the beauty of unconditional love. You don't have to earn it."

"It's not your love I'm worried about," she muttered.

"Oh? Whose love are we talking about, then?"

Ally felt her cheeks go hot. She hadn't meant it that way, but now that he said it, she couldn't help but think it, feel it. "I mean, it's your respect and admiration that concerns me."

She knew her grandfather. The man didn't miss a beat.

"I'm sensing discord in your relationship with Pilot."

She laughed. "You know his name is Tag."

"I know, but it's such a funny story, that you thought his name was pilot. What kind of a name is Tag, anyway? It's not a name—it's a game for children."

"Taggart is his name. It's his mom's maiden name."

"Mmm. Well, that's a little better."

"You have no room to talk—you know that, right? Alsoomse isn't exactly found on every souvenir key chain rack in the country."

The sound of his laughter was such a comfort. "You got me there. But it worked, didn't it? Naming you what I wanted you to be?"

"It did." When it came to her independence, at least, she could be confident.

"Don't think I haven't noticed how you're skirting the issue here. What's up with you and Taggart?"

"Nothing. And I told you before—it's not a relationship."

"You might want to mention that to him."

Ally felt as if her heart had grown crampons and was climbing its way up her throat. "What do you mean?"

"I know we've never had a chance to navigate these waters where dating is concerned. I was always kind of relieved, seeing as how you didn't have your grandmother around. But now

I'm thinking it's unfortunate, because you've been thrown into the deep end, haven't you?"

"What are you talking about?"

"I see the way he looks at you. And the way he looks at poor Davey while *he's* pining after you. It makes me a little afraid for Dave."

No way Tag was jealous of Dave, was he? "Papa, I think you're mistaken. I think your love glasses for me have colored your perception of the situation."

"Is that so? Then am I also imagining the way you look at him?"

CHAPTER NINETEEN

ANOTHER SLEEPLESS NIGHT morphed painfully into Sunday morning, and Tag decided to make himself useful again, this time by fixing breakfast with ingredients he found in Abe's kitchen. Not surprisingly, both the refrigerator and the freezer were well supplied. Stocking up was something most Alaskans were good at, and soon he had bacon sizzling in a skillet while he whisked the eggs for a scramble.

Abe came into the kitchen, looking bright eyed in jeans and a flannel shirt. "Mornin'. Smells delicious." Stepping over to the coffee maker, he filled a mug.

"Good morning. I hope it's okay I'm making myself at home here?"

"Cooking a breakfast like this, you can move on in. It's usually oatmeal around here, I'm afraid."

"How's Zeke?" Tag filled the toaster with whole wheat bread, then poured the eggs into the pan and stirred.

"Doing remarkably well." Abe pulled out

a chair and sat. "The healing power of young people never ceases to amaze me. If only I could bottle it."

"You could save the world." Taking a slice of bread from the toaster, Tag slathered on a pat of butter.

"Don't be shy with the butter there, cowboy. Nah, I'm not interested in saving the world. It's impossible to stop the cycle, you know? My goal is to heal, to ease suffering and make it more pleasant to live in this world. We can all only do as much as we are able. The trick, once you get that helping fever into your blood, is knowing where to draw the line, how much to do, when to stop before draining your own well dry."

Tag paused, then added another swipe of butter to the toast. A stab of longing sliced through him as he was reminded of the time Ally had called him cowboy. He didn't feel like that carefree, risk-taking cowboy lately. He felt more like the toast he was buttering.

After spooning eggs onto a platter, he set all the food on the table and sat down across from Abe. "Ally told me you're a philosopher."

Abe filled his plate and took a bite of eggs. Nodding appreciatively, he said, "Mmm. Delicious. I appreciate a man who knows how not to overcook eggs. It's an art form. Can't let those protein bonds get too hot. I may be something of an amateur philosopher, but I'm a grandfather first, a parent. That line I was referring to earlier? For me, it's Ally."

Tag's bite of eggs turned rubbery. Nervously, he settled in for a conversation that could go many different directions. What had Ally told her grandfather?

Tag gave a casual shrug of one shoulder. "Lucky for me, I have the luxury of not really having a line—not yet, anyway. Meaning I don't have a family of my own, like a wife or kids."

Abe chewed slowly, his brown eyes like hot lasers sighted on Tag's. He swallowed and then took a sip of coffee. In a flat tone nearly identical to Ally's, he said, "Lucky for you, huh?"

Tag realized how much that made him sound like a player, afraid of commitment. "Well, no, not really. Honestly, I wish I had a line." *I wish I had Ally.*

"Hypothetically, if you did have a line, would you be able to not cross it, protect it, cherish it?"

Tag set his fork down and leaned back in his chair. "Okay, Dr. Mowak, I know we don't know each other very well, or at all, really. But I feel like I know you a little through Ally, and I definitely know how much you mean to her.

So, maybe you should just tell me what you're trying to say here?"

"I'm not *trying* to say anything. What I am saying is that I don't appreciate you playing fast and loose with my granddaughter's heart. Despite the way she acts, she feels very deeply. If a person could be accused of having too much compassion, loving too deeply, that would be my Ally. There's nothing she wouldn't do for someone she loves. Probably there's nothing she wouldn't do to protect someone she cares about, either, for that matter."

"Sir, I promise you, it's not like that."

"Not like what?" Abe scooped up another bite of eggs, casual as you please. Tag knew he was anything but. There was so much of this man in Ally.

"I think I know what you're saying. But, uh, I'm the one who is in over my head here."

Abe leaned back a little in his chair, dabbing his mouth with a napkin. With a sad shake of his head, he said, "You know, I'm surprised." Before Tag could respond, he went on, "When Ally told me about you, she said you were smart. I was glad for that. Can't abide the notion of her settling for someone who isn't as intelligent as she is." Squinting slightly, like he was thinking it over, he added, "Eh, I suppose the fact that you're a paramedic and a pilot and a successful businessman confirms your intelligence on one level. The lowest, most basic one."

A mix of amusement and irritation stirred inside Tag, but he held steady. Keeping his feelings to himself, and at bay, was exhausting. He wondered how these two did it all the time.

"Thanks for that, then, I guess."

"You know how old she is, right? And you're, like, what, late thirties?"

Why did everyone keep going for this weak spot? "Yes. But believe me, our age difference was a cause of great concern to me before we ever started dating. Not to Ally, but for me. And I am careful not to forget—"

Brushing a hand through the air to cut him off, Abe said, "It's not that. It's not the *difference* in your ages that I'm talking about here. I don't care about that. I care about Ally being happy. Right now, she's not happy. I think you're to blame."

"Maybe. But not like I think you're thinking. We had a difference of opinion over her… medical beliefs, and then… I don't know if Ally told you, but I'm running for state senate and…" How did he explain how complicated his life was?

Abe was shaking his head again. "I don't

care what you two were disagreeing over. It's no secret that Ally shares my views on medicine. She's used to people questioning that. Differences in opinion can almost always be worked out if you love each other enough. The problem, as I see it, has to do with priorities and honesty, on both sides. Too many of the former are misplaced, however well-meaning, and there's not enough of the latter."

"I've been honest with her from the start," Tag said, and then immediately realized that wasn't true on at least one level. Maybe more, if he counted Kendall. What purpose would it serve to tell her how he felt? Other than breaking his own heart, which already felt battered about with more raw edges than he would have thought possible? As for the priorities, that part was true. But what choice did he have? Running for political office was all about priorities, about putting others' needs ahead of his own. Except where this thing with Kendall was concerned—that he was going to do something about, regardless of what happened with Ally.

"And Ally has been honest with me, too. I know she's not looking for a serious relationship."

More head shaking from Abe left Tag feeling like a wayward teen who'd disappointed his father. "Son, you are sorely lacking when it comes to your knowledge of romantic relationships, aren't you? I'm beginning to think you and Ally are on about the same level when it comes to that kind of experience."

"Well, I can't argue that."

"Can't argue what?" Ally asked in a husky morning voice as she strolled into the kitchen in her baggy flannel pajama bottoms, soft pink T-shirt and leather slippers. She'd secured her sleep-mussed hair away from her face, and a sharp pang of longing shot straight through his bloodstream. A lifetime of Sunday morning images flitted through his brain: him and Ally, kids, cats, coffee and the newspaper, cuddling in front of the fireplace in his house. He needed to…do something. He had to get out of here and away from her before he said something, did something he couldn't take back.

"Argue about bacon," Abe supplied.

Ally spun around from where she was filling a cup with coffee. Lips curving at the corners, she said drily, "Sounds like I've been missing out on some profound and insightful breakfast conversation." Pulling out a chair, she joined them at the table and snagged a piece of bacon from the platter.

Abe's tone was wry, while his gaze was anything but as he pinned it on Tag. "You could say that."

ALLY WAS RELIEVED when Max called later that morning to tell Tag he'd found the part for his plane. The weather had cleared and this meant Tag would be leaving soon. She'd already decided not to fly back with him because, without the distraction of an emergency between them, they'd be forced to talk. She didn't want to talk. She wasn't sure she could have any more conversations about Shay or the campaign—and certainly not about Kendall—and keep her emotions in check.

Then there was the fact that she didn't want to confess that he'd likely been right about her medical discussions getting her fired. She'd been in touch with Flynn, and he'd heard that it wasn't looking good for her.

Tag found her in the living room, where she'd been pretending to read. "Max said his cousin is going to be in the area and can swing by and pick us up. Can you be ready in about thirty minutes?"

"I'm not going with you. My grandpa is flying Zeke to Rankins tomorrow. I'm going to wait and go with him."

"Your grandfather is coming to Rankins?"

"Yep. He, um, he wants to consult with Doc about Zeke. And he has some business to take care of."

"So, you're not coming back with me?"

He phrased the question like he was having a difficult time accepting it. Ally tried not to read too much into it. "No, I already told Flynn. He's going to handle any emergencies."

"Why?"

"Because he knows what to do," she said, purposely misunderstanding the question. "He used to do the job before I was hired."

"No, I mean why aren't you coming with me? I was hoping…" His look told her he knew exactly what she was up to. "Ally, I think we need to talk. I have to leave for Juneau tomorrow, and I won't be back until Wednesday at the earliest."

A rush of relief went through her. If he was leaving tomorrow, there was less chance he'd find out about the hearing. But that also meant it was that much sooner he'd be with Kendall and she'd find out Ally was lying about herself and Tag.

But it didn't matter now, anyway; she and Tag were over. She needed to make that clear, lest she hold on to some pointless hope. She tried to inhale a fortifying breath but her lungs felt caustic and tight, like they were full of campfire smoke.

Her voice was a little low and throaty but she managed a level "No, Tag, it's fine. There's nothing more to talk about. You need to focus on the campaign, and I need to focus on...my job." Or job hunting, more likely.

"Is Dave coming with you to Rankins?"

"What? Dave? No, he's going to cover for my grandpa."

"Mmm. Do you...? Are you guys...? Are you interested in him?"

Ally stared. Was he serious with this? How dare he ask her about Dave after the mauling Kendall gave him on that stage? Enough was enough.

The words bubbled up and burst from her like a volcanic episode. "Are you out of your mind? How could you think that when I'm so clearly—" *in love with you*. She'd almost blurted it out. A sheen of nervous sweat prickled her back. She needed him to get out of here.

"You're what?" he asked, his voice tight and fraught. Tension radiated from his body. "It would be nice to hear you say how you feel, for a change."

Ally froze and then struggled to keep her tone level. "You want to hear how I feel?" Those stampeding words pounded against the back of her throat, clamoring for release. But what difference would it make? There could be no future here. And that's what she wanted: a relationship, a future, a family. If they couldn't have that, what was the point in telling him how she felt? She didn't want to be second on his list. She didn't even think she'd make second place. Probably she was down there around fourth or fifth after the campaign, his family, Kendall, his business… Better to end this, once and for all.

"Ally, tell me how you feel."

Corralling the caribou, she said, "Fine. I feel…fine."

"Hey, uh, Tag?" Dave's voice sounded from down the hall. "Max's cousin Brent is here to pick you up."

"Thanks, Dave," Tag called out. "I'll be right there."

Ally stayed silent.

"That's it?" He stepped toward her. "You're sticking with *fine*? That's how you want to leave this? Us?"

"Yes." A burning sensation erupted inside her rib cage. Excruciating, like her heart was tinder and had been blasted with a blowtorch.

"Can I see you on Wednesday when I get back?"

She managed a casual "I don't see the point."

"I see."

She flinched when he reached out like he was going to touch her cheek. Lowering his hand, he whispered, "Goodbye, Ally."

A sob welled up so quickly she let out a little gasp. She barely managed to swallow it. Like some sort of evil sinkhole, a giant gaping wound formed right in the middle of her soul, taking with it every bit of the joy he'd brought into her life. And more, because now she knew what she was missing. Tears burned behind her eyes and she was afraid to blink for fear they'd come pouring out. All she could manage was a nod before he turned and walked away.

"YOU LOOK LIKE…death warmed over. And then cooled off and warmed again. Are you sick?"

Monday morning, Tag stood in the kitchen of his house scowling at his sister. Upon returning home the evening before, he'd called Kendall, shut his phone off and then tried to sleep. He'd wound up watching infomercials all night. He may or may not now be the proud owner of something called a Quickie Crepe Machine, only $39.99 with shipping and handling. He'd only just dozed off when he heard Iris calling his name. When he hadn't shown up at the office this morning or answered his phone, she'd come over to check on him.

"No." Yes, heartsick. No, it was so much worse than that. Brokenhearted? Crushed-hearted? Was that a thing? He gave up. There were no words to describe the acid-like despair pumping through his veins, shredding him from the inside out with every beat of his aching heart.

"I'm not…sleeping. I haven't slept much in the last few nights." An understatement. Truthfully, he was beginning to fear for his health. He'd realized not long after taking off the previous afternoon that he shouldn't have flown back yesterday, wouldn't have if he'd had passengers.

"You know what? I'm glad. You deserve it."

"What?" He choked on a sip of the coffee she'd made and then poured for him.

"You deserve to be miserable after what you did to Ally."

"What I did?" he asked with a wheeze. "What… You know, you used to be my sweet little sister? And to think I wanted you to come home. I actually missed you. I flew my plane all the way to Anchorage to pick you up."

"Hmmph. What were you thinking, hiring that witch to be your campaign manager?"

"I didn't hire her. Maura did."

"Oh, come on. You could have stopped it."

He supposed that was true. Instead of telling Maura no and directing her to remove Kendall from the short list, he'd told her he'd prefer someone else. *Prefer* did not mean the same thing in political speak as it did regular speak, a fact he was fast becoming all too familiar with.

"It doesn't matter. I have to get ready to go."

"What do you mean? You're not still going to Juneau?" She shifted her stance, hands fisted on her hips, fire shooting from her eyes.

"What is the matter with you? You know I have those meetings."

"But you'll miss the hearing."

"What hearing?"

The sound of his front door crashing open and then slamming drew their attention.

"You're here?" Hannah said, rushing into the room. "Oh, I'm so glad."

"Where have you been?" Shay demanded, hot on Hannah's heels.

"Yep, here. And here. Same answer to both questions. Accosted now by several of my siblings."

"What is the matter with you? Are you sick?" Hannah marched over and put a hand on his forehead.

"Sort of."

"What is it?" Shay scuttled backward a few steps. "Does he have a fever?"

Pointing a finger at Shay, he said, "Ha. You look like a scared crab."

"Is he delirious?" Hannah asked Iris.

"No, well, maybe. Apparently, he hasn't slept much in the last few nights."

Shay blew out a breath of relief and moved forward again. "Oh, that's good. Sign of a guilty conscience."

He scowled. "Why would I have a guilty conscience?"

"Um, Ally, Kendall? Does stringing those two names together ring a bell?"

"Hey!" he cried, bunching his fist into his shirt over his heart. "Ally is the one who broke my heart. Broken, ha. No, I'm pretty sure my heart is dying, a slow and excruciatingly painful death if you must know. I hurt...all over."

"Tag," Iris demanded, "what are you talking about? You slayed her and left her writhing in the middle of the park thanks to that display on Friday with Kendall. Flynn told me that you then flew Ally to Killebrew, where you guys spent the weekend barely speaking. You never even explained yourself to her!"

"I tried. She didn't want to hear it. It doesn't matter now, anyway."

"Of course it matters! You need to explain, apologize, whatever. You need to make this right."

Throwing up his hands, he cried, "It doesn't matter because it's over! And besides, Ally isn't jealous of Kendall."

"Have you turned stupid…er? Ally is crazy about you."

"Trust me, if I had an inkling that she loved me even a fraction as much as I love her, I would try, Iris. I would."

"You're in love?" Hannah asked, her voice a mix of joy and wonder.

"This is great news!" Shay cried.

Iris scowled at him, and Tag could see the wheels spinning in her mind. But she didn't look surprised. Undoubtedly she'd known his feelings before he did.

Peering at him closely, she asked, "Did Ally happen to mention to you the conversation she had with Kendall after the rally?"

"Ally didn't talk to Kendall."

"Oh, yes, she did. I was there. I heard the whole thing."

"What—what did she say?"

"Among other brave, bold and beautifully worded comments that put that awful woman in her place, she told Kendall that she promised you that she'd never make you travel to Juneau without her again, that you'd made her promise never to leave your side."

Hope sprouted inside him. Was this possible? If what Iris was saying was true, it could mean Ally cared more than he thought. It could mean… He needed to talk to Ally. Abe was right. There had to be a way to get over this issue with Shay. He had to find a way to put it aside. He would.

Except, how could they get over it? What happened with Shay was just a symptom of a greater problem. Because there would be more Shays in the future, more cases where they would disagree. And more Gingers, where Ally put concern for herself far below that of the patient. Except eventually she'd go too far.

"There's more to it than that. The night before the rally we had a fight."

"About what?" Hannah asked. "Ally doesn't seem like a fighter."

"She's not. It wasn't really a fight. It was more of an airing of irreconcilable differences. But it was a game changer." He made eye contact with the eldest of his sisters. "About you, Shay."

Eyes wide, mouth open, she looked appalled by the notion, and her words confirmed it. "Me? But I love Ally. I know I was mean about her at first, but that was before I knew her. Before she…"

"Yeah, I know. *Before.* Before she treated you or…whatever you want to call it. I got very angry when I learned that she's been giving you medical advice. It was one thing to give

Hannah tea and herbs and recommend acupuncture or whatever. That stuff felt harmless. But I couldn't stand the thought of her giving you false hope about having a baby. She crossed a line."

"Wait a minute." Iris glared at him. "So, Ally's beliefs are okay so long as *you* approve, as long as *you* believe they're harmless? The omnipotent medical authority on all conditions, Taggart James, gets to decide how much value there is to Ally's vast knowledge and experience? Not to mention the brilliant and respected grandfather doctor who taught her?"

"Iris, I understand what you're saying. It's not that, not necessarily. It's just…this felt… personal. And Shay's situation is different. It's way more serious. It's about who she is."

Shay inhaled deeply before letting her breath whoosh out. "She didn't give me false hope, you well-meaning dolt of a brother. In fact, she didn't give me any medical advice whatsoever."

He turned a frown on Shay. "But when I asked her what was going on with you, she said I should talk to you."

Shay smiled. "Of course she did. Because I told her some things in confidence. All we did was talk. About how you can't change things by worrying about them. You can only change your reaction to situations. And about stress and how bad it is for the body, how it's not a good climate to grow a baby."

Tag sighed and looked at the ceiling.

"Wait, Tag, I know how that sounds. I was going to wait a few more weeks to announce it but today makes three months, and the doctor said if I make it three months there's a very good chance, in my case, that I'll make it nine."

Iris slapped a hand over her mouth and let out a squeal.

Even in his sleep-deprived state, Tag understood what her words meant. A helium-like euphoria expanded inside him. Tears stung his eyes, not tears but joy-filled drops of happiness.

Voice raspy with emotion he said, "Shay... really?"

"Really, Tag, I'm pregnant."

"Oh, my... I'm so... Shay, I'm just... Congratulations." With a clumsy fist, he swiped at his tears.

Much more gracefully, his sister dabbed at her cheeks. "Ally was only trying to help me get over my fear. I needed to find my joy again so I could make a peaceful place to grow our baby. It probably sounds crazy to you, but it worked for me, allowing my brain to accept the possibility that it might actually happen this time. Letting my body accept the baby. And accepting whatever was going to happen, one way or another. I mean, I don't know if it worked scientifically or whatever, but changing my mind-set has made me happy. And I haven't been happy in a while. Too long." Shay's eyes refilled with tears. "I'm so grateful Jonah hasn't divorced me. I haven't been easy to live with."

"Shay!" Hannah admonished. "He would never."

"I know." Shay sniffled on a laugh. "I'm just super emotional. Hormones. You have no idea how good it feels to say that."

Tag walked to his sister and wrapped her in his arms. "You're going to be such a great mom."

"Because I want this so much," she said, nodding. "And I want it for you, too. Someday." She pulled away. "And speaking of that, we're here to talk about Ally. Are you going to the hearing?"

"What hearing? Iris mentioned it earlier, but you guys came in and…" He added a helpless shrug.

"Ally obviously didn't tell you that, either," Iris said.

"Tell me what?"

"Tag," Hannah said, "there's a special hospital board meeting tomorrow, a disciplinary hearing. Dr. Boyd is trying to get Ally fired."

CHAPTER TWENTY

ALLY HELPED ABE get Zeke settled in the hospital and then headed to her office. As far as she was concerned, her job still belonged to her, and she was determined to do everything she could for her patients in the time she had left. The message light was blinking on her in-house phone.

She froze as the voice of Dr. Boyd's secretary boomed from the voicemail requesting that she return the call as soon as possible. Picking up the receiver, she tapped the button to call her back.

"Cora? Hi, it's Ally Mowak."

"Ally, I'm glad you're back. Dr. Boyd would like to meet with you. I went ahead and scheduled it for twelve thirty, hoping you'd be here by then."

Ally glanced at the clock. That left her twenty minutes to spare. She assured Cora she'd be there and then took a few minutes to glance at her email inbox. Expecting a backlog, she was relieved to find only a few and reminded herself that she'd been away only for the weekend.

"Longest weekend of my life," she muttered. She typed out a few responses and headed to Dr. Boyd's office.

Ally walked into the anteroom where Cora sat guarding his inner sanctum. The secretary gave her a tentative, apologetic smile. "He's expecting you," she said and waved her toward his office.

Dr. Boyd, in his white coat, stethoscope draped around his neck, sat with his head bowed. Ally was struck by how ordinary he looked, like a hundred other doctors she'd met in her life. Kindly, if not harmless. Until he lifted his gaze to meet hers, and she saw that the look on his face wasn't harmless at all. It was so full of hatred Ally wanted to wince.

"Hello, Dr. Boyd. You requested to see me?"

"I did, Ms. Mowak. Nice of you to join the rest of us here at work today. I hope you enjoyed your morning off."

"I was out of town on an emergency."

"Yes, with a pilot who is contracted with this hospital but who was able to make it back while you opted to stay behind."

The implication was obvious. "Is that why you asked to see me? Because I took a few hours off this morning? If that's the case, I can assure you that I more than made up the hours in the preceding weeks. You can check my work log."

"I don't like your tone."

"My tone is my voice, Dr. Boyd. If you don't like it, I suggest you get an interpreter or one of those voice alteration devices because this is simply the way I speak."

"Not with patients, it's not."

"I have sympathy, empathy and compassion for my patients. In addition to a desire to help them in any way I can."

One hand spread on the desktop between them, he began a slow thrum of his spider fingers. "See, I don't like that, the way you talk. You very cleverly…imply things. And you're condescending."

She was condescending? What was the point of this? "Are you trying to provoke me into losing my temper, sir? Because I can assure you, you will be disappointed."

"Is that so?"

"Yes."

"Hmm. Interesting. But, no, I don't care about your temper. Don't get me wrong—it would be nice to be able to add that little gem to your file before I send you on your way. But, alas, it's not why I called you in here."

"Then, if you don't mind, I'd like you to get

to the point. Despite your special hearing tomorrow, we both know you, alone, can't fire me. And, at least until then, I have work to do."

"Ah. Yes. I've discovered this to be truer than I realized. That grandfather of yours has tentacles almost as long as mine. Fortunately for you, that means we are not going to have to duke it out at the hearing."

Ally felt a faint stirring of hope but responded with a simple "Oh?"

"I've accepted the fact that I can't have you fired."

"Does this mean there won't be a hearing?"

"Yes, it does, Ms. Mowak. You won't be getting fired tomorrow."

Relief coursed through her. But she wasn't about to give him the satisfaction of seeing how worried she'd been. And she certainly wasn't going to show him even a whisker of gratitude.

"Hopefully, we can find a way to work amicably—"

"Not so fast. You're not going to be fired because you're going to quit."

"Excuse me?"

Arrogant smirk in place, he explained, "I understand you and Tag James are in a relationship." A slight narrowing of her eyes had him bringing a palm up and out as if to halt her response. "It's not a question. I have it on good authority. Let me assure you that I do not care about your private life beyond my ability to use it as leverage."

This time Ally glared at him because she didn't want this man anywhere near her private life. She felt a tiny bit of gratification when she realized that whatever card he thought he had up his sleeve was no good now, not when she and Tag were no longer together.

"I have a complaint all ready to file for the malpractice of medicine, along with a patient who will be compelled to testify if necessary."

Pushing aside her distress at his declaration, Ally thought fast. How could these two points possibly be related? The answer made her body go weak. She knew Tag was upset about Shay, but had he said something to Dr. Boyd? The idea was sickening. But even if he had, she hadn't given Shay any medical advice. And Shay would never file a complaint against her. It didn't matter because there was no way Ally would fall victim to his underhanded strong-arming.

"You know what, Dr. Boyd? I'll take my chances with this complaint."

"I see." He added a patronizing frown and a nod. "Except here's the problem, Ms. Mowak. Those chances are not for you to take."

"What do you mean?"

"The complaint isn't against you. It's against your grandfather."

The blood drained from her head and Ally heard an odd sound inside her skull like the low echoing snarl of a wolf. *Breathe, Ally. Think...* Why was he doing this?

"See these?" He lifted some papers from the desktop before him and dangled them aloft. "This is a list of endorsements and contributions from businesses, organizations and medical professionals, all slated to go to Tag James. Without these, the election is virtually impossible for him to win. It would be a shame to be the reason he didn't win, wouldn't it? You, Ms. Mowak, hold the keys to the futures of the two men you care most about."

"I'd like to see this complaint."

"I'm sure you would. And you will, if you choose to disregard what I'm offering."

"What you're saying is if I quit, then you bury the complaint against my grandfather and Tag gets elected? But if I don't quit you'll file the complaint and do your best to see that Tag loses the election?"

"That's it precisely. You are intelligent—I'll give you that. Too bad you're as misguided and conceited as your grandfather. Now, do we have a deal?"

WHEN THE DOORBELL RANG, Tag couldn't squelch the burst of hope that it was Ally. He didn't bother to hide his disappointment when he opened the door and found Flynn standing on his porch along with Bering and Emily.

Flynn said, "We need to talk to you."

Waving them in, Tag said, "Ramsey, if you're here to lecture me about Ally, my sisters have beaten you to it."

Tag led the way to the kitchen, where Iris and Hannah were now seated at his table drinking all his coffee. Greetings were exchanged, and then Iris said, "Flynn, just like you suspected, Tag didn't know about the hearing. Ally didn't tell him."

Flynn nodded. "Well, things are even worse than I thought."

"What do you mean?" Shay asked.

"Boyd has given her an ultimatum."

"What kind of ultimatum?" Tag asked, even as his stomach dropped.

"The kind where she quits her job to save you."

"Flynn, what are you talking about?" Iris asked.

He went on to explain how Dr. Boyd had threatened to sabotage the election if she didn't resign.

"Can he do that?" Shay asked.

"Yes, he probably could," Bering said. "He can make it very difficult if not impossible for Tag to win. We were already prepared to take some heat over his association with Ally, but he has a lot of clout in the medical community. Who knows what he might say, or make up and who he'll say it to? Espcially if he tried to make her look like a fraud and—"

"Bering, I know you could crush my windpipe with one hand, but if you talk about her like that again, I swear I will—"

"Tag, calm down." Emily stepped forward. "Bering doesn't think that. He's just explaining how it might happen."

A voice sounded from the doorway. "I don't want either of those things to happen."

Tag stared at the woman he loved and wondered how he could have ever believed her to be cold and detached. There was so much emotion flickering in her eyes, they looked as hot and bright as a bonfire. He wished he could identify them—anger, disappointment, fear? He wasn't sure, but he deserved all of those and more, and it took every ounce of self-control not to go to her and beg for forgiveness.

"I wasn't trying to eavesdrop. The door was open." Her gaze traveled around the room before landing on Flynn. "Flynn, did you tell them?"

He nodded. "Yes."

"Good. Tag, I need to talk to you. All of you, probably."

"What do we do now?" Shay asked helplessly.

Bering answered, "I don't know, but we can't lose this election. Tag has to win this."

"Oh, please!" Iris cried. "Why? What's the worst that can happen?"

Bering gaped at her. "Iris, are you serious? If Mammoth Tracks builds a mine in the valley, wildlife habitat will be devastated. They will pollute the Opal River, ruin our air quality and—"

"Stop, stop, stop! I'm not talking about that. I get it. Mammoth Tracks bad. Must be stopped. But why does Tag have to ruin his life in the process? You guys are his family, can't you people see what this is doing to him?"

Tag stared at his little sister, love squeezing his heart so hard his knees went soft. He needed to sit. He sank onto the dining chair nearest him.

"Ally sees it. Don't you, Ally?"

He tried to meet her gaze, but she looked away. The gesture was like a kick to his already bruised and battered spirit.

She answered with a soft "It doesn't matter what I think, Iris."

"I don't agree. But we'll circle back to that. Because first, Tag, I'm going to ask you a question and if you can answer with a resounding, no-hesitating, all-caps yes—and promise you mean it a hundred and ten percent—I'll shut up."

"Iris, don't—"

"Yes, Iris, do," Ally encouraged. "Please."

Iris looked him square in the face. "Do you want to be a senator?"

It took effort to swallow the negative answer. How did his sister know this about him? How did she seem to know everything before he did? He managed a more diplomatic Ally-esque response. "I... It doesn't matter what I want, Iris. What matters is what needs to be done."

Shay bolted to her feet. "No, it doesn't! I mean, it does matter, Tag. If what Iris is suggesting is true, it means everything."

He shook his head. "Shay, I don't think you should be jumping around in your condition."

She grinned and rolled her eyes. "Answer the question."

Bering glowered from the end of the table. "Yes, cousin, answer the question."

"I don't..."

Iris scowled. "If you say you don't know, I will hurt you."

"Fine. No, I don't. I don't want to be a senator." Saying the words felt like a million-pound boulder had been lifted from his chest. It was like he could breathe for the first time in weeks. With the exception of Iris, his family stared in shock and horror. And, just as quickly, the boulder shifted back into place, applying all its pressure.

"But, I'm sure I'll get used to it."

Iris huffed. "No, you won't. And it's ridiculous to try. Everything about this campaign is making you miserable. And it's turning you into someone you're not."

"Tag…?" Bering sighed. "Why didn't you say something if this is how you felt?"

"I couldn't let you down, Bering. Any of you. Don't worry. I know I'm committed. Maybe I can serve one term and then we can find someone else—"

"I'll do it!" Hannah leaped up out of her seat. "Drop out, Tag, and let me run. I'm jealous that you're doing it, anyway. I want to do it. Phew! That felt good."

"Hannah?" Shay cried.

"I would never have taken it away from him, Shay." She turned toward Tag. "But, Tag, if you bow out, I will run. And I will win. And if I don't, it won't be because I didn't try or because I didn't want it."

Tag couldn't help it; he chuckled. Emily was staring at Hannah. Bering looked as shocked as Shay, who was shaking her head.

Emily said, "I think you'd be fantastic, Hannah. And I'd love to be your campaign manager. I don't have political experience, but I know I can do it."

Hannah looked elated. "Emily, no one could do it better. We've already proven we make a great team. You're hired."

Iris was the only one who didn't appear surprised. She grinned, flashed Tag a meaningful look and faced Ally. "Speaking of jealousy— Ally, are you jealous of Kendall?"

"Um…"

"It's okay, you can say it. I already told him."

Ally's gaze slid tentatively toward Tag, and he felt the tiniest glimmer of hope spark inside him.

"Yes," she said.

"Okay." He was instantly on his feet and went to her. "That's… You all need to excuse us for a minute. Ally and I are going to talk outside." With one hand on the small of her back, he led her to the sliding door and out onto the deck.

Facing her, he said, "I'm so sorry about Boyd."

"Is that really what you want to talk about?"

"No. There is so much I want to talk about. But first, I need to apologize for the thing with Shay. I shouldn't have doubted you."

"Thank you. I'll admit that upset me. A lot. Maybe I could have found a way to ease your mind. Sometimes when I feel strongly about something, it's difficult to see options. Period. I don't like to have to explain, to justify my actions... Obviously, sometimes I should. It gets me into trouble. So, for that, I'm sorry, too. And I understand you were emotional because of her history and her pregnancy struggles. What concerns me is that our beliefs might cause more problems in the future."

"But I don't think they will. I mean, they might, in that maybe we'll disagree on certain specific issues. But that's okay. A little debate is healthy, right? We'll both learn. It was my reaction that was the problem. I think I was acting on some of my own fear and disappointment. I wanted Shay to have children because I can't...or something?"

"You make some good points."

"Good." He grinned. "Now I want to talk about Kendall."

"Good." She copied his grin. "Iris is right. I am jealous of Kendall. I hated that photo. I hated seeing her paw you in that photo, and at the Cozy Caribou that night and then again at your rally. I don't know if she told you, but I was rude to her…but only because she insulted me first. Iris is right, she wants you back and she won't stop until—"

"Shh. I know. But I don't want her."

"Then stop letting her manipulate you. That bothers me more than the jealousy."

"I already fired her from my campaign." He grinned, happiness building inside him at the notion. It felt good to take his life back. "My campaign, which no longer exists, apparently."

"Hannah Addison for senate. I'm personally going to go door-to-door."

Tag laughed. "We'll do it together."

Then Ally smiled at him, and a new joy unfurled deep inside him. It was like her happiness had a direct link to his soul, like his own capacity for joy depended on hers. Now, if only he could get her to forgive him, to believe that he had faith in her.

"Why didn't you tell me you were bothered by her? You seemed so…cool about it."

"I don't know… I knew how much the campaign meant to you, how important her parents' contribution would be. I didn't want to add to the stress I could see you struggling with every day. And Flynn told me not to let you know I was jealous. Guys don't like jealous, he said."

Tag shook his head. "There's a reason that guy is still single. Ally, I thought it meant you didn't care. To me, the fact that you weren't jealous meant that I liked you way, way more than you liked me. I mean, no one likes irrational jealousy. Like the kind I had for Gareth and then Dave. It was stupid, but I can see now that I felt that way because I wanted more. And then I thought you wanted to keep your options open and that killed me."

Ally shook her head. "Flynn is the only person I had to talk to about this. I have practically no experience with dating or relationships. You're the first guy I've ever been serious about. The first one I've ever…"

AND THAT WAS the moment the metaphorical herd in Ally's chest broke free. She took a deep breath and said, "I love you, Tag. I'm in love with you."

"You…what? Ally, do you understand what you're saying? You're so young and—"

"Tag!" Frustration tinged her tone, but she didn't care. "You know how much I hate that. And please don't insult me. No, I've never been in love before. I've never even been in a relationship. I might not have any experience in certain areas, but I know love when I feel it, and I just had to say it."

He chuckled. "It's not that. I love you, too."

Ally tried to tamp down her joy. In case there was a *but*. "You don't have to say it because I did."

"For weeks I've been trying my best *not* to say it. I didn't want to pressure you into more of a relationship than you wanted to have."

"But you said you wanted something casual."

"I knew almost immediately that I wanted more than that. But I was afraid..."

"Afraid of what?"

"Of smothering you or going too fast. I know you don't like age to be an issue, but the fact is that it is an issue for me. I'm not saying it's one I can't deal with, but I'm still a little afraid of it, that you're too young to know what you want. But I know what I want."

"What *is* it that you want, exactly? Let's clarify that."

His gaze skittered away for a second before landing right back on her, and the intensity in those many-shades-of-green eyes turned her legs to jelly. Because Papa was right about this, about the way he looked at her. How could she have not seen it before? She realized Tag was pretty good at hiding his feelings, too.

"Everything. Ally. I want everything. With

you. But I don't think it's fair to ask you for this possibility when you're only twenty-two."

"Hmm." Ally gave him her best bland stare.

He puffed out an impatient breath. "Say something. It kills me when you do this."

"Well…" she drawled and purposely paused for way too long. Although this was partially because she was fighting her lips to keep them from twitching. She didn't want to laugh. Yet. "I want some stuff, too."

"What?"

"A lot of things."

"Like?" he asked impatiently.

"A baby. With green eyes and golden specks."

At that moment, Ally truly understood what Ginger had been talking about. She wished with all of her being that she could capture this moment, because although Tag was standing there, still and calm, there was nothing but pure joy and relief shining in his eyes. And love. She could see that, too, and her insides were like warm honey oozing into all the cold, dark places that their days of separation had wrought.

When he finally spoke, his voice was calm and a little flat, and she loved that he was trying to imitate her. "Brown," he countered. "I want a baby girl with dark, dark brown eyes."

"Fine," she said, and her heart felt both light and full, and she thought it might break loose from her rib cage and float away. "Let's have both."

In two steps he closed the distance between them, wrapped his arms around her and lifted her so that their faces were only inches apart. "Ally, are you sure? I'm almost forty, and I don't want to wait long to start a family."

A family. How she wanted one of her own, and she wanted to be a part of his large and loving extended family, too. "Then you better figure out a way to make me your real wife soon. No more pretending."

"No more pretending," he repeated, and she knew he knew that she meant that in all the ways that had caused them to hurt each other.

With a sharp inhale, he buried his face in her neck before lowering her back down. His lips found hers and Ally wouldn't have believed kissing him could be better than before. But this love thing proved her wrong. This had to be why people wanted to say it. That would teach her to try and contain it. Maybe it would teach them both.

When he pulled away, they were both out of breath. Cupping a hand around her jaw, he caressed her cheekbone with his thumb. "I know I'm older and dated more and whatever, but I want you to know that none of it matters. I feel like I was just stumbling around in the dark before I met you. I've never been in love before, either. It's like I've been waiting my entire life for you, only I didn't know it until I found you."

"Tag…"

"And, in light of Shay's struggles, I want you to know that even if we never have kids, that won't change. I know in my heart, Ally, that I will love you, and only you, forever. I want you more than I want anything. All the things I thought were important in my life before I met you pale in comparison. My business, the senate—obviously—even my family and friends. Of course, I love them, too. But from now on, I promise you, you're first. You're all I need to be happy. My love for you is so…intense I can barely think straight sometimes." He lifted his hands from her shoulders and slipped one around the back of her neck. The other he kept on her shoulder. One side of his mouth curled up, and he asked, "Are you scared yet?"

Ally could only shake her head because tears were clouding her eyes and too many words were like a logjam clogging her throat. How could it be possible to love another human being like this?

"Hey," a voice called, accompanied by the sound of the door sliding open. Iris's head appeared. "Looks like you two have got things sorted."

"Pretty much," Tag said.

Ally sniffled and nodded.

"Good. You can sew up the details later. I think I'd make a stunning maid of honor. Tag, you can thank me with a raise and a company car. But right now, we need you guys back in here. Ally, your grandpa is here with Laurel, and apparently we still need to solve another problem."

CHAPTER TWENTY-ONE

BACK INSIDE THE HOUSE, Ally recited the entire conversation she'd had with Dr. Boyd.

"Then he gave me the ultimatum. All I have to do is quit, and it will all go away. He'll make sure the complaint doesn't get filed, and that Tag gets elected."

Throughout the tale, Laurel had been on her phone, only glancing up occasionally. Anyone would have guessed she was barely paying attention until she looked at Ally. "How did you leave it? What answer did you give him?"

"I almost agreed to resign on the spot, but something about this whole situation doesn't sit right. Why does he want me to quit so badly? I mean, I know he doesn't like me, but his attitude toward me has always seemed over the top. I decided to run it by Flynn first. Flynn was having lunch with my grandpa, so I was able to tell them both about the meeting at the same time. Flynn said I needed to talk to Tag and find out if what Dr. Boyd said is true, about the endorsements. And that's as far as we got."

"Boyd likes to believe he has even more power and influence than he does," Flynn supplied. "Before Ally quit, I thought she should make sure he wasn't bluffing."

Bering said, "It is true about the endorsements. With Tag's background as a paramedic and his contract with the hospital, the lack of support from the medical community would raise a lot of questions. And that lack of support, not to mention losing the financial backing, could be enough for Tag to lose the election."

Shay asked, "What does Ally's resignation achieve that having her fired doesn't? And why threaten her with the election?"

"She goes away much more quickly and quietly," Laurel supplied. "No one would think to blame Boyd if she quits. He wants Ally gone and Tag is just additional leverage."

"She's right," Flynn agreed. Pulling out his phone, he began tapping on the screen.

Abe said, "I think this is mostly about me."

"You?" Ally looked at her grandfather.

"Yes. I had a coffee date scheduled with Laurel, and she showed up right after you left. I mentioned this trouble with Boyd, and she gave me some information."

"I believe Abe is right." Laurel explained, "I recently interviewed Kip Patton for a story and learned that Dr. Boyd had formally applied to consult on this medical app that Kip's company is developing. It's one of those apps where a person can enter their symptoms and find out what might be wrong with them. Except Kip wants to have an option where people can see what alternative treatments might be helpful, in addition to a modern medical approach. That is what Kip and Abe have been discussing for some time now."

"That sounds cool," Hannah said.

"Yes, it does. The problem for Boyd is that Kip has just offered the consulting position to Abe. Because of Abe's reputation along with his background in modern and traditional medicine, he can offer both perspectives. Then there's the fact that he's about a million times more personable."

"Wow. Papa, congratulations!" Ally said. "This is amazing. Is this the business meeting you mentioned? It was with Patton? You're going to do it, right?"

Her grandfather grinned at her. "Yep. It is a pretty neat deal. I was going to do it, but I don't want to if it means you're going to lose your job. Boyd has it in for me and you shouldn't suffer because of it."

"You're the one who told me there were lots of jobs, remember? And this is way more important. This app could potentially reach millions of people."

Laurel agreed. "It will. For sure. But, needless to say, if Abe accepts, Dr. Boyd will be out of the picture."

"Not to mention the money Boyd will lose out on," Iris added.

Laurel nodded. "Kip said Boyd is furious about it all. You know what an egomaniac he is. Apparently, he's been spending the money before he's made it. And now he'll do anything to see Abe discredited."

Hannah asked, "But why not just file the complaint? Why force Ally to resign? What does that accomplish?"

"I'm guessing the complaint isn't strong enough or is completely bogus," Laurel supplied. "But he's hoping the threat of it will be enough."

"What do you mean?" Hannah asked.

Tag, who had been quietly absorbing the information until this point, chimed in, "It means he's not going to stop at simply forcing Ally out, is he?"

Laurel answered, "Exactly what I'm afraid of, Tag. His plan seems to hinge on Ally resigning. After which, he's going to leak false information about her use of alternative treatments on a disgruntled patient. She will have already quit, giving credence to the claim and making herself look guilty. Then he'll discredit both Abe and Ally in one fell swoop. This will create a scandal and, if you were still running, your association with Ally would look really bad. It could be disastrous for your campaign."

Shay asked, "What can we do?"

Flynn said, "I have an idea. Ally, remember the patient you sent to me a couple of weeks ago? The young woman?"

"Yes, of course." Gareth's friend, Kyla.

"She told me a story about a doctor who, against her wishes, gave her parents information about her medical condition."

"She told me the same story. It was the reason she was scared to see a doctor."

"Yeah, well, she told me the name of the doctor."

Ally frowned at Flynn. "Flynn, are you saying what I think you are? Because you can't use her name without her permission and she wouldn't give it. And I wouldn't want her to. She's afraid of her father."

"But Boyd doesn't know that. We don't need to use her name. I don't think we even need a formal complaint. If Laurel is right, he doesn't have one, either, not a good, solid one, anyway. I think I should pay him a visit and gently suggest that one could be filed against him as easily as the one he's contrived against Abe."

Ally raised her hands in protest. "Flynn, no. If you go to him with this and threaten him, he will hate you, and I think we've all seen what hatred does to the man. He'll make your life, your job, unbearable. He could find a way to get you fired."

"I don't care."

"I do. You have to finish your internship at the hospital."

Iris agreed. "She's right, Flynn. You have to stay out of it."

"I'll do it," Tag volunteered. "I'll take care of this."

"I'll go with you," Abe said.

Bering stepped forward. "Tag, if you go and threaten him, he'll rescind your contract with the hospital. Even if you're not running for office, he could smear your name over this. Ruin your reputation. He could harm your business, too."

"I could not possibly care less about my business, Bering. Or my reputation. I care about the patients, but if I can't transport them someone else will. No one else can do what Abe and Ally do."

Ally felt a fresh wave of love for the man

standing beside her. If she had any lingering doubts about what he'd told her outside, they were gone now. Despite the crisis raging around them, she was happier than she'd ever been in her life. She knew now that no matter what life threw at them, their love would be more than enough. Tag had just put her first, exactly like he'd vowed. And in the grandest way.

By consensus, it was decided to strike while the iron was hot. A group discussion ensued, dissecting the complexities of the situation. Flynn advised Tag and Abe on how they should handle Boyd. Laurel added her knowledge of what was at stake for Boyd. Shay called Jonah and had him write a letter outlining the unnamed patient's complaint against Boyd. It had no legal teeth, but their goal at this point was to scare him into complying.

TAG WAS EXHAUSTED, running on caffeine, adrenaline, the sheer force of his will and his newly declared love for Ally. The last made him feel like a superhero. He was ready to finish this. Boyd had to be stopped and he wanted to be the one to do it. He wanted Ally happy, and he wanted to start a life with her free of worry and stress. Just the thought of that possibility kept him focused on the task.

Flynn informed them Dr. Boyd was a creature of habit and usually spent about two hours doing paperwork in his office every day after lunch. So, less than two hours later, Tag and Abe entered Dr. Boyd's office suite to find Cora perched on the edge of the sofa. Tag was surprised to see her away from her usual gargoyle-like post behind her desk in front of Boyd's office.

"Hello, Cora. We're here to see Dr. Boyd. Is he in?"

"I'm afraid not, Tag. Dr. Boyd is…gone."

"What do you mean?"

"Well, I don't know what harm it would do to talk about it now. No one told me not to… And I'm just…sitting here, wondering what to do."

Tag sensed bad things brewing. "We would appreciate hearing whatever you feel comfortable telling us, Cora."

"Okay. Well, Mr. Patton came in to see Dr. Boyd this afternoon. They were in the office for about a half hour with the door closed. Mr. Patton came out, told me goodbye, and I thought everything was fine and dandy. But then, a few minutes later, Dr. Boyd came out and asked me to write a resignation letter for him. I did. Then I emailed it to him, and a short time later he came out of his office with the letter in an envelope, a box and his brief-case. He asked me to personally deliver the letter to the board president, which is what I just returned from doing."

"Do you know where he went?"

"No. He didn't say."

"Okay, well, thank you, Cora."

Tag and Abe headed back into the hallway. Silently, they walked until they reached the lobby. They stopped, and Tag turned to Abe. They eyed each other speculatively for a moment before Tag said, "In all the scenarios that played out in my mind about what was going to transpire here today, this wasn't one of them."

Tag expected Abe to wax philosophical at this point about how life rarely went as planned or karma or something.

Instead, he quirked a brow at Tag and said, "Huh. Same goes for me, but I'll take it. I'm getting too old for a dustup, but I'll admit that's where *my* mind was mostly. This guy is a piece of work."

Tag laughed.

"The important thing here, as far as I'm concerned, is that you were willing to do this for Ally."

"I would do anything for her, Dr. Mowak."

"I can see that." Abe grinned. "I'm beginning to think you're not quite as dense as I once feared."

"Thank you. I think. Now, let's go deliver the news."

When they returned to Tag's house, everyone was still there, plus a few extras, Aidan, Janie and Gareth.

"What happened?" Iris demanded.

"Why are you back already?" Shay asked.

Tag held his arms out and let them fall to his sides. "Boyd resigned. Kip Patton beat us to the punch, and I think we have you to thank for that, Laurel."

She shrugged. "Sounds like we have Kip to thank. And he didn't say anything to me about it." Phone in hand, she said, "I'm going to call him."

Tag looked at Ally, and though he spoke to the whole room, the words were for her. "It's over."

His family had questions, which Abe did his best to answer while Tag crossed the room to Ally. Taking her into his arms, he hugged her close.

"Not over," she whispered. "Finally beginning."

The breath he released felt cleansing. "You got that right."

Keeping her hand tucked securely in his,

he faced the room in time to hear Laurel's explanation.

"I just spoke to Kip. Before his company hires a consultant, they do an in-depth background check on the individual. The check revealed that Dr. Boyd and the clinic in Iowa he left before coming to Rankins have recently been named in an ongoing investigation of insurance fraud. Kip has passed this information on to the Alaska Medical Board."

Flynn looked up from his phone. "None of my sources know where he's gone. But since Kip has alerted the authorities, it's only a matter of time before they catch up with him."

Tag listened to the surprised and happy chatter for another few minutes before letting his gaze travel around the room.

"Hey, guys, can I have your attention here?" When the room went quiet, he continued, "Now, I love all of you people and you know I'd do anything for you. Well, except be your senator. Almost anything else, yes. But, right now, I need you all to do something for me."

"I wonder what that could be?" Iris said, giving him a wink and picking up her bag. "Flynn, can I give you ride?"

Tag grinned. "Iris, as usual, knows what I'm thinking. What I need is for you all to get out of my house so I can be alone with the woman I love."

Ally squeezed his hand, and he could *feel* her smile. Love and happiness and exhaustion stirred into him in this oddly perfect way. His body felt light and his eyelids heavy, and for the first time in weeks, peace settled over him as he realized he finally had everything he wanted. Everything he needed. Almost.

"And then," he added, "I'm going to take a nap."

* * * * *